SPECIAL MESSAGE

THE ULVERSCROFT FOUNDATION
(registered UK charity number 264873)
was established in 1972 to provide funds for research, diagnosis and treatment of eye diseases. Examples of major projects funded by the Ulverscroft Foundation are:-

- The Children's Eye Unit at Moorfields Eye Hospital, London
- The Ulverscroft Children's Eye Unit at Great Ormond Street Hospital for Sick Children
- Funding research into eye diseases and treatment at the Department of Ophthalmology, University of Leicester
- The Ulverscroft Vision Research Group, Institute of Child Health
- Twin operating theatres at the Western Ophthalmic Hospital, London
- The Chair of Ophthalmology at the Royal Australian College of Ophthalmologists

You can help further the work of the Foundation by making a donation or leaving a legacy. Every contribution is gratefully received. If you would like to help support the Foundation or require further information, please contact:

THE ULVERSCROFT FOUNDATION
The Green, Bradgate Road, Anstey
Leicester LE7 7FU, England
Tel: (0116) 236 4325

website: www.foundation.ulverscroft.com

James Raven was a journalist for most of his working life. After reporting for local, regional and national newspapers he moved into television in 1982 as a news scriptwriter with TVS television. There he worked his way up to become Director of News across Meridian, Anglia and HTV. When Granada took over most of ITV he became Managing Director of Granada Sport before setting up his own production company. James spends much of his time writing and travelling and also performs magic at various venues across the country. He has three grown-up daughters and is engaged to be married for the second time. *Rollover* is his first novel.

ROLLOVER

It's a rollover week on the National Lottery and the jackpot is a whopping £18 million. Journalist Vince Mayo has picked all six numbers, but before he can celebrate his spectacular win he's battered to death at his home in Hampshire's New Forest. Then Mayo's friend and fellow journalist, Danny Cain, goes on the run when the police suspect him of the murder. But the ticket cannot be cashed whilst Danny, knowing the truth, remains alive. And the killers want their money — whatever it takes. For Danny and his terrified family the odds of survival are stacked against them.

JAMES RAVEN

ROLLOVER

Complete and Unabridged

ULVERSCROFT
Leicester

First published in Great Britain in 2012 by
Robert Hale Limited
London

First Large Print Edition
published 2013
by arrangement with
Robert Hale Limited
London

British Library CIP Data

Raven, James.
  Rollover.
  1. Lottery winners- -Crimes against- -Fiction.
  2. Suspense fiction. 3. Large type books.
  I. Title
  823.9′2–dc23

  ISBN 978–1–4448–1464–4

Published by
F. A. Thorpe (Publishing)
Anstey, Leicestershire

Set by Words & Graphics Ltd.
Anstey, Leicestershire
Printed and bound in Great Britain by
T. J. International Ltd., Padstow, Cornwall

This book is printed on acid-free paper

To the following with love and affection
My fiancée Catherine.
Lyanne, Ellie and Ken, Jodie and Toby,
Lauren, Amy, Jack, Zach and Mya.

Prologue

It was over for me now. That much was obvious.

I was once again at the mercy of the man who was going to kill me. I no longer had the strength to get to my feet, let alone keep on running.

The earth beneath me was cold and damp. I was trapped and disoriented. My lungs were on fire and my breath was coming in great heaving gasps.

The cuffs on my wrists were cutting into the flesh, dripping blood on to the soft dirt and dead, soggy leaves.

I wanted to plead with him to let my wife and daughter live, but I couldn't form the words. Instead, I could only lie where I'd fallen and look up as he approached me. He was still wearing the black ski mask and he was still carrying the knife in his right hand. A carving knife with a serrated blade. Long, shiny and deadly.

I was going to be murdered by this man who had entered our lives just two days ago and whose face I'd never seen.

Two days.

Long enough for the life I had known to be shattered like a light bulb hitting concrete. And I couldn't help but wonder why it had happened to us.

First came the phone call, then the sequence of events that had destroyed our lives and brought me to this god-forsaken place.

'It's the end of the road, Cain,' the man said. 'No point resisting.'

It was as though he was telling me I had to put on a coat or get showered. No emotion. No compassion. Just cold, heartless words.

He was above me now, staring down through the slit in the ski mask. His eyes were black and manic and his voice trembled in his throat. Behind him grey, bloated clouds scudded across a sullen November sky that would soon be dark.

I was too weak to do anything other than brace myself for what was to come. Pain racked my body from the beating I'd taken earlier. Exhaustion numbed my senses and the sheer terror of what was happening had paralysed my mind.

He reached down. Grabbed my shirt front. Pulled me roughly off the ground.

He started speaking again, his mouth wrestling with the fabric of the mask, but his words were now just a jumble of sounds. I felt myself being pulled away from the present into the comfort of my subconscious.

It was a blessed relief. I was suddenly back in our house, back in the familiar surroundings of our loving home.

Back to where it began less than forty-eight hours ago.

1

Two days ago

My wife and I had a row that afternoon. It was over the usual thing — money. Or rather, the lack of it.

We were six weeks away from Christmas and Maggie suddenly decided that we should spend it on a Caribbean cruise. There was a great offer in the paper, she said. We could pay for it on one of our credit cards.

When I pointed out that we'd reached the limit on all of the cards, she suggested we use the last of our savings, a measly £5,000 in a Barclays ISA account.

I said it wasn't a good idea because the way the business was going we'd almost certainly need it in the not too distant future.

And that's when it kicked off.

It was all my fault, she said. If I hadn't been made redundant . . . If I hadn't invested all our money in the news agency . . . If I hadn't talked her out of going back to work when she had that job offer a year ago . . .

Sadly, it was all true, but having it rammed down my throat every time we had words really didn't help the situation or do much for my self-esteem.

Maggie was right to blame me for our current financial woes and I could understand why she was stressed out most of the time. I'd had a great job as a reporter on a national newspaper. An annual salary of over seventy grand. A generous pension. Two foreign holidays a year. Meals out twice a week. We were set to send our six-year-old daughter to a private school. Life was good. Money wasn't a problem.

But then I was made redundant and the cold wind of recession that was blowing through the newspaper industry meant that I couldn't get a job on another paper. There were cutbacks everywhere and it didn't help that I had just turned forty. There were younger, cheaper and frankly brighter journalists out there, eager to fill the few vacancies that did come up.

Deciding to invest my redundancy pot in a news agency with my long time friend Vince Mayo was, with hindsight, not the wisest of moves. Maggie had advised against it, but I had ploughed on regardless and the Southern News Agency was created eighteen months ago.

According to the business plan we should have been turning a healthy profit by now.

But it hadn't worked out so well. We were barely making a living covering court cases for the regional press, flogging occasional features to magazines, and filing human interest stories that too frequently got rejected by the national news editors.

We were still waiting for that big exclusive story that would put the agency firmly on the map and secure us a regular stream of lucrative commissions. There was one story that came close. A police-corruption tale that we sold to the *Mail on Sunday*. But it backfired somewhat after the detective in question committed suicide. His colleagues blamed us and we received a bunch of anonymous hate mail. At the same time the local CID closed ranks and made life difficult for us. It meant that we lost a valuable source of local stories — the lifeblood of a freelance operation. In terms of income it ran into thousands of pounds a year.

So Maggie had every right to feel that I'd let her down. Money was tight and the quality of our life had taken a huge tumble. It had made her increasingly tense. Lately she'd been more off with me than usual and even our sex life had suffered. Headaches. Period pains. Hormonal stuff. She'd been coming up with every kind of excuse to avoid getting intimate with me.

She needed to get a job. Before she married me she'd worked in advertising. But the agencies and the newspaper ad departments were not recruiting. Her frustration was all the more acute because I'd persuaded her to turn down a job offer from an agency in London on the grounds that the commute from our home in Southampton was a killer and it wouldn't be fair on Laura. Now, of course, I wished I'd kept my mouth shut.

The argument that afternoon was mild compared with some we'd had. Raised voices rather than screams and angry rants. But it put a dampener on the day and filled the house with tension.

Luckily, Laura hadn't been around to hear her parents having a go at each other. She'd been out with her grandmother on one of their frequent Saturday excursions into town. By the time they got back Maggie and I were talking again. I'd agreed to think about going away for Christmas, but not on a costly cruise. Maybe a bargain break at a country hotel in Devon or Cornwall. I'd promised to look into it.

After Laura went to bed we settled into our usual Saturday night routine. Light dinner. Bottle of wine. Feet up in front of the television ready for the national lottery draw. The house was calm once again, the friction replaced by feelings of warmth and security. It was how it was meant to be. Cosy, safe, content. The serene face of family life.

⋆ ⋆ ⋆

It was a triple rollover week on the lottery, with an estimated jackpot of £18 million — the biggest prize for several years. Like everyone else I was hoping that this time, despite those incredible odds, our numbers would come up.

'I have a feeling that our luck is about to change, Danny,' Maggie said.

I smiled at the glow of anticipation in her wide green eyes.

'Eighteen million pounds,' I said. 'It'd solve a lot of our problems at a stroke.'

'And we could have that Caribbean cruise after all.'

'Too right we could.'

Maggie laughed and her face lit up. It lifted my spirits to see her looking so relaxed for a change.

She was wearing a black T-shirt and jeans, my favourite combination. They showed off her ample bosom, flat stomach and long, slender legs. She always looked much younger than her thirty-eight years, thanks largely to regular visits to the gym and a strict low-carb diet. Her skin had a brilliant lustre to it and her eyes were the colour of new spring leaves.

We were just a couple of months shy of our eighth wedding anniversary, having met just over nine years ago when she came to work in the advertising department of the *Southampton Evening Post*. Vince and I both fancied the pants off her. But I was the one who asked her out, much to his disappointment.

The courtship was quick and passionate. Cosy dinners, weekend breaks, unbelievable sex. After six months she moved out of her rented flat in Basingstoke and into my two-bedroom house in Southampton. We were married a year later and honeymooned on the glorious island of Santorini. Two years on Laura was born.

I was now keen to have another child, but Maggie said she wasn't ready and that was another issue we sometimes argued about.

'Here we go,' she said. 'Have you got the ticket?'

I held it up. 'Of course.'

On TV the familiar countdown began and the little numbered balls started jumping up and down in that strange perspex contraption. I sat with pencil poised as the lottery numbers were called out.

Five.

I wondered just how many people were

watching the draw with us. Millions, most likely. Many had probably already worked out how they were going to spend the money if they won.

Thirty-one.

I could imagine what people were wishing for. A top-of-the-range car. A new house for mum and dad. A wardrobe of designer clothes from those ludicrously expensive shops in London's Bond Street. A luxury holiday on some exotic island.

Twenty-two.

Some would be hoping to clear their debts. Others would be telling themselves that they would give most of it away to charity.

Nineteen.

And there'd be those who'd be insisting that even £18 million wouldn't change their lives. They'd still aim to get up at the crack of dawn to go to work and act like being rich was no big thing.

Forty-three.

Others would be telling themselves that the odds on their winning were so astronomical that they wished they hadn't wasted the money on the ticket.

Seven.

By now most would realize that their dreams had been shattered, at least until the midweek draw on Wednesday.

The bonus ball was *thirty-nine.*

Cue disappointment.

As always it was over in a flash. A cruel let down. Hopes dashed. I couldn't help feeling like I'd been duped.

I showed the ticket to Maggie, who sat there clutching her glass of wine with a long face.

'Look at that. Five lines and only one of the numbers came up.'

She heaved a sigh. 'So it's not our lucky night after all.'

We hadn't really expected to win, of course, but we'd made ourselves believe that we might. It was all part of the lottery thrill. The great hype.

I leaned over and kissed Maggie on the cheek.

'Don't worry, honey. There's always next time.'

I was doing that a lot lately. Trying to reassure her about the future because I didn't want her to become even more distant and resentful. She gave a smile that dimpled her cheeks. Her teeth were white as mints.

'Of course there is,' she said.

I smiled back. Her eyes were like marbles, clear and round and perfect. But there was also the dull glimmer of disappointment.

And then the phone rang.

'It's probably Mum,' she said. 'Checking to see if we've made up.'

Maggie's mother was a widow who lived alone in Fareham, a few miles east of Southampton. She doted on Laura and fretted if she thought that perfect harmony did not prevail in the Cain household.

Maggie crossed the room to answer the phone. She lifted the receiver and said hello. I watched her smile, then frown. She suddenly drew breath, her eyes flicking towards me.

Then she held out the receiver.

'It's Vince, for you. He says he's won the lottery and he's going to make us rich.'

2

'Is this a wind-up?' I said into the phone.

'No way,' Vince replied. 'It's the truth, honest.'

'Let me get this straight,' I said. 'You're telling me you've got all six numbers on the lottery?'

'Exactly. I've checked and double checked and it's the big one.'

'I don't believe you.'

'I'm not kidding, Danny. I've hit the jackpot. And since you're my best friend and business partner I'm going to make you a millionaire.'

'Are you drunk?'

'Don't be daft. I'm as sober as a judge.'

'Well you sound drunk.'

'That's because I've just won eighteen million quid.'

I still wasn't sure how to react. Could it possibly be true? Had Vince won the grand prize? Or was he having fun at my expense?

'This had better not be a joke,' I warned him.

'I swear on my mother's life it's true. I wouldn't joke about something like this.'

'Your mother is dead, Vince. And so is your father.'

'On *your* life then,' he said. 'You know I wouldn't say that if it wasn't true. So get your arse over here pronto and see for yourself. I'm cracking open the champagne.'

'Are you at home?'

'Of course I'm bloody well at home. Where do you think I'm calling from?'

I hesitated. Vince lived in the New Forest and it was too far to go on a Saturday night for no good reason.

'You won't be wasting your time, Danny,' he said. 'You're like a brother to me and I want to share this moment with you.'

I took a long breath and made up my mind.

'OK, I'll be there in about an hour. But I'll kill you if this is a stitch-up.'

He was chuckling to himself as I hung up the phone and turned to Maggie.

Despite the doubts that raged through me I couldn't suppress the excitement that began plucking at my nerve endings. I actually found it hard to swallow.

'He's adamant,' I said. 'He says his six numbers match.'

We stared at each other. Maggie was breathing heavily through parted lips. Her arms hung stiffly at her sides and her fists were clenched. She was struggling to control herself.

'I'd better go over,' I said.

'Do you want me to come?'

'No. You stay here with Laura. As soon as I know the truth I'll call you. But look, don't hold your breath. Vince could be having a laugh at our expense.'

'But what if he's not kidding? What if he's won eighteen million pounds?'

At last I managed to swallow. It was like a huge lump forcing its way into my throat.

'Even if he has got all the numbers he might not be the only one,' I pointed out. 'There could be dozens of people with the same numbers.'

'But what if there aren't? What if he's won the lot?'

I knew what she meant. A windfall would make a big difference right now, what with my business so crap and money so tight.

At that moment a sound came from upstairs. Laura was calling out. She had obviously woken up and couldn't get back to sleep.

'You get ready,' Maggie said. 'I'll go and see to Laura.'

We both went upstairs. I was wearing an old, stained T-shirt so I put on a clean one and brushed my hair. Pausing briefly in front of the mirror, I noted that I needed a haircut. My light brown hair was sticking out round the ears. I'd also put on weight. Only a few pounds, but enough to convince me that I needed to exercise more and eat fewer takeaways.

Would that be easy to do if I was suddenly a millionaire?

I went into Laura's room with its array of cuddly toys and cartoon-character posters. The carpet was shaggy beige and the walls were of muted lemon. Maggie was sitting on the edge of the bed, stroking Laura's forehead. Laura was lying beneath the duvet, her face bathed in the soft pink glow from the Pooh Bear lamp.

'Is she OK?' I asked.

'She's fine. Woke from a bad dream. Then Max upset her.'

Laura's eyes were barely open but when she saw me she managed a weak smile. As always it made me feel good. I smiled back and pinched her small nose which was slightly upturned and sprinkled with freckles.

'Where is Max, sweetheart?' I asked.

'He's sitting on the chair,' she said sleepily. 'He wants to play but I'm too tired. I just want to go back to sleep.'

'Well I'm sure that if you close your eyes and ignore him he'll go back into the cupboard like he always does.'

'But what if he doesn't?'

'Then you tell him he has to. You're the boss, don't forget.'

Max was Laura's imaginary friend. He'd appeared about a year ago and she'd named him after our pet cat that died about the same time. Maggie was less concerned than I was over the strange, invisible companion who had moved into our house. A child psychiatrist told us it was pretty common and not to worry. She'll grow out of it, he said. Just give her time.

But I'd never been comfortable with Max. I didn't like laying an extra place for him at the table or listening to Laura talk to him like he really existed. To me it was all pretty creepy. Still, Laura seemed happy enough so I played along in the hope that she would soon grow out of this phase in her life.

Maggie leaned over and gave Laura a loud, wet kiss on the cheek. 'Just think what it will mean for this one, Danny. If Vince is going to share his winnings with you then she'll never have to worry about money or getting on the ruddy housing ladder. She'll be set up for life.'

It was a comforting thought, but one I was still reluctant to entertain. I needed rock-solid confirmation before I would allow myself to get too carried away.

'Don't call anyone,' I said. 'Not yet anyway. Let's just wait and see.'

Maggie nodded. She knew what I meant. The temptation to spread the news would be unbearable during the next fifty minutes, which was about how long it would take me to get to Vince's place in the forest.

'Don't forget to call me as soon as you've seen the ticket,' she said.

'Of course I will, but don't be too disappointed if I have to tell you that we're not going to be rich after all.'

'I won't. I promise.'

I gave them both a hug and slipped out of the room.

3

Vince Mayo was indeed my best friend and partner. We'd known each other for fourteen years. He was a thirty-nine-year-old confirmed bachelor who had quite a serious addiction to gambling. He'd had a string of girlfriends, the latest the attractive daughter of a high-ranking police officer in Southampton, and he'd lost a small fortune in betting shops and casinos.

We first met when I joined the *Post* as a reporter. He'd already been there two years, having moved from a local rag in Portsmouth where he allegedly got the married news editor pregnant. We got on well and from the start a rapport developed between us.

Despite his laid-back attitude to life he was a fine writer and a diligent, hard-nosed journalist. But he lacked ambition and never felt inclined, unlike me, to make his name on a national newspaper.

Even when I left to spend five years on the *Daily Mail* we stayed in touch. When I was made redundant he was there to console me. And he was on hand when my failure to get another job took me to the verge of depression.

20

That was when we decided to pool our talents. He was ready for a change and took voluntary redundancy from the *Post*. I had nothing else to do so it seemed like a good idea to launch the Southern News Agency. It was hard work from the start, but fun. Rewarding in the sense that we were working for ourselves and chose what stories to cover and what features to write.

We had an office. Two rooms and a toilet. Prime location in Portswood High Street, about ten minutes from Southampton city centre. We also had a secretary. Her name was Marsha Rowe and she was loyal and efficient and talked endlessly about her husband, who had a drink problem.

But the money just wasn't coming in. Selling stories was much harder to achieve than we had imagined it would be. Which was why I was still driving my five year old 3-series BMW. It was smooth and reliable, but in the past I'd always traded in my cars after three years.

As usual it started first time, though. The tyres rolled over the asphalt driveway and out on to the road.

Home is in a fairly upmarket area of Southampton known as Bassett. Quiet streets, neatly cut lawns, posh detached houses, many with two-car garages and ornate conservatories. It's a ten-minute drive from the city centre and the route takes me past the house I grew up in.

The old place has changed quite a bit since my parents sold it ten years ago so that they could emigrate to Australia. The new owners — a couple of retired doctors — had built an extension on the side and replaced the raggedy hedge at the front with a wrought-iron fence. They'd also put an enormous skylight in the sloping roof.

But the place still evoked fond memories. It was where my father encouraged me to live his dream, the one he had never been able to realize.

Josh Cain had been a successful business-man who always said he chose the wrong profession. His passion was for writing, but after leaving school he had a choice — to join the local newspaper as a trainee reporter on eleven pounds a week or go to work in his uncle's building company and earn three times that.

He opted for the money, and it was a decision he'd always regretted even though he had a long and successful career as a property developer.

'I should have followed my heart instead of my head,' he told me one time. 'I may have earned good money but I was always bored and frustrated.'

He would write endless letters to newspapers just to see his name in print. And he'd write short stories that never got published. He even tried his hand at a novel but didn't actually finish it because he never had the time.

Thanks to my father I gained an appreciation of books and newspapers at an early age. He helped me with my English homework and told me that if I wanted a job that involved excitement, and where no two days were the same, then I should become a journalist.

And so I did. And he was right. I never got bored. I'd travelled the world, reporting on just about everything. I'd covered murder trials and celebrity weddings. I'd investigated corporate corruption and benefits fraud. I'd interviewed ministers of state and members of the royal family. I'd swum with sharks, albeit in a cage, and I'd travelled in Hugh Hefner's private jet.

I'd seen and done more than most people and I had my father to thank for it. That was one of the reasons I missed him so much. We stayed in touch, of course. My mother called once a week and they came to stay with us every other year. We'd been to see them just the once and that was two years ago, when Laura was four.

They live in an apartment complex with a community pool and a view of the famous Sydney harbour. I fell in love with the place the moment I saw it and after I lost my job I tried to persuade Maggie that we should up sticks and move there too. But she wasn't keen. She wouldn't be able to stand the constant heat, she said, or the thought of leaving her mother.

I was hugely disappointed because at the time I was struggling to come to terms with an uncertain future and I was convinced that we'd have a better life down under.

★ ★ ★

As I drove towards the forest my mind switched back to the present and it was difficult to ignore the images that flashed inside my head: a luxury villa by the Med, a brand new car, a world cruise. They could all soon be within our grasp if we were about to get a slice of a mammoth lottery win.

I took a deep breath and told myself to stop jumping the gun. This would probably turn out to be a shattering anticlimax. Instead, I concentrated on the road ahead and the city that surrounded me.

Southampton lies on the south coast between Portsmouth and Bournemouth. It's a short ferry ride across the Solent to the Isle of Wight. The New Forest national park is just west of the city, a great sprawl of ancient woods and open moors, where hundreds of wild ponies graze and attract the tourists.

As it was a Saturday night the city streets were loud and busy. Soon they would be crawling with young people when the pubs turned out and the trouble started. I drove down past the docks and out across the Millbrook flyover towards the forest.

The lights and traffic soon petered out. I cracked open the side window, breathed in the cool breeze that carried the scent of rich soil and pine.

The forest got darker the deeper into it I drove. I skirted the town of Lyndhurst and headed towards the village of Burley. I stayed within the forty mph speed limit because at night you can't see the ubiquitous New Forest ponies until you're almost on top of them. They have right of way and I'm sure they know it. Cars and headlights no longer intimidate them. They move at their own steady pace, which is only slightly faster than a tortoise.

I've always liked the feel of the forest. Day or night you can't help but be touched by its sense of history. It's been an ancient hunting ground for kings of England since just after the Norman conquest and as a boy I'd often come here with my father. We'd walk the vast expanses of heathlands and explore the small villages and towns which to this day bask in legends of witches and smugglers.

The road crossed over a small river where in the summer we took Laura for picnics and paddled in the cold, shallow water. I passed a couple of pubs and a winery, then came to the familiar ruins of an old Norman church. I noticed a car on the grass verge in front of it. I thought I glimpsed someone behind the wheel, but before I could be sure I was turning into the narrow, unlit lane opposite.

It was more a track really, the surface rough and pitted, a mixture of mud, rocks and shingle. On the left a row of tall conifers. On the right two detached cottages, one of which belonged to Vince.

His cottage was at the end of the lane, set back and pretty secluded. I pulled to a stop on the short, paved driveway and killed the engine. His silver Range Rover was parked outside the garage but his house was in darkness. Not a single light burned beyond any of the windows. And that struck me as odd.

It was a small picture-postcard cottage with a thatched roof and whitewashed walls. Even though it was a hundred years old it had been well maintained and Vince adored it. He'd carried out a great deal of renovation inside and in so doing had increased its value by many thousands of pounds.

I switched off the engine and climbed out. The moon looked swollen, fit to burst, and the stars were a blazing trail across the sky. A gentle wind nudged the branches of a nearby tree.

I waited for my eyes to adjust, then walked up to the front door. I expected it to open the moment I stepped on the mat, but it didn't. There was no sound from inside either.

I rang the bell, which was horribly loud, but there was no answer.

I took out my mobile, keyed in Vince's number. A second later I heard the phone ringing inside the house. I waited for him to answer it, but the phone continued to ring until I ended the call.

'What the hell is he playing at?'

I had a spare key to the cottage on my chain because I'd been asked a couple of times to check the place over when Vince was away. I used it now to open the door.

I stepped into the hall, which was really a small vestibule. The house was overheated and I could hear water gurgling through the pipes.

I switched on the light, blinking against the

sudden brightness. The living-room door was directly in front of me, the stairs next to it, the kitchen door to my left.

'Vince, where are you?' I shouted. 'It's me. Stop messing about.'

I stood stock still for several seconds, but the house was as silent as a vault.

I opened the kitchen door. Walked in. Realized that something was out of place even before I flooded the room with light. There was a dark shape on the floor in the middle of the room.

The shape turned out to be Vince. He was lying on his back in a pool of his own blood.

*   *   *

Maggie Cain paced up and down the length of the living room, barely able to contain her excitement. Could it be true? she wondered. Had Vince really won the big prize on the lottery? And if so how much would he give them?

The thought of it made her blood tingle. A rollover sum of eighteen million pounds would give Vince plenty of scope to be generous. He'd told Danny he would make them rich. So what did that mean? A million? Two million? Maybe more!

She found it hard to grasp what was

happening and she prayed that Vince wasn't having a lark. He wasn't averse to playing practical jokes, especially when he'd had too much to drink. But surely this would be a step too far even for him.

Danny should be at the cottage by now. So he'd be calling her any second. She tried to prepare herself for bad news. Told herself there was no way all their financial problems were suddenly going to be solved. Life simply wasn't like that. They had got into a rut and they would not be wrenched out of it by a stroke of incredible luck.

Or would they? It was about time some good fortune came their way. Things had been difficult. Their marriage was under pressure like never before. Maybe a windfall was the answer to all their problems.

Suddenly the phone rang. Their landline. She answered it as quickly as she could, her hand shaking and her heart thumping.

'Is Mr Cain there?' a man's voice said.

She was taken by surprise. Had assumed it would be Danny. Her disappointment was almost palpable.

'No, he's just gone out,' she said. 'This is Mrs Cain. Who is speaking?'

The line went dead and she was left staring at the phone. Who the hell was that? And why had he hung up? She didn't dwell on it for long, though, because Danny often received calls from strangers. And besides, she was too excited to let it distract her.

Instead she went into the kitchen and poured herself a glass of water. She felt hot and sweaty. What on earth was keeping Danny? Why hadn't he phoned?

Just then their doorbell rang. Her heart heaved in her chest again. Was it Danny? Had he come back?

She hurried to the door and pulled it open. She was confronted by a tall figure wearing a black ski mask. Before her brain could even register the danger he had stepped over the threshold and was pushing her back along the hallway.

She started to scream but a large, gloved hand was clamped over her face and the man issued a chilling warning into her ear: 'Make a noise and your daughter will be hurt.'

Maggie had never known such fear. It was like ice-cold liquid passing through her veins. With a firm grip on her arm he marched her into the living room.

'If you stay quiet and do as you're told then you'll be OK.'

He took a roll of duct tape from his pocket and tied her wrists. Then he pushed her back on to the sofa and stood above her, his posture threatening. The ski mask covered his mouth so she could only see his eyes. They were so dark she couldn't tell the difference between the irises and the pupils.

The woollen cloth moved as he spoke. 'I know that your husband has gone to Vince Mayo's house. I also know about the winning lottery ticket. I now need you to tell me if anyone else knows about it.'

The ticket! What was going on? How did this man know about the ticket? Who was he?

He raised his voice. 'Answer the question, Mrs Cain. Have you or your husband told anyone else about the ticket?'

Maggie tried to swallow. She felt her throat lock up. The man reached out and grabbed her by the hair, pulling it until she yelled out in pain.

'I warn you I will hurt you and your child if you don't tell me what I want to know.'

She managed to shake her head.

'Danny told me not to tell anyone,' she said. 'So I didn't.'

After a moment's hesitation, he let go of her hair.

'Where is your phone?'

She nodded towards the table. On top of it rested their landline and her mobile. He crossed the room and picked up the mobile.

'What's your husband's number?' he said.

4

For a long time I couldn't move. The floor swayed violently beneath me and Vince's body with it. In fact, the whole room seemed to be moving as though it were no longer anchored to reality.

Eventually I staggered forward and dropped to a squat beside him. I knew Vince was dead, but I yelled his name anyway. His lifeless eyes bulged open and he stared at a point beyond me.

His skin seemed somehow shrunken and his mouth was pulled back in a rictus of death, revealing those familiar yellow tombstone teeth. But the blood that had spilled from two gaping head wounds was cool to the touch. It soaked his hair and pooled inside his left ear.

Tears blurred my vision but I could clearly see the two wounds. One was just behind the top of his left ear. It looked as though the blow had crushed his skull. His hair and his blood filled the chasm. The other wound was above his right eye. That too was wide and deep and had cracked open his forehead. Some of his blood had spattered over the kitchen cupboards and the inside of the door. It was also spreading out across the lino.

I looked away as a rising tide of emotion and revulsion threatened to overwhelm me. Surely this wasn't real. It couldn't be happening.

I looked around the kitchen. Above me the fluorescent strip light stuttered and hummed on the ceiling. Vince's leather briefcase was on the floor next to the breakfast bar. There was a puddle of clear liquid around it. At first I assumed it was water, but then I saw an open bottle of champagne on the smart granite worktop and wondered if that had caused the mess. Next to the champagne something else caught my eye. A wad of cash. The top note was a twenty.

What the hell had been going on here?

The room suddenly started to move again and soon it was spinning around me. I shut my eyes and took deep, shaky breaths.

Vince was dead.

As I struggled to my feet the stark reality of what had happened hit me. My friend and partner was lying at my feet, soaked in blood, his head crushed.

Murdered.

The word slammed into me like a gust of cold wind. No way was this an accident. He hadn't fallen over and hit his head on anything. That was obvious. Someone — some callous monster — had done this to him.

Fear suddenly wrapped itself around my chest like steel bands.

The killer might still be here, I thought. After all, Vince had been alive just over an hour ago when I spoke to him on the phone. Maybe that was why there'd been no lights on in the house. The killer — or killers even — heard me coming and switched them off.

Shit.

If there was more than one I'd had it. I too could soon be lying dead on the floor with my head splattered open like a coconut.

But anger and grief made me blind to the danger. I spun round. Pulled open the cutlery drawer. Rummaged around until I found a large carving knife.

Clutching it in my right hand, I went into the living room. Empty. As always it seemed to be heavy with the scent of lemon, as though it had just been cleaned. Nothing struck me as unusual. Nothing out of place. A newspaper on the coffee table. A mug half-filled with tea or coffee on the floor next to the sofa. A TV remote control on the armchair. Books neatly packed on shelves.

I stepped back out of the room and mounted the narrow staircase slowly, pangs of fear rippling through my muscles. At the top was a small landing with three doors leading off it.

I switched on the light, moved cautiously towards Vince's study. On reaching the door I pushed at it gently with trembling fingers. Then I swallowed the fear that was climbing out of me and reached in to switch on the light.

This room too was empty. The desk was cluttered with notebooks and more newspapers. The PC screen was glowing with a Windows desktop.

My eyes moved to a framed photograph on the wall. It had been taken last summer. The occasion was a barbecue in Vince's garden. There was Maggie, Laura and me standing with Vince. Jennifer, his girlfriend, had taken the picture and it showed us all smiling and enjoying the sun.

I stood back, took tentative steps along the landing, hearing nothing but the torrent of blood racing through my ears.

But the other rooms were also empty and it didn't look as though they had been ransacked.

I dashed back downstairs and into the kitchen. I was shocked and stunned all over again by the sight of Vince lying on the floor.

I went to the sink, dropped the knife into it, splashed water on my face. My head was spinning again and the emotions were rolling inside me. I had to get a grip before calling the police. I needed to be coherent when I told them what had happened.

Suddenly my mobile went off. I plucked it out of the front pocket of my jeans. Maggie's ID flashed at me.

I stalled for a couple of seconds as I tried to summon the courage to tell her what I'd found. My hand shook and my breath was coming in short, sharp gasps.

I swallowed hard, flipped the phone open, said, 'Maggie.'

A brief pause on the line and then a man's voice. 'This isn't Maggie.'

My whole body tensed.

'Who are you?' I said. 'Where's my wife?'

'Your wife and daughter are with me,' he said. 'I'm about to take them out of the house.'

A raw, sick feeling churned the acid in the pit of my stomach.

'What are you talking about?' I managed.

'If you do as you are told then no harm will come to them,' he said. 'If you don't then they'll be killed just like your friend.'

★ ★ ★

A searing lance of pain erupted in my chest. I started to speak but a strangled sound came out.

'Listen carefully,' the man said, his voice husky and neutral. 'I'm only going to say this once.'

'Who the fuck are you?' I yelled. 'What's going on?'

'Calm down, Cain. It won't help anyone if you lose your head now. You need to stay strong and focused for the sake of your family. Do you understand?'

No, I didn't understand. How could I? My best friend had been murdered and my wife and daughter were apparently being kid-napped. It made no sense at all. It was crazy. Ridiculous. Stupid. Totally fucking unreal.

'I said do you understand?'

Who was this guy? How did he know my name and where I lived? What was he planning to do to my family?

'If you harm my wife and daughter so help me I'll — '

'You'll what, Cain? Come after me. I don't see how that would be possible since you have no idea who I am. So don't bother to make idle threats. It'll just sap your strength and that won't help you in the days ahead.'

I fought the urge to scream into the phone. I closed my eyes and said, 'I want to speak to my wife.'

'Later,' he said. 'Right now I want you to confirm that you understand what I just told you — of the need to stay strong and do as you're told.'

I sucked in air and felt bile burn my throat. Blood pounded through me at a rate of knots.

'All right,' I said. 'I understand. Just don't hurt them. Please.'

'That's good. Very sensible. You obviously love your wife and daughter a great deal.'

'Of course I do. They mean everything to me.'

'I realize that. It's why I'm convinced you'll co-operate.'

'So what do you want me to do?'

He left it a beat and said, 'I want you to keep your mouth shut about your partner's ticket.'

'His what?'

'The lottery ticket, Cain. I know he told you about it. But you must not tell anyone else. Certainly not the police. If anyone finds out you'll never see your wife and kid again.'

The lottery ticket. I'd forgotten all about it. It was the reason I'd come rushing over to Vince's place and naturally it had vanished from my thoughts the moment I stepped into the kitchen.

'Is that what this is about?' I said incredulously. 'Is that why you killed Vince? Because of the ticket?'

'There's no time to explain,' he said.

'But I don't have the ticket.'

38

'I know that. I have it.'

'So how the hell did you know about it? He only just called me.'

'That's not important right now. What's important is that you follow my instructions.'

'Look, I don't care about the money,' I said. 'I only care about my family.'

'That's what I'm counting on, Cain. And later you'll be reunited with them. In the meantime you have to ensure that the police don't find out what has happened to your partner. They can't be involved.'

'So why can't I meet you now? I can drive straight home.'

'Two reasons,' he said. 'First there's a risk that you'll panic and call the law. And second I've already got my hands full with your wife and daughter. Once they're in a safe place I can sort you out.'

'But it's insane.'

'Just leave the cottage, come back here to your house, and wait for my call. You're being watched so don't try to be clever. And if you talk to the police I'll know within minutes from a contact on the inside.'

'But what you're asking me to do is not possible.'

'I'm not expecting you to bury him, for fuck's sake. Just leave him there. Nobody has to know.'

'Then let me speak to Maggie. I need to know that she's all right.'

'Later,' he said. 'But only if you keep your trap shut.'

'You'll never get away with this. It's monstrous.'

'Just do what I've told you, Cain. If you don't, they die.'

And with that he cleared the line.

5

Nausea rolled in my throat. My head swam. My lungs burned. My mind struggled to hold on to reality.

I dashed out of the cottage, pushing the door to behind me. I fumbled with the key in the ignition, got it started, stamped on the accelerator.

I raced along the lane and skidded to a stop opposite the church. I noticed that the car that had been parked on the verge when I arrived was now gone. So I probably had seen someone behind the wheel. Who could it have been? And why had they been parked there with the lights off at such a late hour?

As I pulled out on to the road I tried to recall what type of car it had been, but I couldn't conjure up an image because I hadn't paid attention to it. Now I wished I had because the driver might well have been the person who killed Vince.

This chilling thought stayed with me as I drove like a man possessed. The tyres screeched around every corner. More than once I came close to sliding off the road. I kept seeing Vince's blood-soaked body on the kitchen floor, the gashes in his head. The image was burned on to the back of my retinas.

And I kept imagining Maggie and Laura, scared witless and wondering why the hell I wasn't there to save them. What exactly was happening and why? Who was the man on the phone? How did he know about the lottery ticket? How did he know about Maggie and me and Laura?

And what about the car parked outside the church? Was it just a coincidence? Had the driver simply stopped to take a pee or have a nap? Or was the explanation far more sinister?

I sped past traffic and drew angry stares from other drivers. The streets were busier now. More cars. More Saturday-night drunks stepping off the kerbs. Slurred shouting and cold laughter. Queues at the burger stalls. Not a good night to be in a hurry.

But thankfully I made it all the way home without encountering a cop, although I did jump three red lights and mount the pavement twice.

I leapt out of the car and let myself in.

'Maggie. Laura.'

I stood in the hall waiting for them to respond. They didn't.

Feeling sick with dread, I burst into the

living room. The TV was still on and our wine glasses were still on the table. No Maggie. No Laura.

Upstairs the bedrooms were empty. Laura's duvet was piled on the floor beside her bed. Next to that her lime-green nightdress.

Back downstairs I stood in the living room, half crushed under the weight of terror. My mouth was dry and my heart was racing.

I had this desperate urge to call the police. They could be here in minutes and begin a frantic search for my family. Patrols all over the county would be alerted and maybe road blocks set up.

But I knew I had to resist. I couldn't take the chance. Whoever had killed Vince and taken Maggie and Laura hostage was ruthless in the extreme. I had to assume that he — or they — would carry out the threat to commit more murders.

I felt helpless and alone. My life had been shattered. The evil and violence in the world that I had written about for years had suddenly consumed me. This time I wasn't a detached observer — I was a victim.

I lost it then and started to cry. I was completely overwhelmed by fear, remorse and even guilt. I should have been here for Maggie and Laura when that monster came to call. I could only imagine the terror that my little girl must have experienced.

The sobbing eventually subsided, by which time my chest hurt and my head throbbed. I knew I couldn't afford to lose control. I had to stay calm and alert for their sakes.

I poured a large whisky, slumped on the sofa. Laura smiled at me from a framed photo above the television. It had been taken on her last birthday. Her sixth. We went to the zoo and she rode on a camel. She talked about it for weeks afterwards and I often heard her telling Max what a great day it had been.

Time passed slowly. I sat there checking my watch every couple of minutes. As midnight approached I felt panic well up inside me. When would the kidnapper call again? What was happening to my family? Had I turned off all the lights in the cottage? For the life of me I couldn't remember. I also couldn't remember locking the front door.

The whisky burned its way down my throat, but it didn't make me feel any better. There was nothing I could do to help my family. They were at the mercy of a man who had already demonstrated how ruthless he was.

I paced the room, in desperate need of a distraction. I flicked through the television. Sky News. A story about a near miss involving two passenger planes over the English Channel. I was only half-aware of what was being said when the newscaster mentioned the lottery draw. Suddenly the television had my full attention.

'And finally we can confirm that there's just one winning ticket for tonight's eighteen million pound triple rollover lottery jackpot. It was purchased in the south of England by an extremely lucky punter who hasn't yet come forward to claim the prize.'

A huge ball of fear formed in my solar plexus and I suddenly found it hard to breathe.

6

A grey Mercedes with tinted windows eased its way up the driveway of a house four miles outside Southampton. It was approaching midnight and the moon threw a cold, hard light on to the ground. That same light created myriad shadows out of the edges of the woods that bordered three sides of the property.

The driver cut the engine and switched off the lights. He sat for a short while staring at the house through the windscreen. It was supposed to be empty, but he wanted to be sure that it was before he went any further.

The house was a two-storey affair that had been erected in the fifties. Grey and characterless. A high chimney. A flat-roofed garage that had been attached as though as an afterthought. The place was in need of a makeover.

He had never set foot inside it before, but it was the only place he could think of using at such short notice. It was by no means completely safe, but he was in no position to be choosy. There was no time to think things through. He had to go with his instincts and trust that his spur-of-the moment decisions were the right ones.

Outwardly he might have looked calm but his insides were coiled up like a spring. But that was to be expected. After all, what had happened tonight had changed his life forever. He could never return to what he'd had. Vince Mayo's death had jerked him out of his comfort zone and flung him into the eye of a storm.

Now it was up to him to hold his nerve and see this thing through. He could not bring himself to consider the alternative.

There were no lights on inside the house. No other cars in sight. The man got out of the car and walked up to the front door. He rang the bell. Slammed the heavy brass knocker. Waited a couple of minutes before exhaling a long sigh of relief. The house was unoccupied. Just as he knew it would be. The owners were still on the other side of the world, blissfully unaware that their home was about to be violated.

He stood back and studied the front door. Dark wood with frosted-glass panels. He raised his right foot and kicked out with his walking boot, smashing one of the panels. There was no burglar alarm. That was lucky, although not a surprise. People would never learn. He reached in and fiddled with the lock but couldn't get the door open. There was a window to his right, but too high to aim a kick at. He looked around. In a nearby flower bed he spotted several stone animals. A duck, a badger, a hedgehog. He picked up the duck and used it to smash the window. He reached in through the broken glass, found the handle and opened the frame. He hauled himself up with ease and climbed through it.

Then he was inside, exploring the house, safe in the knowledge that he was alone. He barely knew Peter and Anne Salmon, but it was the sort of house he would have imagined they lived in. Boring. Uninspiring. Totally lacking in imagination.

The cherrywood furniture was old and for the most part ugly. The colours were overbearing. The place felt closed-in and claustrophobic.

He checked all the rooms. On the upstairs landing he saw a wooden pole that was used to open the loft hatch. It gave him an idea. He picked it up and lowered the ladder, then stepped gingerly up it. There was a light switch attached to a joist inside the loft. He flicked it on and a single bulb suspended from a cord came to life.

Perfect, he thought.

The loft ran the length of the house. Grim

and dusty. Shadows jostling for attention. A floor of chipboard sections had been laid over parts of it. About fifteen feet above the floor the angled rafters met to form an apex. The space felt damp and airless but it would suit his purpose.

He hurried back downstairs, searched the kitchen until he found a bunch of keys, including one for the front door. Then he went looking for some rope. But in the garage he came across something better.

Chains.

There were five of them, each one about six feet in length. Peter Salmon probably used them during bad winters to give his tyres more grip. He rolled up the chains and stuffed them into the rucksack.

Next he found some blankets in a bedroom drawer and took them up to the loft. Then he went back out to the car. The ski mask that he often wore on his long winter walks was lying on the front passenger seat. He slipped it over his head again. It felt tight against his skin.

Then he leaned against the car door and flared up a cigarette to steady his nerves. He blew out a long kiss of smoke that was taken away on a gentle breeze. His hands were shaking and his heart was pounding. He knew it was going to be a long and dangerous *night. He would have to be careful but at the same time ruthlessly determined.*

He dropped the cigarette butt and ground it into the gravel with a sharp twist of his ankle.

It was time to get the woman and child.

7

Detective Chief Inspector Jeff Temple was not a happy man. It was gone midnight and he was knackered. As he stared down at the corpse on the kitchen floor he just knew that he wouldn't be getting to bed any time soon.

It had been a long day. As usual the chronic shortage of CID officers in Southampton meant that the weekend shift was a struggle. There'd been an off-licence robbery, a mugging and three acts of mindless vandalism.

Temple had managed to get home just after ten and had been about to crawl into bed just as the phone rang. He knew instinctively who it would be because no one else ever called him at home except his daughter and it was the last thing she would think of doing on a Saturday night.

When his wife had been alive she would urge him not to answer the late-evening calls and tell him to let them find someone else. But work was all he had now. It kept him going and staved off the loneliness. So without hesitation he'd picked up the receiver.

'There's been a murder,' he was told by the controller. 'In the forest. Can you go?'

So here he was, standing in the kitchen of a secluded cottage wearing white paper overalls so as not to contaminate the crime scene.

Detective Sergeant Angelica Metcalfe — or Angel as she was known to her colleagues — had arrived at the scene before him. She was the latest addition to the team, having moved down south from the Met four months ago. According to gossip it was because of a break-up with her boyfriend and a desire to start a new life away from the Smoke.

She had short brown hair and brown eyes. Attractive but not pretty. Tonight, as ever, she was dressed like a smart business-woman. Grey trouser suit, white blouse of some silky loose material, navy-blue raincoat. This was only the second time that she and Temple had attended the same crime scene, but he was looking forward to working with her because she was smart and savvy and nice to look at.

'I gather you knew the victim, guv,' she said.

Temple nodded. He'd been given the name on the way over. The first thing he did was try to contact his boss, Superintendent Lloyd Priest. But Priest didn't answer his phone — probably because he was tucked up in bed

— so he'd left a voice message.

'Vince Mayo,' Temple said. 'A local freelance reporter. He runs — or rather he ran — a news agency with his partner.'

'Is there something I should know about him, guv?' Angel said. 'Only I just overheard one of the uniforms describe him as a little shit who got what he deserved at last.'

Temple was concentrating on Mayo's face. The bulbous eyes, exposed teeth, streaks of blood across his forehead.

He looked up and said, 'I'll tell you in a bit. What have you gleaned?'

Angel gave him a puzzled look before consulting her notes.

'Mr Mayo has lived here alone for the past five years according to his only neighbour. I've had a quick look round and there's no sign of a break-in and all his belongings appear to be in order. The neighbour did see a car leave here earlier that might have belonged to the killer. But don't get excited. He didn't manage to get the registration or even the make.'

'Any sign of a weapon?'

'Not as yet.'

Temple peered more closely at the body. The pathologist, Frank Matherson, was already kneeling on the floor beside it.

'What have we got, Frank?' Temple asked.

Matheson threw a glance over his shoulder. He had short, pewter-grey hair and grey eyes, with deep wrinkles radiating out from them.

'Two blows to the head,' he said. 'Front and back. No question it was deliberate. Victim is somewhere in his late thirties, I'd say.'

'Is it too soon to give me a time of death?'

'Well, rigor has only just started to set in so this didn't happen very long ago. Few hours at most. Say between eight and ten. We're lucky the body was discovered so soon.'

'And the weapon?'

Matherson thought about it. 'A heavy blunt instrument of some kind. Those wounds are deep but also pretty smooth. The impact areas are wide, too.'

'What about defensive wounds?'

'There don't seem to be any. Doesn't look to me like this bloke struggled. Maybe he was taken by surprise.'

There were smudged footprints in the pool of blood that had spread across the lino. Temple drew Angel's attention to them.

'The neighbour who found the body swears he didn't get close enough to step in the blood,' she said.

'Any of our lot responsible?'

'No.'

'So it's fair to assume that the killer made a mess.'

'It looks that way. As you saw coming in there's a blood trail on the hallway carpet and up the stairs. There are also traces out on the driveway. It could have been an attempted robbery. Mayo surprised the thieves and they clobbered him. Then they panicked and ran without taking anything. Maybe related to that spate of burglaries in and around Lyndhurst a month ago. If you recall, the thieves targeted houses in remote locations.'

'That's something we need to give thought to,' Temple said.

He looked around the kitchen, spotted a bottle of champagne on the worktop, uncorked.

'What do you make of that?'

'I'm not sure,' Angel said. 'There are no glasses out to go with it. I checked the other rooms and the dishwasher. You can also see where some of it spilled on to the floor and over the briefcase. Mayo's briefcase by the looks of it.'

Temple stepped carefully up to the worktop and examined at close quarters the champagne bottle.

'I wonder what the occasion was,' he said.

'Well, whatever it was it was short-lived,' Angel said.

'Any prints?'

'The bottle's been wiped clean apparently.'

Something else on the worktop caught Temple's eye. A large granite mortar bowl that would have been used with a pestle for grinding and pounding herbs. He had one just like it at home, only smaller.

He looked around the kitchen for the heavy, bat-shaped pestle, but didn't see it.

'There's no pestle,' he said.

'What?' Matherson got up to have a look.

'The pestle is missing,' Temple said. 'You don't often see a mortar without a pestle.'

Matherson nodded. 'You're right about that.'

'Which raises the possibility that the pestle might have been used as the murder weapon.'

Matherson chewed at the corner of his lower lip. 'It's a sound theory. In fact I worked on a case once where a guy used a heavy pestle to smash open his wife's skull. And that there is a hellishly big mortar, so the pestle that goes with it must be sizeable.'

'We'd better look for it then,' Temple said and Angel immediately instructed one of the officers in the hallway to spread the word.

Temple moved into the living room. He noted that the cottage was furnished in a style that was in keeping with its age: an old over-stuffed sofa, a studded leather armchair, an antique table, bookshelf. Temple flicked through the titles. Reference books, diction-aries, a Thesaurus, a large collection of paperback novels, some hardback fiction by the likes of Michael Collins and James Lee Burke.

Upstairs there were two bedrooms, both with double beds. All the usual stuff such as wardrobes and drawers and pleasant pictures on the walls. Most of the pictures were paintings or photographs of the New Forest. Landscapes. Wildlife. Village scenes. But there was one in Mayo's office that caught Temple's eye. It showed Mayo with two other adults and a little girl. They were standing in front of a barbecue with the cottage in the background.

Temple pointed to the other man in the picture. 'That's Mayo's business partner,' he said. 'Danny Cain. I reckon that must be Cain's wife and daughter.'

Temple had met Cain, but not the wife. In fact he knew very little about either Cain or Mayo even though, like almost everyone in CID, he harboured a grudge against them. It was something he would have to keep in check. And so would everyone else who'd be working on this case.

'That's interesting,' Angel said. 'I checked Mayo's landline when I got here and the last call he made was at eight forty-five this evening. It was to a number registered to a Danny Cain.'

Temple arched his brow. 'Is that so?'

They went back downstairs, checked the utility room, then the garden. The air outside had a crisp bite to it. The moon's insipid glow washed over the tear-shaped lawn. There was a wall at the back, and some trelliswork entwined with honeysuckle and some kind of fern. The wall kept the creeping forest at bay.

Back inside, Temple said, 'So who found the body?'

'Guy who lives next door,' Angel said. 'He's outside. I told him you'd want a word.'

Temple took off his forensic suit, asked Angel to look around some more and went outside.

★ ★ ★

Bill Nadelson was about sixty-five with grey hair and a weathered face. He had a sharp chin and prominent, aquiline nose. He was breathing hoarsely though his mouth and wearing a heavy dark coat.

Temple introduced himself.

'Are you feeling all right, Mr Nadelson? You look awfully pale. Perhaps you should see a doctor.'

Nadelson shook his head. 'There's no need for that. It was just a shock to find Vince like that. I think I just need a strong cup of tea.'

'Why don't we chat in your house then?' Temple said. 'I'm sure you'll be more comfortable there and we can both have a cuppa.'

Nadelson lived in a cottage not unlike Mayo's. But inside it was much smaller, with a low beamed ceiling and too much bulky furniture. Temple followed him into the kitchen where Nadelson started talking as he put the kettle on.

'Vince was a great neighbour,' he said. 'We got on well. My wife died two years ago and he was very supportive.'

'So what happened tonight? How did you come to find the body?'

Nadelson took off his coat and sat at the kitchen table, opposite the detective. Temple noted that he was lean and fit looking. Heavy chest. Toned skin.

'I'd been out all day at my son's house in Cadnam,' he said. 'I got back slightly before ten. I'd just unlocked the front door and was stepping into the hall when suddenly a car screeched out of Vince's driveway and tore along the lane with a roar that shocked me.'

'Did you recognize the vehicle?'

'No, it was too dark. But I think it was black or dark blue. And it was a nice-looking car. Shiny too. Maybe an Audi or a BMW.'

'So what then?'

He shrugged. 'Well, it was pretty unusual

and curiosity got the better of me. I stepped into the lane and noticed that Vince's car was in the driveway and the lights were on in the cottage. I decided to pop over and check that everything was all right.'

The kettle boiled and Temple gestured for Nadelson to stay put. He got up to pour the teas. Nadelson had put out two chunky earthenware mugs with tea bags and milk in them.

'When I got to the cottage I rang the bell but there was no answer,' Nadelson said. 'So I called for Vince but he didn't respond. I got a little worried so I tried the front door and discovered it wasn't actually shut properly. I called out and went in. The kitchen is to the left of the hall and the light was on. That's when I saw him.'

Temple put both mugs on the table and sat back down.

'So what did you do?' he asked.

Nadelson cupped his hands around his mug, lifted it to his lips and took a sip of tea. 'I went in to see if he was alive, but it was obvious that he wasn't. I was careful not to tread in the blood. I saw his wounds and realized that he hadn't died of natural causes. I knew better than to touch anything so I immediately ran home and phoned nine nine nine.'

'Did you go upstairs?'

'No I didn't. I just wanted to get out of there. It was horrible.'

'Did you touch anything in the kitchen?'

'No, nothing.'

Temple took him through it again and made notes. Then he said, 'So what can you tell me about Mr Mayo?'

Nadelson described Vince Mayo as a quiet, respectful man whose only vice seemed to be gambling. He enjoyed a flutter on the horses and was a frequent visitor to the casinos in town.

'He's had several girlfriends,' Nadelson said. 'Currently there's a pretty young woman named Jennifer. She sometimes stayed over-night in the cottage. A lovely girl. Always smiling.'

'Was she here today?'

'She was this morning so she must have stayed over on Friday night.'

'How do you know? Did you talk to her?'

'No, but I saw her briefly when I dropped in on Vince this morning. She was coming down the stairs and she was still in her dressing-gown. She said hello but I was in a hurry so I didn't go in.'

'Was that the last time you saw Mr Mayo alive?'

'I'm afraid it was.'

'So why'd you go over to his place?'

'I'd been to the shop in town and bought Vince's lottery tickets for him.'

'Is that something you often did?'

He nodded. 'Every Saturday morning. It became a routine after I offered to do it once. He always had ten lucky dips so it didn't take me long to get an extra ticket for him in addition to my own. He always paid me of course.'

Temple ploughed on with more questions. Did Mayo have many visitors? Had the cottage ever been broken into? Had he spotted any strangers hanging around recently? Did Mayo have any enemies that he knew of? Who were his friends?

Nadelson said he didn't know if Mayo had any enemies, but his closest friend was another journalist named Danny Cain, who was also his business partner in the news agency.

'How often does Cain come here?' Temple asked.

'Very occasionally. I've met him a couple of times. He has a charming wife and a delightful daughter. I last saw them at Vince's barbecue in the summer.'

'Any problems between Mr Mayo and Mr Cain?'

'I wouldn't know, Inspector. I never talked to Vince about his business life.'

Finally, Temple said, 'I'm afraid we'll have to take up some more of your time, Mr Nadelson. We need to take a formal statement.'

'That's not a problem.'

'We also need your fingerprints and I'll have a forensic officer check your clothes and shoes.'

Nadelson's face registered alarm. His hands jerked and some of the tea spilled over the rim of the mug on to the table.

'It's just routine,' Temple assured him. 'For elimination purposes.'

Nadelson put his mug down. His eyes narrowed and his lips pressed tight together.

'Is there something you're not telling me, Mr Nadelson?' Temple asked, puzzled by the man's reaction. 'Something that might be relevant?'

Nadelson made an effort to compose himself. He straightened his back and sucked nervously on the inside of his bottom lip.

After a beat, he said, 'No, I'm finding it all a bit overwhelming, that's all. This is a ghastly experience.'

Temple regarded him for a few seconds and put his reaction down to shock.

'Are you sure that you don't want me to arrange for a doctor to drop by?' he said.

'I'm sure, Inspector. I'll be OK. Really.'

Temple finished his tea, thanked Nadelson and walked back along the lane to Mayo's place. There were no other houses in sight. They were in the heart of the New Forest and therefore it was unlikely that anyone else had seen anything tonight.

He stared up at the cottage, wondering at its history. What dramas had been played out within its thick uneven walls over the years? Was this the first murder? The cottage was the type you see in the tourist brochures aimed at attracting people to the forest. Squat, quaint, picturesque. A cosy retreat from the real world, buried as it was in a corner of this ancient woodland. Not a place where blood should be spilled, Temple thought.

So what had happened here tonight? Who had shattered the tranquillity and destroyed the sense of peace?

He sucked the cold air into his throat and gave a shudder. It was at times like this that he wished he hadn't given up smoking. But six months ago he'd finally heeded the advice of his doctor, who was concerned about the raspy voice he'd developed over the years and the bouts of coughing that were becoming more frequent and troublesome.

Angel emerged from the cottage and came striding over, her knee-length raincoat billowing like a cape.

'We've got something,' she said. 'A shoeprint in the blood on the kitchen floor. Quite distinctive. Almost certainly male and size nine.'

'A careless killer,' Temple said. 'My favourite kind.'

'What about Mr Nadelson?' she asked. 'Is he a suspect?'

'Everyone is at this stage, although I can't in all honesty imagine him killing anyone. Still, he did get flustered when I said we'd need to take his prints. So we should check him out. Get someone to have a longer chat with him and get a statement.'

'Will do,' she said. Then, 'So come on, guv. It's time you filled me in on Vince Mayo. Why did the lads have a problem with him?'

'Vince Mayo was not popular among your colleagues,' Temple said. 'The same goes for his partner, Cain. And that fact alone is going to ensure that this case will attract a lot of unwanted media attention.'

Angel took out a cigarette and lit up, much to Temple's annoyance. Staying off the weed was a struggle at the best of times, but it was sheer torture if smoke was being blown in your face.

'Care to explain, guv?' she said, sensing that he was drifting into his thoughts.

He took a step back and turned away from

her. He looked up at the cottage which was teeming with scene of crime officers. A flash-light exploded. A police radio crackled. Somehow it didn't seem right that this should happen out here in the forest. This was a place that ought to have been immune from the horrors of the outside world.

'Those two set up a news agency a couple of years ago,' he said. 'Before that they worked on the local evening paper, although Cain did spend a few years away from here in London. Anyway, Mayo especially had lots of contacts in the area. He came up with quite a few exclusive stories, a couple of which shed a bad light on the constabulary.

'One of those stories broke about a year ago. It involved a detective inspector named George Banks. A good friend of mine. Worked out of Southampton CID for fifteen years.'

'The name rings a bell,' Angel said. 'I've heard the lads mention him.'

Temple took a deep breath through his nose, enjoying the second-hand smoke that was caressing the back of his throat.

'Mayo and Cain got a tip-off that George had gone bad. They were told that he was recycling seized drugs and selling them to his brother-in-law, who is a bit of a lowlife.'

'Was it true?'

Temple nodded. 'George has a son named Warren. He was diagnosed with a rare form of liver cancer. New drugs that would have helped him were not available on the NHS. So George had to raise the money himself. He found it impossible even though he sold almost everything he owned. As a last resort he helped himself to some of the drugs we confiscated. Like a fool he didn't think anyone would notice.

'Anyway, someone got wind of it and tipped off Mayo and Cain. They went to work on the story. They called George for a quote and he pleaded with them not to sell it. He called me and I went to see them in the hope of talking them out of it. I explained the situation. George only did it once and the amount of drugs was relatively small. I said I would see to it that George was dealt with. But because of the extenuating circumstances I was hoping to keep it low key and avoid a prosecution. I appealed to Cain and Mayo to drop the story.'

'But they didn't,' Angel said.

Temple shook his head. 'They gave me the usual bullshit about it being in the public interest and police corruption was an epidemic that had to be curtailed. Mayo was more aggressive than Cain, who I think might have been persuaded. But in the end it went ahead.'

'And I take it the story destroyed George Banks's career?'

'That's right,' Temple said. 'We were forced to suspend him and he was facing charges. But before it got to court he topped himself.'

'My God.'

'It's why we virtually blacklisted those two reporters. Technically they'd exposed a corrupt police officer and had done nothing wrong. But that's not how his colleagues saw it. There's been a lot of ill-feeling. Still is. Some of the guys have always felt they had a score to settle.'

'What happened to the son?'

'Warren is OK for the moment,' Temple said. 'He's nine now and responding to the new treatment. A fund was set up after George's death. A lot of money was raised and then three months ago the NHS agreed to supply the drug free of charge.'

They both fell silent. Temple tried to remember the last time he had dropped in on George's widow, Beth. Surely he was due to pay another visit.

'Sounds to me like maybe Danny Cain is a good starting point for this investigation,' Angel said. 'What do you think, guv?'

'I think you're right,' Temple said. 'I know where he lives. We'll leave DC Patel in charge here and go right over. But before we do there's something else you ought to know about this case.'

Angel tilted her head to one side and arched her brow.

'It concerns our boss,' Temple said. 'Superintendent Priest.'

8

'I'm scared,' Laura said. 'I want Daddy.'

Maggie Cain pulled her daughter close to her with her free hand. Her little face was red from crying. Her eyes were dull and unfocused.

'Daddy will find us soon, sweetheart. Everything will be all right.' Saliva cracked at the back of Maggie's throat as she spoke.

'But why does that man want to hurt us?' Laura said.

'I don't know, sweetheart, but I swear I won't let him harm you. Trust me on that.'

'Max says the man is going to kill us.'

Maggie was suddenly furious with Max, which of course was absurd since he was a figment of her child's imagination.

'Max doesn't know what he's talking about. I suggest you tell him to be quiet. Or maybe you can get him to tell you a story. Take your mind off what's happening.'

'He didn't bring any of his books. He forgot them when he chased out of the house after us.'

'Then why don't you tell *him* a story? He's probably as scared as you are and that will cheer him up.'

Laura started whispering, which was her way of communicating with her imaginary friend. That's good, Maggie thought. It'll focus her mind on something other than the terrifying reality of their situation.

Maggie chewed her bottom lip and rested her head against the wall behind her. They were sitting on the floor of a freezing loft, or attic, or whatever it was called. One ring of a pair of metal handcuffs was attached to Maggie's left wrist and the other ring to a short length of chain that encircled a wooden stanchion.

The loft was large and gloomy and there were lots of timber supports. Between them spiders had woven dozens of webs. It hadn't been fully converted. There was a makeshift floor of chip-board sections that had been nailed on to the joists, although they didn't cover the whole area. There were gaps where the insulation obscured the top of the ceiling below. Light welled softly from a naked bulb suspended from above. The walls were bare brick and there was a noisy water tank in one corner.

Their own loft at home was filled with junk. Cardboard boxes, spare pillows, old photo albums. But this space was empty.

Maggie closed her eyes and prayed that the nightmare would soon be over and that no harm would come to them. But she was scared. Desperately scared.

If only she hadn't opened the door. But then how was she to know that it would prove to be the biggest mistake she had ever made? She just wasn't thinking. The prospect of sharing in a massive lottery win had unsettled her.

After the man in the balaclava had taken Maggie's phone he called Danny. And as she listened to what he said to her husband it became clear to her that Vince was dead and that this man was a cruel, sadistic killer.

After the call he forced her upstairs to wake Laura. Her daughter was naturally terrified and clung desperately to her mother as she got out of bed. The man allowed them both to dress. Before leaving the house he wrapped a scarf around Maggie's head to cover her eyes. He led them outside and into the boot of a car.

They were in the car for almost an hour. They stopped several times. The third time she heard him get out of the car. Then she heard glass breaking near by. This was followed by a long silence. After another twenty minutes or so they were allowed out of the boot. He didn't make her put the scarf back over her eyes. It was too dark to see much anyway other than a large house partly surrounded by trees. The man was still wearing the ski mask and was also carrying a rucksack on his back.

'That way,' he said. 'Go.'

They walked across a gravel driveway to the front door. Inside, the house felt empty and cold.

The man led them up some stairs to a short, dingy landing. Bare floorboards. Yellowing wallpaper. Muted lighting from an old-fashioned wall lamp.

An aluminium loft ladder had been lowered from the ceiling hatch. He ordered them to climb it, Maggie first.

'There's a light up there,' he said. 'And some blankets.'

'You're going to leave us here?'

'You'll be all right. I won't let you starve to death.'

'What about my husband?'

'He'll be joining you later.'

After securing her to the stanchion, he took a second set of cuffs and a chain from his rucksack and attached them to a joist. He used a key from a bunch to lock the cuffs.

'That's for your husband,' he said. 'I won't bother to restrain your daughter, but I suggest you keep her close to you. It's dangerous to walk around up here.'

Then he left without saying another word,

closing the hatch behind him.

Now Maggie opened her eyes and looked down at Laura's head. She ran her fingers through her curls in the hope that it would provide some comfort to her daughter.

Then she mouthed another silent prayer.

Please don't let him hurt her. Please save us from this madman.

She told herself she had to remain positive. It wasn't easy, though, especially when her mind turned to Vince and she wondered how and why he had been killed.

And what about Danny? He'd be frantic with worry and she feared he might ignore the kidnapper's warning and go to the police. And if he did, what then? Would the man in the mask be true to his word and kill them?

Just then the hatch was raised and the ladder was lowered. Then the man appeared as a dark, hooded figure framed by the light from the hall below.

Maggie wanted to scream but she didn't dare. And besides, she very much doubted that anyone would hear her. Instead, she straightened her back and stuck out her chin. She also tightened her grip on Laura. She wouldn't give in to the bastard without a fight. She'd scratch, gouge, bite and do whatever else it took to protect her daughter.

But her determination to resist did nothing

to diminish the strength of the fear that gripped her body: a fear borne out of the simple truth that they were completely at his mercy.

'Your bastard husband has fucked up,' the man said, his voice jagged, harsh. 'You heard me warn him not to involve the police. I told him what would happen. Well they're now crawling all over Vince Mayo's cottage.'

Maggie's heart leapt into her mouth. She felt a rush of blood cascade through her veins.

'Please don't do anything to us,' she pleaded. 'I beg you.'

She shifted position and put the cuffed arm around Laura. Then clenched her free hand into a fist and held her breath. This is it, she thought. Be ready. Go for the eyes or the throat. At least make sure you hurt this maniac before he can hurt you.

'I need to find out what that idiot has told them,' he said. 'And I want you to remind him what's at stake here. Understand?'

The man stepped towards them and she saw that he was holding a mobile phone. *Her* mobile phone.

9

There was blood on my shoes. I hadn't noticed it before, but I suddenly became aware of the dark stains on the brown leather toes. There were also tiny pools in the crevices of both rubber soles. I'd been trampling Vince's blood all over the place, for God's sake. The thought of it made me cringe.

I took off the shoes and put them in a plastic bag which I stuffed into the cupboard under the sink. Out of sight. Then I started pacing the room again, trying to stop my mind from imploding. Sky News remained on in the background, reminding me every so often that there was only one winner of the eighteen million pounds lottery jackpot.

And unbeknown to the rest of the world that winner had been Vince.

He really did have all six numbers, and to one of the biggest UK lottery prizes in years. But he must have known it for only a matter of minutes — time enough to get excited and then phone me with the news.

Before he was butchered.

Talk about a dramatic reversal of fortune. I couldn't imagine a more cruel twist of fate.

One moment you're the luckiest person on earth with a fabulous life to look forward to. Then the next moment you're dead. How was that possible? How could it be justified in the grand scheme of things?

And who the hell was responsible? The bastard on the phone had killed my friend and kidnapped my family. Yet I had no idea who he was or how he had come to appear on the scene so suddenly. But what I did know was that eighteen million pounds is a strong motive for murder. The kind of mind-boggling figure that can turn a law-abiding person into a cold-blooded killer. And for that reason I had no choice but to take the threat to my family seriously. There was no question but that they were in mortal danger. And for that matter so was I.

I started pouring myself another drink just as my mobile rang. Maggie's name appeared on the illuminated screen, causing my scalp to tighten against my skull.

Hands shaking, I snapped open the cover.

'Maggie — is that you?'

'I thought you cared about your family, Cain.'

It was him. The voice was louder and more threatening than the last time I'd heard it. I felt a dramatic change in the rhythm of my heartbeat.

'I told you not to involve the police,' he said. 'I told you what would happen to your wife and kid if you did.'

'I didn't call them,' I said. 'I swear.'

'Then why are they at your partner's place?'

'They can't be. The cottage was empty when I left it.'

'Well it's not empty now. There's a whole army of filth there.'

'How do you know?'

'I told you I have contacts.'

'But I did exactly what you told me to do. I left the cottage and came home. I've been waiting for you to call. Someone must have gone there after me.'

A pause. His heavy breathing scraped across my eardrum.

'I'm telling the truth,' I said.' Please don't do anything to my family. I didn't contact the police.'

'I'll soon know if you did,' he said. 'I'm going to make a call. If I find you're lying I'm going to slit their throats. You got that?'

I mumbled something that sounded like a yes. There was another long pause.

Then: 'Danny?'

Oh sweet Jesus, it was Maggie. I could barely contain myself.

'Babe, are you OK?'

She cleared her throat and spoke in a hurried, tearful voice. 'For now I am. But look, you mustn't tell anyone about the lottery ticket. Promise me you won't.'

'I promise,' I said. 'Is Laura all right?'

'She's coping, but only just.'

'Is she hurt? Are you hurt?'

'No, but we're scared, Danny. And cold.' She started to sob.

'You have to keep it together, honey. Be strong.'

'I'll try, but he's threatening to kill us and I know that he killed Vince. He says he won't let us go until he has the money. Please don't stop it from happening. Please don't involve the police.'

'I won't,' I said. 'You have to believe that.'

'I do, but I'm not sure if . . . '

He must have snatched the phone away from her because he was suddenly back on the line.

'That's enough,' he said. 'Get this, Cain. I'll soon know the truth about what happened tonight. If you've lied so help me they die.'

'I haven't lied. I really don't know why the police are at the cottage.'

'Well they are, and they'll soon drop in on you.'

'But they don't know that I was there tonight.'

'It won't take them long to find out and I don't want you talking to them.'

'So what should I do?'

'Leave your house now, like this minute,' he said. 'Go somewhere out of harm's way. And don't answer the phone unless it's me calling on your wife's mobile. I'll be in touch soon.'

'How soon?'

'I don't know. A few hours. Or maybe never if it turns out you're fucking with me.'

There was a click as he severed the connection. I listened to the silence for a moment before hanging up.

★ ★ ★

Hearing Maggie's voice gave me hope. She was still alive and appeared to be unharmed. But her situation was even more perilous now because the police were apparently involved. How had that happened? Who had tipped them off? Had someone turned up at the cottage after I left?

Maybe it was the neighbour. What was his name? Bill something or other. A retired jeweller who was always dropping in on Vince unannounced. The last time I'd seen him was at the summer barbecue.

Not that it mattered now who alerted the cops. The damage was done and I could only pray that the kidnapper would find out for himself that I was not to blame.

My watch said 1 a.m. I had to get moving. If the police did come to the house then I couldn't afford to be here. If they started to question me then I was bound to give the game away and that might well prove to be catastrophic.

The kidnapper's objective was clear to me now. He wanted to submit Vince's lottery ticket and claim the money. But in order to do that he had to be sure that no one else knew about it. I was the loose end: the one person who could derail his plan by telling the police. They'd then make sure he didn't collect the money. Or even if he managed to do so they'd make sure he didn't get to spend it. So he had to rein me in quickly.

But then what? Would he let us all go once he had the money? I wanted to believe that he would, but I knew it was unlikely. He'd want us out of the way.

I couldn't allow myself to dwell on this hellish scenario, though. I had to get to Maggie and Laura. A step at a time. It was the only way.

I rushed upstairs and put on my trainers, then discarded the sweat-soaked T-shirt for a jumper. The sight of Maggie's pale-blue dressing-gown on the bed sent a shiver of fear racing through me right into my stomach. I just stood there for several seconds, unable to move as the pounding blood in my head slowly came to the boil. I'd told Maggie to be strong. Now I had to tell it to myself. It meant I'd have to control the fear and not allow it to overwhelm me. Easier said than done when your wife and daughter are facing such a grave threat.

I took several deep breaths to help me regain my composure. Then I turned off the light and was about to leave the room when I heard something outside. A chill shot through me as I swivelled round to peer through the window.

Twin headlights were coming up the driveway. A car I didn't recognize. I stood, transfixed, as it came to a stop. The front doors opened and a man and a woman stepped out. There was just enough light to see their faces. The woman I didn't recognize, but her colleague was familiar to me.

DCI Jeff Temple. The man who once described me as a hack without a conscience. He believed I'd helped drive his best friend to suicide. Great. That was all I needed.

I rushed downstairs. Grabbed my windbreaker off its hook in the hall. Entered the kitchen just as the doorbell rang. I paused to consider my options, but it took only seconds for me to conclude that I had to avoid being confronted by the police. I couldn't afford to ignore what the man had said, not as long as he was holding Maggie and Laura hostage.

As the doorbell rang a second time, I unlocked the kitchen door and stepped out on to the rear patio. Then I eased the door shut behind me and launched myself into the night.

10

'Are you sure you saw someone?' Temple said.

Angel nodded. 'A figure moved across an upstairs window. I'm certain of it.'

Temple rang Cain's doorbell for the third time. This is odd, he thought. There are lights on inside the house, a car on the driveway, and Angel saw movement inside. So why is there no response? He looked again at the car. A blue BMW. Was it the car that Mr Nadelson saw speeding along the lane away from Vince Mayo's house? Temple couldn't help but wonder.

He rapped his knuckles on the front door. Called out Cain's name. Angel stepped over to a window, peered inside.

'The light's on in the living room,' she said. 'It's empty, but there are two wine glasses on the coffee table.'

Temple pressed his thumb against the bell again. No answer.

'I'll check around the back,' he said. 'You stay here.'

The rear lawn rolled away from the house towards a low hedge. There was a small wooden gate set to one side. Blackness beyond it.

Temple stepped on to the patio, looked through the French doors into a smartly furnished living room: three-piece suite, flat screen TV on a stand, a glass dining-table. A comfortable, well-maintained home. He tried to open the doors but they were locked. He moved on to the door that gave access to the kitchen. No light here. He stuck his face to the window and saw that the room was empty. Then he grasped the knob, turned it slowly and pushed to see if it was locked. It wasn't.

Strictly speaking he should not have ventured in without a warrant, but he decided to throw caution to the wind. He stepped inside and called out Cain's name again, then waited for a response that didn't come. He switched on the kitchen light, looked around at the bright, modern interior and then went into the hall. The house was dead quiet, eerily so.

He walked up to the front door and opened it. Angel was still right outside. She furrowed her brow at him.

'The kitchen door was open,' he said. 'C'mon, let's have a quick look. I've got a seriously bad feeling about this.'

They went upstairs together, announcing their presence just in case Cain and his family were in their beds. But the upstairs rooms were empty, although in the child's room the bed looked as though it had been recently slept in. There was a little girl's nightdress on the floor.

Temple picked up a framed photo from on top of a chest of drawers in the main bedroom. He showed it to Angel, saying, 'Here's another picture of Cain and his wife.'

This photo had been taken in front of a castle. They were a good-looking couple, especially Mrs Cain, who had a nice smile and glowing teeth. Her dusty blond hair cascaded over her shoulders. Her husband was tall and lean with high cheekbones and a wide mouth. Late thirties or early forties.

There were other photographs in the room of their daughter. Curly hair, round face, full lips. Five or six years old. A sweet-looking child who would surely grow up to be the image of her mother.

They quickly searched all the other rooms in the house. The place was empty.

'What do you think?' Angel said.

Temple shrugged. 'I think we shouldn't jump to a conclusion. Could be the family popped out for a perfectly good reason.'

'Except it's the middle of the night, guv. And at least one of them was here when we arrived.'

Temple chewed the inside of his cheek. 'Let's get Cain's mobile phone number and call him. We might be able to solve this mystery quickly.'

As Angel reached for her phone Temple went back into the garden and walked over to the fence. The gate was unlocked. He stepped through it into a small wood. He could see streetlights through the trees and set off towards them.

He trudged over a rough bed of soggy leaves and fallen branches. On the other side of the wood was a quiet residential street. Cars were parked outside a row of detached houses. No sign of life. He walked about twenty yards along the street to the left. Then he backtracked and went the same distance to the right. He saw no one.

Back at the house Temple told Angel about the road.

'Someone could easily have done a runner through the wood,' he said.

'I know I'm not mistaken, guv. This house was occupied when we arrived.'

Temple's phone rang. He snatched it from his pocket.

'DCI Temple.'

'Jeff, it's Priest. I got your message. What's up?'

Temple hesitated before speaking. He

wasn't sure what reaction to expect.

'Have you heard about the murder in the New Forest, sir?'

'Not the details,' Priest said. 'I heard only that a body was found and they were going to call you out. Why? Is there a problem?'

Temple swallowed. 'The dead man is Vincent Mayo, sir.'

There was a screaming silence on the line. Then Priest said, 'Are you absolutely sure?'

'No question, sir. That's why I'm calling. I thought you should know.'

Another pause, longer this time. Temple heard Priest breathing into the phone.

'How was he killed?' he asked at length.

'Two blows to the head,' Temple said. 'Pretty messy. We've not yet found a murder weapon, but it could have been a granite pestle that's missing from its mortar bowl in the kitchen. That's where the body was found and almost certainly where the murder took place.'

'Any leads?'

'Not really. The last phone call he made this evening was to his partner, Danny Cain. We're at his house now but he's not in.'

'When did it happen?'

'We think between eight and ten. The body was discovered by a neighbour.'

'This is unbelievable.'

'The same neighbour told us that your daughter stayed in the cottage last night,' Temple said.

'That's right,' Priest said. 'She left this afternoon to come here. Arrived about four. We had dinner and watched some television.'

'Is she still with you, sir?'

'No, she went home about eleven. I wanted her to stay but she said she had things to do at home. She was planning to call Vince before she went to bed. I don't know if she did.'

'I need to talk to her, sir.'

'Of course, but I'd like to be the one to break the news.'

'I think that's a good idea.' Temple looked at his watch. 'I have her address. I can be there in twenty minutes.'

'Make it forty-five minutes,' Priest said. 'It'll take me that long to get dressed and over to Jen's flat.'

Temple said that was OK and hung up. He'd filled Angel in back at the cottage. He'd explained that Jennifer Priest had been going out with Vince Mayo for about a year and a half, a situation that her father was not happy about, but had become resigned to. She'd met Mayo before the scandal involving George Banks, and her father had found himself in a difficult position. But to his

89

credit Priest had made an effort to get to know Mayo. More than once he'd told Temple that the journalist was a decent bloke, despite what had happened to Banks.

'I reckon we're going to have our work cut out for us,' Angel said. 'Priest will pile on the pressure. He'll want a quick result on this one.'

'And so would I in his position,' Temple said.

His own daughter, Tanya, was twenty and at university. Her boyfriend was a laconic nerd named Ben Creelman. Temple knew that if Ben turned up dead like Vince Mayo then Tanya would simply fall apart.

'You stay here and check the place out,' he said. 'Try to find out where the Cains are. I'll go see Jennifer Priest. We'll meet back at the nick later and get the team sorted.'

11

The streets around my home were near deserted. I was therefore totally conspicuous. I tried as much as possible to stay in the shadows, ducking into doorways and behind hedges when a car approached.

I part walked and part jogged towards the city centre. It was crazy. My best friend had been murdered and my family kidnapped. And yet I was the one running from the police.

As I moved through the streets I told myself that I had to hold on to the belief that Maggie and Laura would not be killed or otherwise harmed. I couldn't allow myself to think the worst or to imagine them suffering any form of abuse. That would only drag me down and paralyse me with fear and dread.

Laura was a sensitive child, and shy. An ordeal as terrifying as this would almost certainly scar her mentally for life, even if it turned out not to be protracted. Maggie, on the other hand, had never been shy and sensitive. She could be headstrong and opinionated. And that bothered me. She might conceivably try to make things difficult for the kidnapper and in so doing make him even more dangerous.

A picture of Maggie entered my head. It was of the day I first set eyes on her. She walked into the office with the advertising manager who was taking her on a tour of the building to introduce her to the staff. It wasn't actually love at first sight, but it was close to it, I'm sure. She looked magnificent in a white summer blouse and black, hip-hugging trousers. When I shook her hand I made up my mind to find out everything I could about her. And later, when Vince told me that she'd had the same effect on him, I resolved to be the first to ask her out.

But I couldn't hold on to that picture of Maggie because my resistance cracked and I was suddenly confronted by an image that showed her lying on a cold, concrete floor in the semi dark, her face wet with tears, her eyes filled with terror. The image caused a hard knot to twist inside my chest.

What was actually happening to her now? I wondered. Was she in pain? Bleeding? Crying? Unconscious? I had no way of knowing and it was tearing a hole inside me.

And what of Laura? What kind of state must she be in? Six years old, for Christ's sake. Innocent. Vulnerable. Naive. And trapped inside a real nightmare. In my mind's eye I saw her curled up on the floor paralysed by fear. It was awful.

But thankfully the shriek of a police siren wrenched my thoughts back to my own plight and the image faded. I ducked down behind a parked van as the patrol car screamed by, going in the direction of my house. Then I was on the move again, a stitch in my side slowing me down. I knew these streets, but they seemed strangely unfamiliar. Darker and more foreboding than I remembered. I felt like I was intruding. As a young reporter I had gained an extensive knowledge of the city and its people. I'd written about the social problems on the council estates, I'd profiled the recession-hit home-owners, I'd covered the planning issues, the business failures, the in-flux of immigrants. And yet now I felt like an outsider who wasn't welcome. It was just a feeling, but it had seized every fibre of my being.

The nearer I got to the city centre the more people and cars there were. Saturday-night revellers heading home or waiting on pavements for taxis. I began to feel less conspicuous, but at the same time I felt more alone than at any time in my entire life. There was no one to go to for help, no one to share my desperate concern for my family, no one to tell me what to do. I had little choice but to follow the kidnapper's instructions.

I came to the Bargate, a large archway that used to be the main entrance to the medieval walled city of Southampton. The high street opened up at this point and there were a few people hanging around, clearly drunk and in no hurry to go home.

I looked around for a temporary sanctuary, somewhere I could go to collect my fractured thoughts and catch my breath.

But at that moment my phone rang, shooting me with adrenaline.

I whipped it out and hurried towards the shadows of the Bargate. In the gloom of the archway I peered at the screen and experienced a surge of disappointment when the words 'anonymous caller' flashed at me.

It wasn't Maggie's phone. So who the hell was calling me at this hour? The kidnapper had warned me not to answer unless the call was from my wife's phone.

I stood with my back against the cold, ancient stones of the Bargate walls, staring at the pulsating letters.

It dawned on me then that it must be the police. Having found the house empty DCI Temple and his colleague were now trying to contact me. Obviously they wanted to talk to me about Vince. Did I know he was dead? When had I last seen him? Why was I not at home at this ungodly hour?

'Shut that fucking thing off.'

The voice barked at me from the shadows on the other side of the archway. For the first time I noticed that there were two figures standing in a narrow alcove about ten feet from me. Their faces were just visible in the soft glow from lighted cigarettes, or maybe they were joints. They both had cropped hair and were wearing short jackets over jeans.

'Did you hear what I said, you fucking moron?' one of them shouted.

A cold sweat leapt all over my body. My phone was still ringing and I didn't want to switch it off because I didn't want the police to know that I had it.

I thrust it into my jeans pocket and mumbled an apology. This prompted one of the youths to say, 'Why don't you answer the bloody thing?'

I didn't respond and that proved to be a mistake.

'You trying to be funny?' one of the youths said as they both stepped out of the shadows and started towards me.

The phone stopped ringing but now my heart was hammering so fast that I swear I could hear it slamming against my ribcage. I felt threatened suddenly. The youths were obviously drunk or off their heads on drugs. I was about to say something but thought better of it. Instead, I started to turn, intending to run away, but I wasn't quick enough. Both youths came at me suddenly like tigers leaping on their prey.

The first blow caught me on the left side of my face. The fist hammered into my cheekbone, hurling me against the wall. Then I felt a hard boot make contact with my left shin bone and my leg buckled. I stumbled sideways as both my attackers started yelling abuse at me. The next blow was a heavy punch to the back of the head. I lost my balance and fell to the ground. This was followed by a sharp kick to my stomach.

I tried to get to my feet but the blows came thick and fast. I didn't stand a chance. I resorted to curling up on the ground in the hope that the attackers would quickly tire or be scared off by a passer-by.

But they were in a frenzy and I didn't have the strength or the cunning to escape. So I just lay there as the blows rained down. It seemed to last for ever, although it was probably less than a minute.

'He's had enough,' one of them said at last. 'Let's fuck off.'

'Grab his phone,' the other responded. 'And see if he's got any cash.'

I felt them searching me, rough hands

thrusting into my pockets, and I tried to resist. But my arms were heavy and painful and I couldn't keep their claws at bay.

After a few seconds I sensed them step back from me. One of them stamped on my chest for good measure, forcing a searing gasp of air from my lungs.

I opened my mouth to plead with them not to take my phone, but the words that came out were barely intelligible. I rolled on to my front and watched helplessly as they bolted away from the Bargate down the high street.

I was suddenly oblivious to the pain that was exploding all over my body and the blood that was pounding in my head. All I could think about was my phone. It was my only link to the kidnapper and my family.

And it was gone.

12

Jennifer Priest lived in a small block of modern flats close to the city's football stadium. Each flat had a balcony and a bay window overlooking the road out front. Some of the balconies had pot plants. Others had small bistro tables and chairs.

Before going inside Temple phoned Angel for an update. She told him they'd got Danny Cain's mobile number and had called it, but there was no answer.

'Keep trying,' he said. 'Has DC Patel got anything new to report from the cottage?'

'I just spoke to him,' Angel said. 'There's nothing yet, but he has it under control. I'll call you as soon as I have something.'

'So what have you turned up at the Cain house?'

'I checked the garage,' she said. 'There's a second car inside. A Mini. Probably the wife's.'

'That's curious,' Temple said. 'The family vanish but without their own transport. What about neighbours?'

'The uniforms are doing the rounds now, but so far there's been no joy.'

'All right, keep at it. We'll talk later.'

Jennifer Priest's flat was on the second floor. Her father, Superintendent Priest, answered the door to Temple and showed him into a compact living room that had off-white walls and was packed with trendy Ikea furniture, including a huge crimson rug and a round glass coffee table.

Priest looked pale and worried. His features were taut and his brow was deeply furrowed. He was a heavy set man in his mid fifties with broad shoulders and a thick neck. He had receding grey hair and a prominent brow.

Priest was an old-school copper. Gruff, cynical, dedicated to the job. Temple was able to relate to him for that very reason. He considered that they were from the same mould, shared the same values and fought the same battles with bureaucracy.

Priest was essentially a private man and Temple was one of only a few officers who socialized with him outside work. Neither of them was into big, raucous CID get-togethers down the pub, preferring instead a quiet chat over a glass of Chablis in the nearest wine bar.

They both liked football and occasionally went along to the St Mary's stadium to see the Saints play. And they were both interested in firearms. Priest had an impressive collection of replica guns, including a valuable Western revolver that he'd bought at auction for £3,000. Temple just liked firing the things down at the range. They gave him a buzz and had earned him the nickname *Billy*, as in Billy the Kid.

Over the past year, as Priest went through a bitter divorce, their get-togethers had become more frequent: two fifty-something men putting the world to rights and dreading the prospect of retirement. Priest was still recovering mentally and financially from a long-drawn-out and bitter divorce. Temple was still trying to come to terms with being a widower and having no kind of life outside work. They found a curious comfort in each other's company.

Temple knew that Priest would be badly shaken by what had happened. He often talked about his daughter and clearly worshipped her. He would take Vince Mayo's murder personally, that was for sure.

'You want tea or coffee?' Priest said.

Temple shook his head. 'I'm fine, sir. Mind if I sit down?'

'Go ahead. Jennifer will be out shortly. She's in the bathroom. I'm afraid there have been a lot of tears.'

Temple sat on a black leather sofa while

Priest, dressed in loose-fitting jumper and Wrangler jeans, stood in front of the fire, his face gaunt with concern, his cheeks flat. The air of authority that always commanded so much respect had disappeared.

'What's your take on this, Jeff?' he asked, his tone sombre. 'Was this a premeditated murder or what?'

Temple leaned forward, elbows on knees. 'It's too soon to call, sir. However, there were no obvious signs of a break-in at Mayo's cottage, and his belongings appeared to be in order. It doesn't mean, of course, that we should rule out a burglar or burglars.'

Priest sucked in a lungful of air and exhaled slowly with a hissing sound through his teeth.

'As you know, I didn't approve of Vince as Jennifer's boyfriend,' he said. 'I felt the same way about him as you and the others did after George Banks died. But my daughter adored him and wouldn't hear a bad word said against him. In fact, when the Banks story was published we argued about it and she defended Mayo to the hilt. Said she didn't understand why George's colleagues, including me, were so outraged since he was clearly in the wrong when he took the drugs.'

'How have you been getting on with him recently?' Temple asked.

'Just fine,' Priest said. 'Can't say I saw much of him, but then that was OK because I was always worried that he was discreetly pumping me for information, even though I made it clear at the outset that I wouldn't be his source inside the service. Always had to be careful what I said, though. But he wasn't a bad lad, to be fair.'

'So was your daughter's relationship with him pretty serious?' Temple asked.

'Oh, for sure. He hadn't actually asked her to move in with him but she was hoping that he would. And who knows? Perhaps it would have led to wedding bells. I know that Jennifer is ready for that. She's anxious to start a family.'

'You say your daughter went to your house during the afternoon?'

'That's right. She usually comes over every other weekend. Sometimes with Vince, but mostly by herself.'

'Did she have any contact with Mayo while she was with you?'

'No, she didn't.'

Temple took out his notebook and started scrawling.

'How old is Jennifer, sir?'

'She's twenty-seven.'

'And her occupation?'

'A sales rep for a cosmetics company.'

'And she and Mayo have been together for how long?'

'About fourteen months. They met at a local gym where they were both members.'

'How long has she lived here?'

'Two years. She moved to Southampton from Andover after her mother and I split up.'

'And has she any idea who might have killed Mayo?'

Priest gestured towards the door. 'Why don't you ask her yourself? Jen, this is Detective Chief Inspector Jeff Temple.'

Jennifer Priest was wearing a beige towelling robe that swamped her slender frame. She had long, straw-coloured hair tied back from a pale, pretty face. She wasn't wearing make-up and the flesh around her smoky-grey eyes was red and puffy. She had her father's nose, straight and pert, with slightly flared nostrils.

'Hello, Miss Priest,' Temple said, rising to his feet.

She gave a slight nod and shuffled further into the room. Priest put an arm around his daughter and led her over to an armchair. She sat down, hands in lap, and began rolling a soggy tissue between her fingers.

'The inspector is in charge of the case,' Priest told her. 'He needs to ask you some questions. They're likely to be the same as those I've already asked but you have to answer them.'

Jennifer lifted her head and looked at Temple. Her eyes searched his face. They were brimming with tears, but there was a hardness in her expression too.

'Are you one of the officers who refused to have anything to do with Vince after he exposed that crook George Banks?' she said.

Temple blinked in surprise. For a moment he was lost for words.

'I told you not to go there, Jen,' Priest said to his daughter. 'Now is not the time to bring this stuff up.'

'Yes it is,' she said 'Because I want to be sure that your people will do all they can to find whoever did this. I know they all harbour a grudge and I wouldn't be surprised if certain people are pleased that this has happened.'

'You have nothing to worry about, Miss Priest,' Temple said. 'We'll treat this crime as we do every other. I can assure you that any ill feeling towards Mr Mayo among officers in Southampton evaporated a long time ago. Your father can testify to that.'

'Vince showed me the letters,' she said. 'All the hate mail.'

'As I remember they were anonymous,' Temple said.

'Yeah, right. We both know who sent them.'

There was an awkward silence. After a few seconds Priest cleared his throat and said, 'Look, Jen, I know you're upset and felt the need to make a point. Well, you've made it. Will you now please answer the inspector's questions?'

She blew her nose and rubbed her eyes. Then said, 'Can you tell me what happened to Vince?'

Temple sat up straight and took a breath. 'He was attacked in his home and suffered two fatal blows to his head.'

Jennifer swallowed and wiped her face with her sleeve.

'Where was he found?' she asked.

'In the kitchen. That's almost certainly where the attack took place. His body was discovered by his neighbour, Mr Nadelson.'

Jennifer closed her eyes briefly.

'Do you mind if I ask what car you drive, Miss Priest?'

She opened her eyes, but other than that there was no emotional reaction to the question.

'It's a Peugeot 207.'

'And the colour?'

'White. Why do you want to know?'

'Mr Nadelson saw a car driving away from Mr Mayo's cottage about ten o'clock last evening. A dark vehicle, perhaps an Audi or

BMW. Does that description mean anything to you?'

'No, it doesn't. And besides, I was nowhere near the cottage last night. I thought my father told you that.'

'He did, Miss Priest. It's just that I have to ask certain questions anyway, even though I might already know the answers.'

Jennifer looked at him doubtfully and lowered her eyes.

Temple could see that she was on the verge of losing it. A single tear slipped out of her right eye and trickled down her cheek.

'Do you know of anyone who might have wanted to see Mr Mayo dead?' Temple asked.

She raised her eyes. 'But I assumed it was robbery. That he was killed by burglars.'

'That's a possibility, Miss Priest. But there were no signs of a break-in. It could be that he knew his killer.'

This shocked her. She looked at her father and started sobbing.

Priest stood behind her, placing both hands on her shoulders. It looked to Temple as though he too might be about to break down.

'I know this is difficult for you, Miss Priest,' Temple said. 'But I have to ask you more questions.'

Jennifer blew her nose again and cleared her throat.

'I know,' she said. 'I'm all right.'

He allowed her time to compose herself, then went on, 'I gather you stayed at Mr Mayo's cottage on Friday evening?'

She nodded. 'Yes. We watched a film, *Mama Mia.*'

'Mr Nadelson said he saw you briefly this morning.'

'He popped over with Vince's lottery tickets. Vince invited him in for a cup of coffee but he was in a hurry so he didn't come in.'

'So what did you and Mr Mayo do during the rest of the day?'

'Not much really. By the time we'd had breakfast and got ready it was almost lunchtime. Vince did some work and I read a book and watched television. Then in the afternoon I went to my dad's house for dinner.'

'And Mr Mayo stayed at home?'

'That's right, but that wasn't unusual. Vince liked my father but he always felt a little awkward spending time with him. On this occasion he had a proper excuse, though. He said he had to wait in because a man he owed money to was coming to the cottage to collect some of it. It was part of his gambling debt.'

'Was Mr Mayo a serious gambler, then?'

'Very serious,' she said. 'Trouble was he wasn't very good at it. That's why he was in so much debt.'

'Do you know how much he owed?'

'Not exactly, but it was well over twenty thousand pounds.'

Temple and Priest looked at each other. Priest shrugged his shoulders, as if to say that it was news to him.

'So who was the man who was coming to collect the money?'

'His name is Dessler,' she said. 'Joe Dessler. I know because Vince mentioned him a few times.'

Temple glanced at Priest. 'There's a Joe Dessler on the patch, sir. He's a small-time pimp and loan shark.'

'I know of him,' Priest said. 'The vice lads have had him in from time to time. I'm sure he's got form.'

Temple turned back to Jennifer. 'So what do you know about Dessler, Miss Priest?'

'I know that Vince didn't like him much,' she said. 'And I know that he and Danny were planning to do some kind of exposé on him through the news agency.'

'What do you mean?'

She shrugged. 'That's all I know really. He talked to Danny about it a few times when I was with him.'

'You mean Danny Cain, his partner?'

'That's right.'

'So tell me about this exposé they were working on. What's it all about?'

'Well, apparently Dessler wanted his money back from Vince and had made some threats against him,' she said. 'But Vince was always short of cash and on one occasion he even borrowed from me to service his debts. So he came up with the idea of doing a story on Dessler and selling it to a Sunday newspaper. Vince was keen on it because he thought it might solve his cash problems if Dessler got put away. I know Danny was a bit worried about it but as far as I know he didn't object.'

'So why didn't you tell me about this?' Priest said, aggrieved.

Jennifer looked up at her father. 'Vince told me not to mention it to anyone, especially you.'

Priest turned to Temple. 'We need to talk to Cain about this article. It could be significant.'

'We will when we find him,' Temple said.

'Is he not at home, then?'

'His house was empty when we got there, although the lights were on. There was also a car on the driveway and DS Angel swore she saw someone moving around inside as we arrived.'

'What are you saying, Jeff? That you think he did a runner?'

'I don't know, sir. He might have ducked out the back. He has a wife and daughter and they're not around either.'

'Do you know if there were any problems between Vince and his partner?' Priest asked his daughter.

Jennifer shook her head. 'Not that I'm aware of. They always seemed to get on.'

'What do you know about Danny Cain?' Temple asked.

'He's a nice man,' she said. 'A family man.'

'Has he or his wife got any relatives in this area? Parents or siblings?'

'I think Danny's wife has a mother who lives close by. I don't know where.'

A few beats of silence. Jennifer seemed to shrink further into the chair under the weight of her grief.

'Did you talk to Mr Mayo at any point after you left the cottage?' Temple asked.

'I wish I had,' she said. 'I tried calling him when I got home, just before I went to bed. I wanted to say goodnight. But there was no answer on his mobile or landline.'

'Did that not worry you?'

'Not really. I assumed he was either in bed or had gone to one of the casinos in town. He often did that when he wasn't with me.'

'Did it occur to you that he might have a problem if the man who'd been threatening him was going to his home?'

'He didn't seem worried about it. In fact he told me that Dessler was happy to get at least some of his money back. Plus I heard them talking on the phone. It was fairly amicable. Vince was sure there wouldn't be any trouble.' She paused there, took a breath and then her jaw dropped. 'Oh, my God, do you think Dessler killed Vince? Is that what you think?'

'We have no idea, Miss Priest,' Temple said. 'At the moment there's no evidence to suggest that he did but we will be talking to him. By the way, do you know if Mr Mayo kept any valuables in the cottage? Something that might be of interest to thieves?'

She shook her head. 'He sold off everything of value to pay for his gambling, except for his mother's jewellery, that is. He told me he would never part with that.'

'How much jewellery?'

'I'm not sure exactly. He kept it in a leather jewellery box in his bedside drawer. I told him he should put it in a safer place but he said he wanted it close to him for sentimental reasons.'

'Can you describe what was in the box?'

'He showed me once but it's all a bit vague

111

now. There were some necklaces and a couple of brooches. That sort of thing. He said he'd had them valued and they were worth a tidy sum. Thousands of pounds, in fact.'

'And there was nothing else of value as far as you know?'

'There was the cash.'

'Cash?'

'The money for Dessler. Vince left it on the worktop in the kitchen. All in notes.'

'How much?'

'Three thousand pounds.'

Temple turned to Priest. 'There was no money in the kitchen. I checked the worktop myself.'

'So whoever killed Vince must have taken it.'

'Looks that way.'

At that point Jennifer lost it again and started to cry into a wad of tissues.

Her father squeezed her shoulders. 'Let's leave it at that, Jeff. My daughter's not going anywhere, so she can answer more questions later. I'll stay here with her for now and call you if she thinks of anything that might help the investigation.'

'Fair enough,' Temple said. He put his notebook away and got to his feet.

Jennifer held up her hands and forced herself to stop crying.

'There's something else you should know,' she said. 'I just remembered. It might not be relevant, but I think you ought to know.'

She swallowed. Breathed through her mouth. Swallowed again.

'Just over a week ago I saw a man watching the cottage,' she said. 'It was early evening and he was standing on the edge of the wood out back. He had binoculars.'

'Are you sure?' Temple said.

She nodded. 'I only saw him because I was upstairs in Vince's study and happened to look out of the window. He was standing next to a tree, staring at the cottage. I watched him for about a minute and then rushed downstairs to tell Vince. But when Vince went outside there was no sign of the man.'

'When exactly was this, Miss Priest?'

She looked up at the ceiling, searching her memory through the fog of grief and shock. 'The Friday before last, about four o'clock. I know because it was almost dark and I'd just arrived at the cottage having left work early.'

'Can you describe this man?'

'Not in detail,' she said. 'But he had a shaved head and ears that poked out. He was wearing a sheepskin coat. I remember that much. If I saw him again I'd recognize him.'

'How old?'

'In his thirties maybe.'

'Anything else you can tell us? Was he tall or short, fat or thin?'

She shrugged. 'Normal height, I think. It was difficult to tell.'

'I don't understand, Jen,' Priest said. 'Why didn't you mention this to me? I'm a policeman, for Christ's sake, as well as being your father.'

'I didn't think, Dad. Vince said not to worry about it so I didn't. I'm sorry.'

Priest shook his head, clearly put out, but anxious at the same time not to add to his daughter's anguish by making a deal of it.

'Did Mr Mayo have any idea who the man might be?' Temple asked.

She shook her head. 'He wasn't familiar with anyone who looked like the description I gave.'

'I'd like you to help us produce a photofit,' Temple said. 'Would that be all right?'

She nodded.

'I'll get it sorted then.' Temple looked at his watch. 'I'd better go now. But before I do there's one last question, Miss Priest. Have you any idea why Mr Mayo might have opened a bottle of champagne last night?'

She looked at him, puzzled.

'No, not at all. Why do you ask?'

'Well, there was a bottle in the kitchen. It'd been opened, but it didn't look as though any of it had been drunk.'

'Well, he didn't open it before I left. And I can't imagine what he might have had to celebrate.'

Priest showed Temple out. At the door, Priest said, 'Dessler has to be a prime suspect. I want you to find him now and grill the bastard.'

'I intend to, sir.'

'And pull out all the stops. I don't care what it costs. Use as many bodies as you need to. I'll sanction any overtime.'

'That's good to know, sir.'

Priest clapped Temple on the back. 'Now get out there and find the bastard who just screwed up my daughter's life.'

13

Half an hour after the youths attacked me I was still wandering aimlessly around the city centre. It had taken me five minutes to haul myself to my feet back at the Bargate. My legs still felt like jelly. My head swayed violently and a deluge of vomit had burned its way up through my gullet. I was bruised and bleeding and shaking all over.

I passed a few people, most of them boozed-up youngsters, but they barely seemed to notice me. I got a few strange looks, giggles from a group of drunken girls. Their reaction — or lack of it — was both shocking and sad, but at the same time I welcomed being left alone. I needed to move and to think.

Things had now gone from bad to worse. The kidnapper had no way of contacting me. The lifeline to my family was severed. I had no idea what Maggie's mobile number was. I'd never had to memorize it. So what would happen now? How would he respond when he failed to get through?

Pain gnawed at my bones. I must have looked like a wino who had been rolled over for his last cigarette. A huge swelling had come up on my forehead. Blood trickled down my left cheek. My ribs hurt and my muscles throbbed.

How in God's name had it come to this? In a matter of hours the life I'd known and loved had been shattered like a beach-hut in a tsunami.

The sheer gravity of the situation was overwhelming. As I hobbled along the empty streets, wincing with pain, the drumming of despair inside my head grew into a deafening crescendo.

The reporter inside me yearned to know what was going on. The events of the past few hours made for a cracking story. But my journalistic curiosity was tempered by the fear that curdled in my stomach. I just didn't know what to do or where to go.

Alongside the fear there was guilt. I felt that I'd let Maggie and Laura down, just as I had done too often in the past. They would be counting on me to hold it together. But I'd failed, and now it was likely they'd pay a terrible price.

I turned down a side street leading towards the docks. There were warehouses along one side, derelict shops and offices along the other. It seemed colder here and even less friendly. Weeds reared up through gaping cracks in the pavements. I heard creatures scurrying in the shadows. The air smelled of motor oil and rotting fish.

I came to a junction and looked to the left before stepping into the road. And that was when I saw the police car. It was about fifty yards away and parked at the kerb under a streetlight.

Maggie's words rang in my ears. She'd pleaded with me not to involve the cops. The kidnapper had warned me that if I did then he would kill my family. But what choice did I have? I needed help now and I needed to act quickly. So I broke into a run. And as I ran my head started to clear and I forgot about the aches and pains that racked my body.

I was about to share my terrible burden and that at least would surely bring me some relief.

★ ★ ★

Maggie was listening for any sounds. But all she could hear was the wind whistling through the eaves above her.

The kidnapper had disappeared downstairs straight after he called Danny. Minutes later she heard a car start up outside and since then there had been silence.

Thankfully Laura had fallen asleep whilst

gibbering away to Max. The man had given them four smelly blankets and Laura was curled up beneath two of them. She had whispered to her invisible friend for almost half an hour before eventually dropping off. She told Max she was scared but that her father would soon be here to save them and sort out the nasty man in the funny mask.

Maggie wasn't able to sleep. Her mind was a maelstrom of ugly thoughts and images. The fear was like a living thing inside her. Every time she was distracted by something it moved, wrenching her back to the horrible reality of the situation.

A while ago she had urinated and the warm liquid had filled her knickers and stained the front of her jeans. She actually welcomed the sensation because briefly a small part of her didn't feel so cold.

She sat with her knees pulled up in front of her, covered by the other two blankets, her head against the wall. She kept telling herself that Danny would be with them soon and the man would go and get the lottery money. Then they'd be set free to resume their lives.

The trouble was she didn't believe it. She knew that once the man submitted Vince's lottery ticket he'd have to decide what to do with them, if he hadn't already made up his mind. And that was where it got scary.

It was likely that she, Danny and the kidnapper were the only people who knew about the ticket. Once Danny was safely ensconced in the loft the kidnapper could claim the winnings and nobody else would know the truth.

But of course he might not get to spend any of the money if he let them go. So it followed that he would almost certainly murder them all, just like he'd murdered Vince.

Danny, then, was their only hope, but this thought served only to increase her sense of despair. Her husband was no Bruce Willis. He was fit and intelligent, but he wasn't a man of action. He wouldn't, therefore, come bounding to their rescue like a movie-star hero. In fact he would probably mess things up. Just as he'd messed up their lives by losing his job. And then by sinking their savings into a stupid freelance news agency that was going nowhere and would eventually disappear without trace.

So how would he disappoint this time? she wondered. Despite what he'd said on the phone she was pretty sure that he'd panic and alert the police. And that would be disastrous. Maggie tried but failed to hold back a flood of tears. The tide of emotion she experienced was overwhelming. A mixture of fear, despair, frustration, anger and grief for Vince. But there was also a great deal of guilt. And it struck her suddenly that she was trying to assuage that guilt by blaming Danny.

But he wasn't responsible for what was happening. She realized that now. If anyone was to blame it was she. She was the one who had stepped over the line five months ago. What she had done was unforgivable and she should have known that it would end in disaster.

This was payback time. Divine retribution. The terrible consequence of her own selfish actions.

Vince was dead and the lives of her husband and daughter were now at risk.

And Maggie was convinced that she was to blame.

Please God, she whispered through a deluge of hot tears. *Please forgive me for what I've done and don't make my family suffer because of it.*

★   ★   ★

I was about twenty yards from the police car when I came to a sudden stop. I stared in amazement.

In the sodium glow from a nearby street lamp I could see the two feral youths who

121

had mugged me. The bastards who had my phone. They were being questioned by a couple of policemen in luminous jackets.

My heart pumped and my mouth dried up.

I moved to the left behind a pillar box, from where I watched and listened. It was a typical late-night scene, as depicted in scores of reality cop shows; part of the fight against street crime where suspicious youths are stopped and searched, and often arrested.

I strained to hear what was being said, but I was too far away and I didn't dare move closer for fear of being seen.

The youths were probably being asked to account for their movements. Where were they going? Where had they been? Were they carrying knives or drugs?

I was debating whether to approach the group when the two officers got back in the car.

Decision time. Should I break cover and catch the cops before they drove away? Or should I go for it alone and try to retrieve the situation? What course of action offered the best odds of saving my family?

The police car's engine turned over. I started to move forward — and then held back. Decision made.

The patrol car drove off, leaving the youths on the pavement. One of them lit up a cigarette before they both started walking along the street away from me.

My mind whirred and my pulse raced. Needless to say I didn't have a plan. I just had an objective which was to get my phone back. And right now that seemed like an impossible task.

I knew I had to act pretty quickly. If I followed them for any length of time I'd be spotted. The streets were more or less deserted and in this part of town they were fairly well lit.

These were two hulking lads who could handle themselves. I knew that from personal experience. So how was I meant to prise the phone away from them? Diplomacy was out of the question. Approaching them would invite another beating. No, there was only one thing for it. I was going to have to jump them and hope that the element of surprise would give me an advantage.

I'm not a violent person. In fact I had not been involved in fisticuffs since leaving school. But right now I had no choice. Not if I wanted to see my wife and daughter again.

I watched from the shadows as the two youths turned a corner. I broke into a trot to catch up. I needed a weapon of some kind because without one I wouldn't stand a chance. These guys were serious hardcases.

They knew how to fight. I didn't.

I reached the corner and stopped to check their whereabouts. They were still walking at a casual pace, chatting to one another like two innocents out enjoying a late evening stroll. The anger welled up inside me.

I knew the area they were heading into: St Mary's. The most insalubrious district of Southampton. Here buildings were run down and shops boarded up. Pavements were busted. Everything was ugly and tainted with neglect. Even the graffiti was poor quality. Crude rather than artistic. An air of desperation hung over the area like a toxic cloud.

The pair crossed a road towards an estate of high-rise council flats. I came up behind a builder's skip that was jutting out on to the pavement from between two empty buildings. A pile of rubble inside the skip contained bricks, chunks of wood and slabs of plasterboard. I peered more closely, looking for something to use as a weapon.

And it didn't take me long to spot it. An iron bar poking out of the debris.

I reached up, stretched out, managed to get a purchase on the exposed end, jerking it free. The bar was about four feet long, three inches in diameter. It was hard and heavy and more than capable of cracking open a skull. Or two.

Having a weapon bolstered my confidence. Gripping it tightly in my right hand I shuffled across the road and started to close the gap. The youths hadn't yet bothered to look behind them. I prayed that they wouldn't choose this moment to do so. They stepped on to a path that would take them across a patch of dead grass to one of the blocks of flats. There was no one else around. I quickened my pace, then bolted towards them. They heard me when I was about six yards away and they both turned, as though sensing a threat. I was psyched up by this time, the fury in me having gathered power and momentum.

'Who the fuck . . . ?'

That was all one of them managed to say before I was on top of them, yelling like a maniac and flailing the bar wildly at their heads.

A crack of bone. A pitiful cry as the first blow struck one of them full in the face. The other youth ducked but he wasn't quick enough to avoid the downward thrust of my arm. The bar made contact with the back of his skull. He let out a yelp as he fell to the ground.

I turned my attention back to the other one. He was on his feet still, but disoriented. He was holding his face in his hands and

125

moaning. So this time I took aim at his knees and gave them an almighty wallop. The moaning turned into a full throttle scream and he keeled over.

Back to yob number two, and by now I was in my stride and eager to vent my anger and frustration on these two scumbags. A kind of madness, bred of desperation, had come over me. I whacked him across the head and neck and then shoved one end of the bar into his face.

And I didn't let up for at least half a minute, giving neither youth time to retaliate.

Blood spattered all over the pathway. Some of it sprayed across my face and clothes.

When it became obvious that they were no longer a threat, I dropped the bar on to the ground and started going through their pockets.

It was strange, because I felt totally calm. Sure, I was hot, sweaty and gasping for breath, but at the same time I didn't feel like I had done anything wrong. In fact I was feeling what I can only describe as a deep sense of elation.

And this feeling reached a new level when I found my phone in one of the pockets. I checked it quickly. No missed calls, thank God. I didn't find my wallet but that had probably been dumped soon after they swiped it.

I stood up and took one last look at the youths, who were both struggling to haul up their battered bodies. I felt the urge to inflict more pain but decided there was no time. Instead, I turned and ran towards the road.

14

Ten minutes after the attack on the youths I was seized by a bad case of the shakes. I was crossing a road near the old city walls when it happened. I managed to reach the pavement and lower myself unsteadily to the kerb, where I sat hunched over with my face in my hands.

My head spun and cold sweat sprang from every pore on my face. This was a delayed reaction to what I'd done. I should have expected it, but it took me completely by surprise. It was a weird and unpleasant feeling and it was at least two full minutes before my body stilled and the sensation passed.

Then I was hit by a wave of nausea that had me retching wildly. I started sucking in great chunks of the chilled night air. It was laced with petrol fumes and salt water from the nearby docks.

Gradually I got control of my breathing and my stomach settled. I'd suffered a massive shock to the system. I'm a reporter, not a thug. I can't smash someone's head in with an iron bar and not experience an extreme charge of adrenaline.

But I'd got the phone back. That was the main thing and it justified my actions. At least that was the way I chose to look at it.

I zipped up the windbreaker and stood up from the kerb. My muscles were tired and sore. The swelling on my forehead had grown bigger and more painful. I felt wretched.

I walked for a bit, avoiding the main streets and fighting the burn of gastric acid in my stomach. Eventually I found myself down by the waterfront, close to the old stone walls that once protected the city of Southampton in medieval times. Now they're proud ruins that cast huge dark shadows.

So I moved quickly from one shadow to the next, then up on to the crumbling ramparts, where I had a bird's-eye view of the dockside roads. Ships' horns blasted plaintively out in the docks. Someone let off a firework. Shrieking sirens continued to shatter the early hours of this cold Sunday morning.

I watched and listened and wondered how long the kidnapper would prolong the agony. What was he doing? Why couldn't he just come and get me? After all, that was his objective — to seize me so that I was no longer a threat to his plan.

I thought about Maggie, longed for her warm body, the comfort of her voice. Would I ever again feel the soft brush of her lips against mine or the tender touch of her fingers across my brow?

Already it seemed as though an eternity had passed since I last saw her. At least we were on speaking terms when our lives were brutally disrupted. It would have been even harder to bear if we hadn't made up when we did.

It was bad enough knowing that we had wasted a lot of time over the past few months. Things had not been right. The tension. The awkward moments. The stilted conversations. How I wished now that I had made more of an effort to get to the bottom of the problem and sort it out. Regrets. They were already piling up and stabbing at my conscience. Adding to my burden.

And what about Laura? My little angel. I would have given anything to hold her in my arms and read her a bedtime story. I'd even be happy to lay a place at the dinner table for Max.

I felt sick now with worry and dread, not knowing if I would ever see my family again. My head ached and my mind was in chaos.

I thought about Vince. My only true friend. I had lots of acquaintances. Guys I would pass the time of day with and call from time to time to see how they were doing. Former colleagues. Old school friends. But over the years I'd lost touch with all of those whose friendships I'd valued. But that's what happens when you get married and devote yourself to family life.

Vince, though, had been ever present. Friend, business partner and confidante. It was a pity I couldn't mourn him. He deserved that. But grief was an emotion I couldn't indulge right now. I had to focus all my energy and all my thoughts on saving my family.

The cold had reached every part of my body and I was starting to shake again. The sea air that came in over the docks had a hard bite to it. I could feel it burning my lungs with every intake of breath. And I was still in pain. Bruises and swellings pulsed annoyingly across my head, chest and arms.

Time dragged on. The roads below me became virtually deserted. I sat huddled against a wall to try to keep warm, but the longer I waited there the colder I became.

I considered finding somewhere else to hide, somewhere warmer, but decided not to because up here on the ramparts I felt safe. No one could see me. I was invisible.

The minutes turned into an hour and I was actually on the verge of falling asleep when the phone rang at last.

And this time, thankfully, Maggie's name flashed at me when I flipped back the cover.

15

'Joe Dessler is relatively new on the scene,' DC Dave Brayshaw told Temple when he got back to the station. 'He hails from Manchester and runs an escort agency that operates between Southampton and Ports-mouth. He's also a loan shark with a nasty streak. We hauled him in seven months ago after a guy claimed that Dessler beat him up because he couldn't pay a debt. But then the victim withdrew the complaint, so nothing came of it.'

Brayshaw was sitting on the edge of Temple's desk. Catalogue Man they called him in the nick. He was tall, lean and ruggedly good-looking, just like the male models in fashion catalogues. The ones who wear the smart suits, tight shirts and revealing Y-fronts.

'Dessler keeps a low profile, but he's well known to Vice,' Brayshaw said. 'He makes every effort to stay out of trouble. But he does have one conviction for ABH. Clob-bered someone outside a club in London and did twelve months. That was back in 2000.'

'How long has he been pimping?'

Brayshaw consulted his notes. 'The Blue Tequila escort agency was set up about eighteen months ago. That's when he took out his first ad in the local evening paper. He runs it as a legit business, keeps accounts and files tax returns.'

Southampton, in common with other major cities, has a thriving prostitution business, despite government attempts to curb the trade. There's no law against so-called escort agencies so long as they don't overtly offer sex to the punters. But once a punter hires an escort through the agency, the girl is at liberty to do whatever she wants.

'I'll go back to Vice,' Brayshaw said. 'See what else I can dig up on Dessler.'

'You do that. And I'd like you to get the team together for a briefing as soon as I get back.'

A patrol car was waiting for Temple in front of the station. He sat in the back behind the two uniforms. The moment they were on the move he closed his eyes. But sleep was waiting to draw him under so he opened them again and stared out of the window at the near-empty streets of Southampton.

He wondered if it had been another hectic Saturday night and Sunday morning. The city centre had got much worse over the past five years. More drunks. More fights. More stabbings. More racial tension. He supposed it was no different from any other city in the UK.

'Much trouble tonight?' he asked without turning from the window.

'Oh, the usual stuff,' the driver answered. 'Savages on the rampage. A clubber claims she was raped in Mayflower Park. Then we just heard that two youths got beaten to a pulp by a crazy man with an iron bar down St Mary's. You ask me I reckon the world's gone mad.'

He wasn't far wrong, Temple thought. A rape, a vicious assault and a murder. And the government had the temerity to insist that crime was under control.

Temple pushed back against the headrest. It was time to reflect on the case. Already there were lots of questions. Who killed Vince Mayo and why? Had Mayo known his killer and let him or her into the cottage? Was there more than one killer? Would Joe Dessler kill a man who owed him money? Where the hell was Danny Cain and his family and did he know that his best friend had been beaten to death?

He thought about Joe Dessler. Small time escort agency boss and moneylender. An unsavoury character with a criminal record for violent behaviour. But was he a killer?

134

He had motive — a debt that he wanted paid. But one way to ensure that it would never be paid was to kill Mayo. Not very sensible. Unless he wanted to make an example of him. So maybe he went to the cottage to give Mayo a final warning and things got out of hand.

And what of Danny Cain? There were certainly grounds for suspicion there. Why had Mayo phoned him shortly before he was killed? And why was his house empty even though his car was on the driveway and Angel saw movement through one of the upstairs windows?

Very sus, especially when the car — a blue BMW — matched the description of the one that Bill Nadelson spotted tearing along the lane shortly after the murder was committed.

Temple recalled his one and only meeting with Cain and Mayo together. Cain was the quieter of the two and at the time it was clear that his conscience had been pricked by George Banks's situation. But he was also a typical journalist, obsessed with what he regarded as a great story and determined to see it in print regardless of the consequences. And those consequences had been tragic. George Banks had been one of the most popular guys in the Hampshire Constabulary. He and Temple had been friends for years.

They often went fishing together, had dinner at each other's homes, shared the same concerns about the state of the modern police service.

Despite what he said to Jennifer Priest there was still a lot of ill feeling towards Mayo and Cain. It was as strong as ever because the officers would frequently come into contact with one or both of them at crime scenes and court sessions. It made it difficult for them to forget what had happened to George.

Temple understood their anger but he didn't share it. After all, George had committed a crime and had decided he couldn't live with the consequences. Cain and Mayo were not to blame — although they were guilty of a lack of compassion.

Temple could well remember the day he arrived at George's house to pick him up. They were on a late shift together and George's wife had taken the car.

Temple honked the horn and when George didn't appear he got out of his car and rang the doorbell. There was no answer so he peered through the letterbox and was about to yell for George when he saw a pair of legs dangling in mid air above the stairs.

George had gone to the trouble of getting dressed before hanging himself from the upstairs banisters with an electric cable.

* * *

Dessler lived in a penthouse flat overlooking Southampton's prestigious Ocean Village marina. It had been one of his late wife's favourite places; he and Erin used to go there to admire the luxury yachts and cruise from the open-air restaurants along the quayside.

As the patrol car turned into the complex Temple could see the white-hulled boats bobbing at their moorings. Around them were a few upmarket blocks of flats and a handful of trendy restaurants, including Erin's favourite. He could actually recall the last meal they had there. It was to celebrate her promotion at the school where she taught — and it was precisely a year before she succumbed to the cancer that had ravaged her stomach.

Dessler's block had its own security man at the entrance, who woke from his slumber with a start when Temple rapped on the glass door. He sat up behind his desk and buzzed them in.

'We've come to see Mr Joe Dessler,' Temple said. 'Which floor does he live on?'

'Seventh floor, sir. The top. Number eighty-eight.'

'Is he in?'

'I believe so, but I expect he's in bed. He

arrived back here late this evening.'

'How late?' Temple asked.

'About midnight, I think. Do you want me to call up and tell him that you're here?'

'No, I'd rather it was a surprise.'

They went up in the lift, walked along a corridor with a sumptuous green carpet and sepia prints of yachts on the Solent. Who says crime doesn't pay? Temple thought. This was high-end luxury. He could almost smell the money.

They got to the flat and Temple rang the bell. He thought he would have to ring it several times before he got an answer. But not so. The door opened within seconds and a tall, surly-looking man was standing there. He had olive skin and would have been quite handsome if it were not for the scar that ran from one corner of his mouth to just below his ear. It was dark and deep and distorted the side of his face.

Temple was somewhat surprised to see that Dessler was fully dressed in a black polo sweater, jeans and heavy boots. He wondered instinctively if there was any blood on the soles of the boots.

'Are you Joe Dessler?' Temple asked.

'Who wants to know?' The hint of a northern accent.

Temple flashed his ID. 'I'm Detective Chief

138

Inspector Jeff Temple, Hampshire Major Crime Department. Mind if we come in for a chat?'

Dessler eyed the two uniforms. His hair was coal-black and short and he had thin colourless lips.

'I do actually,' he said. 'It's late. What's this about?'

'Caught you at a bad time, have we?' Temple asked.

'I was just going out.'

Temple looked at his watch. 'At three in the morning? For your information the shops aren't open yet.'

'Very funny.'

Temple shrugged. 'Look, I know this is a cliché, but we can talk to you here or take you down to the station. What's it to be?'

Dessler gritted his teeth and stood back to let them in.

The flat was bright, spacious. Two large windows in the living area offered impressive views of the marina and beyond it to the Solent and the Isle of Wight. A long L-shaped sofa and two armchairs surrounded a marble coffee table. There was an Andy Warhol poster on one wall and a top-of-the-range Bang and Olufsen stereo system on another.

The two uniforms stood just inside the door. Temple cast an approving eye over the decor before turning his attention to the owner, or maybe he was merely the tenant.

'So I take it you are Joe Dessler?'

'That's right.'

'Do you live here alone?'

'Most of the time.'

Dessler was in his late thirties and had about him an air of unbridled arrogance. Clearly he worked out and looked as though he could handle himself. He had a thick chest and pronounced biceps.

'Mind if I sit down?' Temple asked.

Dessler merely shrugged.

So Temple lowered himself on to an armchair and gestured for Dessler to sit opposite him on the sofa. Dessler did so with obvious reluctance.

Temple fixed him with a look and said nothing for several seconds. He wanted to get a handle on the man, gauge whether he was nervous and intimidated. But he didn't show it if he was. He simply sat there, crossed his legs and waited for Temple to break the silence.

'So why aren't you in your jimjams, Mr Dessler? Most people are tucked up in bed at this time of the day.'

'What I do with my time is my business,' Dessler said.

'Not if you're breaking the law it isn't.'

'So what law are you accusing me of breaking?'

'I'm not sure yet, but I expect there's more than one.'

Dessler rolled his eyes. 'Look, what the fuck do you want with me? I'm a respectable local businessman and I resent your attitude.'

Temple held it a beat, then said, 'We're investigating the murder of Vince Mayo.'

Dessler swallowed and Temple saw the cords in his neck move, but it was impossible to tell whether he was genuinely surprised or putting on an act.

'Are you serious?' he said.

'Mr Mayo was killed at his cottage in the New Forest a few hours ago,' Temple said. 'He was bludgeoned to death. We know he owed you money and that you've been making threats against him. We also know that you went to his cottage this evening. So naturally we're very suspicious.'

'I didn't go to the cottage,' Dessler said. 'In fact I've never been to his place.'

'Then why did he tell his girlfriend that he was expecting you there? You were going there to collect some money. He'd even got the cash out ready for when you turned up.'

Dessler gave a finger massage to the bridge of his nose. 'I did plan to go to his place. The bastard owed me over twenty grand, but I got tied up. I called earlier in the evening to tell him I wouldn't be showing up and that I'd see him on Monday.'

'In that case you must have an alibi,' Temple said. 'I'm particularly interested to know where you were and what you were doing between eight and ten.'

'I was at the casino,' Dessler said. 'Got back here about midnight. I was just about to leave to go there again. It closes at five and I want to win back some of the money I lost.'

'Which casino? There are three in Southampton.'

'The Grand. There were plenty of witnesses, so you can check.'

'We will,' Temple said. 'And you were there all evening?'

'Correct. I'm a regular. They know me well enough. So you'd better look for someone else to blame for Mayo's murder. He probably owed money to a string of other people. He had a serious gambling problem.'

'And you helped him fund it.'

'I lent him the cash as a one off,' Dessler said. 'I don't make a habit of it. I'm not a loan shark if that's what you're suggesting.'

'Of course you are,' Temple said. 'You charge astronomical rates of interest and you prey on the vulnerable.'

'I lent him the money as a favour. If he was

alive he'd tell you that himself.'

Temple pursed his lips. 'So why don't you tell me about the threats you made against him.'

'I didn't threaten him. I just made it clear I wanted my money.'

'And you told him you would hurt him if he didn't give it to you.'

'Don't be ridiculous. I'm a businessman, not a thug. I don't need to go around threatening people.'

Temple almost smiled at that one.

'So you're saying that you didn't go to Mayo's cottage and beat him to death?'

Dessler's mouth curled into an unsightly smile, revealing perfectly straight white teeth. 'Do I look that stupid, Inspector? If the guy owed me money then the last thing I'd want is to see him dead.'

'What if you knew he was writing a story about you and your nefarious activities? A story that would be published in a Sunday red top and would likely land you in prison.'

Dessler frowned. 'What are you on about?'

'As you know, Mr Mayo was a journalist and a partner in a freelance news agency,' Temple said. 'We have reason to believe he was writing an article exposing you as a crook.'

Dessler grinned again, this time a little nervously.

'Firstly I'm not a crook,' he said. 'And secondly I know nothing about any article.'

'Well, I'm sure it'll make interesting reading,' Temple said. 'After all, as well as the loan sharking there are the girls and the brothels and whatever else you've got your dirty mitts in.'

'You're flailing in the dark, Inspector. You've got nothing on me and you know it. I run a legitimate escort agency. I bring people together. It's all above board. Your friends in Vice have tried to stitch me up often enough and they've always wound up looking like the Keystone Kops.'

'Well I don't work in Vice,' Temple said. 'And I'm not interested in your sleazy business dealings. But I am keen to know if you've graduated from pimping to murder.'

Dessler blinked twice. 'I told you. I had nothing to do with it and I've got an alibi. Now if you want to ask any more questions I want my lawyer present.'

'In that case I'll have to take you down to the nick.'

Dessler puffed out his cheeks. 'This is fucking ridiculous. I've done nothing wrong.'

'Well, if you really are innocent then I'm sure you won't mind us looking around this flat,' Temple said.

'Nice try, Inspector, but unless you've got a

search warrant you can piss off. I'm not going to let you fit me up.'

'At least show me the soles of your boots,' he said.

Dessler's eyes popped. 'What for?'

'Because there was a lot of blood at the scene of the murder and quite a few shoeprints.'

Dessler gave a pinched smile. 'And you think I'd be stupid enough to still be wearing the shoes if it was me who did it?'

Temple shrugged. 'Even sadistic killers make stupid mistakes.'

Dessler shook his head, then surprised Temple by sitting back and lifting his legs. The soles of his shoes were clean.

'Happy?' Dessler said.

Temple was about to respond when his phone rang. He turned his back on Dessler to answer it.

'It's me, guv,' Angel said. 'Where are you?'

'Interviewing Joe Dessler at his flat,' he told her. 'He claims he didn't go to the cottage this evening and has an alibi. But I think I'll bring him in anyway and get a search warrant for the flat.'

'I don't think he's our man, guv,' she said.

'Oh? Why's that?'

'We've found something that implicates Danny Cain in the murder of Vince Mayo.'

'Are you positive?'

'Absolutely, sir. It's firm evidence.'

'So you're saying we can put Dessler on the back burner?'

'I think so, guv. For now at least.'

'In that case I'll come straight back.'

Temple hung up the phone and turned to Dessler, 'OK, Mr Dessler, we're done for now, but I will want to talk to you later. So give me your contact numbers and don't make it difficult for me to reach you.'

'Why would I do that? I've got nothing to hide.'

Temple got to his feet, gave Dessler a contemptuous look. 'The last smart arse who said that to me ended up going down for five years,' he said.

16

The incriminating piece of evidence that Angel had referred to on the phone was a pair of shoes with blood on them. They'd been hidden away in a plastic bag that had been placed in a kitchen cupboard at Danny Cain's house.

Although the blood hadn't yet been analysed in the lab, the forensic technician who examined it confirmed that it was fresh. He was also convinced that the shoes would match the print found in the pool of Mayo's blood.

In addition, blood had been found on the front carpet and pedals of Cain's BMW.

The investigating team, consisting of six detectives and four uniformed officers, had gathered in the CID briefing room. They were all young and ambitious, at least half of them graduates. Average age thirty-three. They were often far too eager to make an impression, but Temple rated them all pretty highly. It meant a lot to him that he had their respect too, even though he knew that some of them thought he was a bit long in the tooth and too set in his ways.

The room smelled of strong coffee, stale sweat and hangovers. Once upon a time you couldn't breathe for cigarette smoke. Back then Temple was on thirty fags a day and George Banks was never without his pipe. Most of the other officers were smokers too, so the place resembled an opium den.

Angel had kicked off the session by delivering the news about the shoes. It was a significant breakthrough, but it wasn't by any means the only lead to have emerged.

'The door-to-door along the road behind the Cain house turned up a resident who said he was out walking his dog after midnight when he saw a man matching Cain's description run past him.'

And according to Cain's immediate neighbours the family were in during the afternoon. But no one seemed to know where they were now.

Angel then told the team that a granite pestle might have been used as the murder weapon. She explained about the mortar and said that the matching pestle had not been found in a search of the cottage.

'So a possible scenario is this,' Temple said. 'Cain goes to Mayo's house for whatever reason and kills him with the pestle. But he makes a mess of it. Then he gets in his car and the neighbour, Mr Nadelson, sees him

148

speeding away from the cottage. Cain drives home, leaving a trail of blood, and then does a runner when we show up.'

'What about the wife and daughter?' Brayshaw asked.

Temple looked at him. 'Good question, but we don't know the answer. Either they were not at home or they fled with Cain, which seems unlikely since they weren't spotted by the dog walker.'

Temple turned to Angel. 'Tell us about the phone calls,' he said.

Angel nodded. 'We think that Cain might have gone to the cottage in response to a call that Mayo made at about eight forty-five. The call has shown up on his landline log.'

'Did Mayo make and receive any other calls last night?' Temple asked.

'There was one from Jennifer Priest at eleven thirty. She also called his mobile. And there was another one earlier at about seven. We checked the number and it turns out it was a pub in Lordshill.'

'Dessler told me he called Mayo to tell him he wouldn't be dropping by,' Temple said. 'So that could have been him. Except he claims he was in the Grand Casino. That was his alibi. I think we need to check the pub. Find out what's going on there.'

The log of calls to Cain's landline threw up

another mystery. Someone phoned the house at 9.50 p.m. It had been answered but the call lasted only a couple of seconds.

'So who made that call?' Temple asked.

'We don't know, sir,' Angel said. 'But here's the odd thing. The call came from a public phone box in the same street as the Cain house.'

Temple arched his brow. 'So who the hell would phone the house from down the street? And why?'

A sudden spate of phone calls around the time Mayo was murdered. That had to be significant. But how?

Temple moved on to give a brief rundown of his conversation with Dessler.

After a short Q&A he asked Brayshaw to check Dessler's alibi with the casino. He then briefed them all on the situation with Jennifer Priest, but they already knew who her father was.

'It doesn't stop us treating her like everyone else,' he said. 'Just be sensitive. The super's very upset about this. That means it's personal. He wants a quick result and is prepared to throw resources at it. So expect some overtime.'

He chose this point to raise the issue of Cain and Mayo's relationship with the police.

'I know how most of you feel about those

two guys,' he said. 'But that must not intrude on this case.'

'That'll be easier said than done, guv,' Brayshaw said with a sour grin. 'We can't help thinking that the bastard at last got what was coming to him for what he did to Banksy.'

Temple gave him a withering look.

'I don't want to hear that kind of talk. It's unprofessional and downright fucking dangerous. Let's be clear: Vince Mayo deserves as much respect as any other murder victim. And Danny Cain deserves to be treated fairly regardless of what happened in the past. Is that understood?'

'If you say so,' Brayshaw said grudgingly.

'I do,' Temple said. 'And if any of you have a problem with that, tell me now and I'll reassign you. This case is going to attract a lot of attention. And remember that as far as the media are concerned Cain is one of their own. If they sense that we're not a hundred per cent committed to finding out the truth they'll crucify us.'

Temple paused to let his words sink in. He noted the shared looks and the rustle of bodies. George Banks had been highly respected and liked by all of them, with the exception of Angel who hadn't been around then. They understood and sympathized with George's reasons for crossing the line. After all, he had only been trying to keep his desperately ill son alive. They'd therefore condemned Cain and Mayo for exposing the wrongdoing. And Temple didn't doubt that right now they were thinking that it would be poetic justice if Mayo had indeed been murdered by his own partner.

But Temple knew he had to do his best to steer them away from such thoughts. They could only lead to complacency and mistakes.

So he moved on with alacrity to the mystery man mentioned by Jennifer Priest.

'We need to find out who this bloke is,' he said. 'If he's a thief it could be he was casing the cottage. So let's check up on all the local tea leaves. I also want someone to arrange for an artist to go over to Jennifer's flat and get a photofit done, then get it into circulation.'

'Leave that to me,' Brayshaw said. 'I'll get it sorted.'

Temple went on to talk about the article that Mayo was writing on Dessler's activities.

'We've taken computers from both houses,' he said. 'So hopefully we'll soon know exactly what they came up with and whether or not it's useful to us. Do we know if this agency has an office?'

'We're on it, guv,' Angel said. 'We got the address from Mayo's contacts book. It's in Portswood.'

'Well, see what you can come up with there and find out if they have any staff.'

Temple asked if any cash had been found at the cottage. He explained that Mayo had left it out to pay Dessler. But no money was found, according to Officer Patel, who had been in overall charge of the search.

'What about jewellery?' Temple said. 'According to Miss Priest he kept his mother's jewellery in a leather box inside his bedside drawer. It's quite valuable, apparently.'

Patel confirmed that he himself searched both bedrooms in the cottage and had not come across any women's jewellery. Or *any* jewellery for that matter, save for a watch and some cufflinks.

'So carry out another thorough search of the cottage,' Temple said. 'If the cash and jewellery aren't found then we have to consider robbery as a motive.'

The door to the briefing room was suddenly flung open and the duty sergeant came rushing in. Her name was Ruth Logan. She was as thin as a fishing rod and wore thick-rimmed glasses that magnified her large, soulful face. She was clearly excited about something, and as she addressed herself to Temple she spoke loud enough for all to hear.

'There's been a development, sir. According to Cain's mobile phone service provider he's been receiving calls from a mobile that belongs to his wife.'

'Then ask the provider to put a trace on both phones,' Temple said. 'If they're switched on they can get the latest triangulated locations.'

Logan's smile had the slightest trace to smugness. 'I already did that, sir.'

'And?'

'We've just got their positions. Apparently both phones are close together and they're right in the city centre.'

'Are you kidding?'

'Definitely not, sir. The phones are both located at this precise time in Palmerston Park. It's just off the High Street.'

'I know where it is,' Temple said, grabbing his coat off the back of a chair. 'Put an alert out and get me a car.'

As he headed for the door he gestured for Angel to follow.

17

The risk he was taking was huge, the implications profound. But there was no going back now. He was committed to a course of action that would change his life for ever.

But before he could start making plans he had to decide what to do with the Cains. If he allowed them to live they would talk and he'd be exposed. It would mean prison or a life on the run in some foreign country where £18 million would buy anonymity. Maybe.

But if he killed them he'd secure a comfortable future as a multimillionaire, safe in the knowledge that no one would ever know the truth.

The downside would be living with what he had done. A family of innocents slaughtered. An act of gross wickedness that right now he was not convinced he could go through with.

He held up the pink lottery slip and examined it in the red glow from the dashboard gauges. £18 million. A massive fortune. But was it enough to temper the pain of a ravaged conscience?

He read the numbers out loud to himself for perhaps the twentieth time. 5,31,22,19,43,7. He still couldn't believe that this was the winning combination. It brought a smile to his face. Caused his hands to tremble slightly.

So much money and so much he could do with it. The possibilities were endless. It would buy security, peace of mind, a life of sheer luxury. He'd now get to see all the places he had dreamed of seeing. Do all the things he never thought he'd get around to doing. And the irony was not lost on him. Since the National Lottery had first been introduced in the UK he had never once purchased a ticket. For him the odds were always so great that he considered it a complete waste of time and money.

But now he had the winning ticket. And as soon as it was safe to do so he would submit it and claim the money. But there was still a way to go yet. Danny Cain continued to be a liability. He had to be neutralized and fast, before he told someone what was happening.

The kidnapper glanced through the side window of the Mercedes. He could see Cain on the other side of the small city centre park. A desolate figure who was a little too conspicuous.

But he was alone. The kidnapper was sure of that, having watched him and the surrounding area for the past half an hour.

It was therefore time to make his move.

* * *

The call from the kidnapper had been short and sweet.

'Where are you?' he said.

'The old city walls,' I told him. 'I'm hiding up on the ramparts. The police — they came to the house.'

'I knew they would.'

'So what now?' I asked.

'Do you know Palmerston Park?'

'In the city centre?'

'That's the one. There's a small car park between the park and the high street. It's behind a public toilet.'

'I know it.'

'Then be there in half an hour.'

'What about my wife and daughter? Are they all right?'

'So far they are. But be warned. If you try to be clever they won't live to see the sunrise.'

The line went dead.

That had been an hour ago and I was still in the car park freezing my nuts off. I could feel the anger twisting my stomach. The rest of me still ached from my ordeal with the two youths.

Why was he late? Was it a test? Was he watching me? Or had something gone wrong?

There were four cars in the car park and no sign of life in any of them. I stood with my spine against the brick wall of the public toilet. From here I had a view of the park, which even at this hour was not entirely deserted. I could see a few shadowy figures moving along the pathways and huddled beneath the occasional halogen lamp.

This whole thing was completely surreal. Like it was happening to someone else and I was watching the action from above.

My thoughts turned to the identity of the man I was about to meet, the creature who had turned my life into a nightmare.

Who was he? Had Vince known him? Had he been at the cottage when Vince discovered he had won the lottery? Did they open a bottle of champagne with the intention of sharing it? Or did he suddenly appear on the scene after Vince called me? And what was with the pile of cash on the worktop?

I recalled the conversation on the phone. Vince was naturally excited. But he said nothing to suggest that there was someone in the house with him.

Vince did not have many friends and certainly the ones he did have could not be described as killers or kidnappers. But he had some enemies. No doubt about that. Among them most of Southampton CID. But Vince's addiction to gambling had also introduced him to a world that was full of shady and desperate people.

I knew of at least one who had threatened Vince.

Joe Dessler.

Vince owed him a large sum of money and because he couldn't pay it back he had started snooping on Dessler in the hope of digging up enough dirt for a story. It was an area of journalism that Vince excelled at. He was a tenacious operator with good contacts and a ferret-like mentality for finding out the facts. So it was no surprise to me that he managed to find the evidence to prove that Dessler was involved in at least two illegal brothels.

But Vince had also stumbled on something else by chance. Something explosive. It was a relationship that Dessler had with a bent copper. Vince had told me about him a couple of weeks ago and claimed that Dessler had him on a retainer.

'*He's a detective,*' Vince had said. '*I've never met the guy but apparently he's an arrogant bastard.*'

The officer kept the law away from Dessler and tipped him off if a raid on one of his properties was in the offing. Vince had been told about the relationship and was aiming to get some photos next. It was a process we knew only too well. It was how we proved that George Banks was selling drugs. Catch them in the act. Secure irrefutable evidence. It was good investigative journalism and police corruption was a legitimate target, especially as the latest official statistics showed a huge increase in corrupt activities during the past three years. There were more incidents of cash being stolen during raids, illegal use of police computers, the taking of bribes, fabrication of evidence and the passing of sensitive information to criminals.

Criminals like Joe Dessler.

So was *he* involved in this? Was he the mystery man who was hoping to be £18 million richer after submitting Vince's lottery ticket?

If you talk to the police I'll know within minutes from a contact on the inside.

That's what the kidnapper had said when I answered the phone to him at the cottage, minutes after I stumbled on Vince's body.

A contact on the inside. Could that be the corrupt detective Vince had got wind of? It was an uncomfortable thought knowing that the kidnapper had someone inside the police helping him out. It made my position more precarious and made me realize that terrible things were going to happen to my family if I didn't get an opportunity to save them.

And how likely was that? The kidnapper was in control. I was just a pawn, doing what he told me to do. Once he took me out of circulation I'd be at his mercy, along with Maggie and Laura. And so my mind circled around this thought: *For how long would he keep us alive?*

Would he claim the lottery money before deciding when and how to finish us off? Or would he rush to do to us what he had done to Vince?

A wave of dread travelled up and down my spine. Whoever this bastard was he was cruel and calculating. He probably wouldn't make any mistakes with so much money riding on the success of his outrageous plan.

The panic started to rise in me just as something else seized my attention. A car was approaching along the road, its nearside hugging the kerb. I couldn't tell what make. The headlights were on full beam. It was crawling along at a snail's pace. I stopped breathing as I watched its progress. My pulse accelerated to an alarming rate. My stomach muscles contracted.

Then the car stopped about five yards away from me. The twin beams pinned me against the wall, causing me to shield my eyes with my hands.

I waited.

After a few seconds the driver's door opened. I took a step forward. Saw a figure emerge on to the pavement. I couldn't see his face beyond the brightness. Suddenly every nerve ending in my body came alive.

I took another step and a strangely muffled voice said, 'Is that you, Cain?'

'It's me,' I replied. 'I've been here for an hour. I want to see my wife and daughter. You said you'd take me to them.'

The man moved to the left and I got to see him. He was dressed in dark clothes and his face was concealed beneath a ski mask.

'Start walking towards me,' he said. 'I have a gun in my pocket and I won't hesitate to use it if you try to be a hero.'

The kidnapper stepped away from the door as I got close, but not before opening the boot. I tried to ascertain the make of the car, but it wasn't instantly recognizable and I didn't have the mental capacity to concentrate. My focus was on the menacing figure in front of me. The movie image of a terrorist or bank robber. But this was real and the sight of him chilled me to the bone. Sinister. Malevolent. Threatening. All words I could have used to describe him.

'Get inside,' he said. 'And be quick about it.'

I hesitated. There was a good chance the bastard did not have a gun in his pocket, so if I jumped him I might bring him down. But what purpose would that serve? I needed him to take me to Maggie and Laura. That was the whole point of following his instructions, even though the likely outcome didn't bear thinking about.

'This is the only way you'll get to see your family again,' he said. 'So get in the fucking boot.'

'How do I know you'll take me to them?' I said.

'You'll just have to trust me, won't you? Not that you have much choice.'

I looked around. The street was still empty. The park seemed even darker. I could no longer see any other people. The knot of anticipation in my stomach tightened. The masked man was right. I didn't really have a choice. He was pulling my strings.

I stepped towards the gaping boot and put one foot in. That was when he pulled something from his pocket and cracked it across the back of my head. There was a blast of pain and I felt myself falling forward into the cavernous boot.

Before the blackness consumed me I heard the squeal of a siren, coming closer and growing louder.

18

'The mobile service provider says the location of both phones has just changed,' said a disembodied voice over the patrol car radio. 'They're together still but on the move.'

Temple didn't like the way this was shaping up. He knew that desperate men tend to resort to desperate measures. And if Cain had indeed killed Vince Mayo then he might well have flipped altogether. This made Temple more than a little anxious about what was happening.

'It sounds like Cain has met up with his wife,' he said. 'Maybe his daughter is with them too. It's a scary thought. If he has lost it completely then they could be in danger.'

As the squad car sped through the city, siren blaring, Temple felt his heart gathering pace. They were closing in according to the voice on the radio. The phone signal placed their quarry in London Road, then Winchester Road, then The Avenue.

'They're heading for the motorway,' the driver said.

Temple leaned forward and grabbed the radio. He started barking out orders. He wanted the northbound carriageway of the

M3 closed off. He also wanted all cars to converge on the area.

'And remind everyone that this man is likely to be extremely dangerous and could be armed,' he said.

Seconds later they were told that the phones were no longer moving. They were stopped at a petrol station just before the start of the motorway.

'That's just two minutes from here,' Temple yelled at the driver. 'For Christ's sake put your foot down.'

The driver was good, but he was also nervous because Temple was breathing down his neck. He almost lost it at one point when he went too fast into a bend. The nearside wheels lifted off the road and they came dangerously close to rolling over.

But they got to the station in less than a minute, and were the first to arrive at the scene. The forecourt was deserted except for a white transit van parked next to the pumps.

The police car screeched to a halt beside it and Temple, Angel and the two uniforms jumped out. It took Temple just a moment to size up the situation. No one in the van. He could see through the wind-screen into the back. Empty.

But he saw that there was a man inside the shop at the counter. The man and the cashier were looking at them and Temple wondered what the hell was going on. It was clear that the man buying petrol was not Danny Cain.

So had the service provider cocked it up? Had they been following a rogue signal?

'Come and look at this, guv.'

It was Angel. She had moved to the back of the van and was staring at something.

Temple walked over. A plastic Tesco shopping bag was hanging from the rear door handle. With something inside it.

'Are you thinking what I'm thinking?' Angel said.

Temple reached for the bag and unhooked it from the handle. Inside he found two mobile phones.

★ ★ ★

Maggie was holding Laura to her chest. Her daughter had woken up suddenly and was now having what appeared to be a panic attack. Her little body was shivering violently and her anxious face was dripping with sweat despite the low temperature in the loft.

'Calm down, sweetheart,' Maggie said, caressing Laura's brow with her fingertips. 'We'll get out of here. I promise.'

'Where's Daddy?' Laura said. 'You told me that Daddy was coming.'

'He is, sweetheart. It won't be long now.'

'But we don't like it here. I want to go home and so does Max. We're both cold.'

Maggie clenched her jaw and fought back tears. She couldn't bear the thought that her daughter was in grave danger. The fear that gripped her was compounded by her own sense of guilt. This was God's punishment for what she had done. She was convinced of it. She was a bad mother and a terrible wife. The old adage that you don't know what you've got until it's gone had never rung so true.

She'd had it all. A loyal husband. A precious child. A wonderful home. And yet it had not been enough. Discontentment had grown like a cancer inside her over the past few years. She had blamed everyone but herself. She recalled what her GP had said:

It could be a form of mild depression, Mrs Cain. It's fairly common. You feel stressed out, you're increasingly worried about finan-cial matters, the spark has gone out of your marriage, you resent your husband for not being more successful. And you're bored. You should talk it through with your husband. He probably has no idea how you feel.

And he didn't. Danny, bless him, remained blissfully unaware that she was putting on an act for much of the time. She had chosen to hide her true feelings because she assumed they would eventually go away and she would feel herself again. But instead she'd continued to feel that there was something missing in her life. It was something she couldn't put her finger on and yet it blighted her happiness and stifled her contentment. Then five months ago she did something that made her feel better about herself. She embarked on an extra-marital affair. It was sudden and unexpected, but as a result she became less moody and more patient with Danny. Their money worries were no longer at the forefront of her mind. She was no longer bored with her mundane existence. Suddenly she had a distraction.

But, of course, she chose not to confront the brutal fact that the affair couldn't last. Had she done so she would have seen that it could only end in tears. Or much worse.

'Did you hear that, Mummy?'

Laura's brittle voice jerked Maggie away from her dark thoughts.

'What was that, sweetheart?'

'I heard something,' Laura said. 'Outside.'

Maggie stilled herself, strained her ears to listen.

Then she heard it. A car's engine. Tyres on gravel.

A spasm of sheer terror shot up her spine. The man in the ski mask was back.

19

The car came to a juddering halt. I heard the grinding of brakes and then the engine was turned off.

It was pitch black in the boot so I couldn't see the face of my watch. I had no idea how many minutes or hours had passed since I was hit over the head.

I'd regained consciousness a short time ago and it had been like waking up inside a drum. The pain pounded my brain in rhythm with the manic beating of my heart. I had tried to move, only to find that my wrists were bound together with duct tape. I tried now to focus on what was happening. It wasn't easy. My head felt like it was being squeezed in a vice.

I heard a car door open and then slam shut. Was he coming for me? Was this the moment of truth? Had he brought me to the place where he was keeping my family? Or was I at the end of some deserted road where he would finish me off and dump the body?

My mind swirled. The darkness taunted me. I felt cold and sick.

Then the boot was jerked open. I was on my back, tethered hands resting on my chest, knees bent. I looked up at the sky, dotted with stars. The darker shape of the man in the mask stepped into view, like a black cloud sweeping across my vision.

'We're here,' he said. 'Get out.'

It was easier said than done. I rolled on to my side, lifted my right leg over the side of the boot, then tried to haul my body out. But I didn't have the strength. So the kidnapper grabbed my windbreaker and pulled me. He was rough and the process was painful. I hurt both my knees and my chest. And when I was at last clear of the boot my legs gave way and I fell on to the damp gravel.

'Don't be pathetic, Cain. Stand up.'

This time he didn't help me. He closed the boot and stood there watching as I struggled to my feet. Once up I was hit by a wave of dizziness and had to steady myself by leaning against the car.

I looked at him in the pale glow from an almost full moon. I could just see the whites of his eyes. And I could also see that he was holding something in his right hand. A revolver. Its dark metal glinted suddenly in the moonlight.

'Where are we?' I said.

'A house,' he replied. 'It's empty, except for your wife and daughter. And you're about to join them, just like I promised.'

I looked at the two-storey building ahead of me. No lights were on. All I could see was a large, black shape in the night.

'Who are you?' I asked him.

'You don't need to know that.'

'But why are you doing this?'

'Isn't that obvious?'

'Not to me.'

'Well, it should be,' he said. 'There are eighteen million reasons.'

He gripped my arm and steered me away from the car.

'Start walking towards the house,' he said. 'And keep quiet.'

My knees felt weak and the thudding inside my head impaired my sense of balance. I swayed from side to side like a drunk.

'Are you really prepared to kill us just so you can get the lottery money?' I asked him.

'I didn't say I was going to kill you,' he said. 'At least, not if you co-operate.'

'So what happens when you hand in Vince's ticket and claim the money?'

'I set you free and disappear.'

'And you expect me to believe that?'

He poked me in the back with the muzzle of the gun. 'Just stop talking and up the pace. The sooner you're in the house the sooner you'll be reunited with your family.'

* ★ *

The house was secluded. That became clear as I shuffled towards it. We were in the countryside, in an elevated position. I could make out a steep hill to my left, beyond the gravel driveway. Some distance away a pair of lone headlights moved slowly along a road. Beyond the road the earth met the sky on an inky canvas. It was dotted with tiny lights from remote homes and small hamlets.

Trees were clustered around the back and sides of the house and through them I glimpsed some lights, but it was impossible to tell how far away they were. There was a flat-roofed garage attached to the property and an army of rampant weeds were sprouting up through the gravel. The front door was made of shiny dark wood. It had two square glass panels and one of them was broken.

'The door's unlocked,' the kidnapper said. 'Go inside.'

I opened the door and stepped into a dark hallway. The kidnapper followed me in and switched on the light. Patterned carpet and plain, papered walls were revealed. A small, cherry-wood unit stood next to the stairs. A framed print above it showed a seascape at dusk. The place looked old and unlived in. A musty smell hung heavy in the air. The top of the unit was covered in dust.

The kidnapper nudged me to one side with the gun and shut the door behind us.

I turned to look at him. He was even more intimidating in the light. The ski mask was black, along with the heavy duffel coat he was wearing over jeans. He also had on a pair of thick, brown leather walking-boots and I noticed for the first time that there was a canvas rucksack on his back.

'So where are my wife and daughter?'

He flicked his head towards the stairs.

'In the loft,' he said. 'Go on. They're waiting for you.'

I started up the stairs, my heart pumping in anticipation. The kidnapper followed me, his gun pointing at my back. There was no carpet on the upstairs landing, just wooden floorboards of polished oak. All the doors were closed. When I saw the loft hatch my spirits lifted.

He ordered me to step aside while he picked up a short wooden pole that was resting against the wall. He raised it to the hatch, hooked the end through a ring and pulled it downwards. The hatch opened and an aluminium ladder slid gracefully out.

He pulled it to the floor. 'I'll go first. Stand well back.'

He moved quickly and a little awkwardly. He was carrying a fair amount of weight, I noticed. Bulkier than me but not by much. I watched him mount the ladder quickly. When he was in the loft he beckoned me to follow with a quick flick of his wrist.

My entire body buzzed with trepidation as I climbed up. But the moment I stepped into the loft space I saw Maggie and Laura. They were cowering against a wall, their bodies bathed in the soft, orange glow from a single naked light bulb.

When Maggie saw me she called out my name. The relief surged through me like a wave of molten lava.

★ ★ ★

As Maggie rose to her feet I saw that she was chained to one of the wooden uprights. It was a gut-wrenching sight. My wife chained up like an animal. It made me want to throw myself at the monster responsible.

Instead, I stepped gingerly across the patchwork of chipboard floor sections to my wife and daughter.

Maggie sobbed when I reached her. 'Oh my God, Danny. I didn't think I would ever see you again.'

The tape around my wrists stopped me

from embracing her, so she did the honours, throwing her arms around me and pulling me against her.

We both cried uncontrollably for about half a minute and I became completely lost in the explosion of emotion. Then I felt something tugging at my trouser leg. Looking down, I saw my daughter's pale, tear-soaked face staring up at me. I dropped to my knees and she threw herself at me, burying her head against my sternum. It was a feeling the like of which I had never experienced. Intense and overwhelming. We were back together as a family.

'Daddy's here now, sweetheart,' I said. 'Don't you worry. Everything will be all right.'

Her little body shuddered and she tried unsuccessfully to speak as she cried. Maggie dropped to her knees to join us, sweeping us both up in her arms. The three of us clung to one another and sobbed. But the wave of euphoria didn't last long. The kidnapper destroyed the moment, just as I knew he would.

'There's a chain hanging from the upright to your left,' he said. 'A pair of handcuffs attached. Get your wife to snap one cuff over your wrist. Then you can remove the tape.'

I briefly considered not doing it because I

knew that once I was cuffed our chances of surviving this were greatly diminished. The only alternative was to rush him, but that didn't seem sensible, seeing that he was holding a gun and my hands were tied. So we complied. Maggie snapped the cuff on my left wrist; thankfully the chain was a good five feet in length which allowed me some movement.

Maggie got the tape off using her teeth and nails, then I embraced them both, squeezing them so hard that at any other time they would have complained that I was too rough.

'Here's some food and water,' the kidnapper said. He threw the rucksack across the loft. It landed next to us with a heavy thud.

'I'll be back soon,' he said. 'Meanwhile, you can scream your lungs out but there's nobody around to hear.'

The light from the hall below washed up over his body, creating the most frightening image I had ever seen.

'What are you going to do with us?' I asked.

He stepped back towards the open hatch and put one foot down on to the top rung of the ladder.

'I told you, I'm going to keep you here until I decide it's safe to claim the lottery winnings. Then I'm going to let you go.'

'But if you let us go now I give you my word we won't say anything to the police,' I said. 'We don't care about the money.'

'But I *do* care about it,' he said. 'And I want to make sure I get to spend it.'

'The police are not stupid,' I said, the anger rising in me. 'They'll find you. The cottage was a mess and I guarantee that you left a shit-load of clues.'

He gave a caustic laugh. 'If that's the case then why are you their number one suspect?'

On that note he lowered himself through the hatch and pulled the cover down behind him.

20

In the briefing room there were now photos pinned to presentation boards of Vince Mayo's body. All in gory colour. Various notes were scribbled above and below them.

More officers had been roused from their beds and called in. Murders were rare in Southampton and the excitement they generated was intense. But this case was bigger and more emotive than most. It was already causing a stir way beyond anything the team had experienced in years.

After returning from the service station Temple called everyone together. He filled them in on what had just happened with the mobile phones. There were murmurs of disbelief.

'The bastard must have known that we were homing in on them,' Brayshaw said.

'He was playing safe is my guess,' Temple said. 'It's common knowledge these days that we can pinpoint a phone's position.'

Brayshaw shook his head. 'Even so it was pretty smart of him.'

'The important thing is we now have to assume that Cain and his wife are back together,' Temple said. 'But we don't know in what circumstances. She might be a party to what's going on or she might be in the gravest danger, along with the child.'

He pointed to one of the pictures from the Cain house. 'This is Laura Cain. She's six years old.'

It was the kind of photograph that all parents cherish. A little girl wearing a pretty dress and a huge natural smile.

'She hasn't been seen since her grandmother dropped her back at home at about five o'clock,' Temple said. 'There's growing cause for concern for both her and her mother.'

Temple then asked for updates. He was told that no cash or jewellery had been found in Mayo's cottage during a second search of the place. Did that mean the killer had made off with them?

Temple was told that Maggie Cain's mother lived in Fareham, close to Southampton. A car was on its way there now. However, there was still no word on any of Danny Cain's blood relatives, or Mayo's next of kin.

Temple then divided the officers into teams of two and gave them specific tasks, one task being a trawl of CCTV cameras around the murder scene and Cain's house.

'This case is developing fast,' he said. 'The

evidence is so far suggesting that Cain killed his partner. Now he's leading us a merry dance. We need to find him quickly because God only knows what state of mind he's in and what level of threat he poses to his family and everyone else.'

★ ★ ★

Marsha Rowe was the only employee of the Southern News Agency. She was a frumpy, overweight woman in her forties with a narrow face and prematurely greying hair that was tied up in a bun at the back of her head. She looked tired and nervous and had clearly been crying.

Temple thanked her for coming to the station at such an early hour and escorted her to his office. Once she was seated, a uniformed officer was dispatched to fetch her a cup of tea.

'Please don't be nervous, Mrs Rowe,' Temple said. 'This is very informal. I just want to ask you some questions about Mr Mayo.'

'It's Miss,' she said in a low, nasally voice. 'I'm not married.'

Temple apologized.

'The policeman who came to get me told me that Vince had been murdered,' she said. 'Is it true?'

'It happened at his cottage in the New Forest,' Temple said. 'Last evening between about eight and ten.'

She put the cup down. Closed her eyes briefly and breathed deeply through her nose. 'It's awful,' she said. 'A tragedy.'

'Were you close to Mr Mayo?' Temple asked.

'As close as a secretary can be. I've worked for the agency since it started. I do all the admin and answer the phone, not that it rings that often. They've been good to me.' She paused as a thought struck her. 'Oh, Lord. Does Danny know yet? He'll be beside himself.'

'Were they close, Miss Rowe? Mr Cain and Mr Mayo.'

She nodded. 'They were like brothers. Very rarely argued, except when Danny lectured Vince about his gambling.'

'We're trying to trace Mr Cain to tell him what's happened,' Temple said. 'But he's not at home and he's not answering his phone. Have you any idea where he and his family might be?'

She looked puzzled. 'No, not unless they're at Maggie's mother's. She lives in the area.'

'Any other relatives or friends they might be with?'

She thought about it and shook her head.

181

'Danny's parents emigrated to Australia some years ago. I don't actually know if he has any brothers or sisters.'

'What about Mr Mayo? We'd like to trace his next of kin.'

'I know his parents are both dead,' she said. 'And he has a sister who lives abroad somewhere. But I don't know her name or her address.'

'When was the last time you saw Mr Mayo?'

'On Friday. He left early, which was unusual. I think he'd had some bad news or something.'

'What makes you say that?'

'Well, that morning when I arrived for work there was a large manila envelope under the office door,' she said. 'It was addressed to Vince and marked strictly private. There were no stamps, so somebody must have slipped it under the door. I left it on his desk and I was in the room when he opened it. I remember how he seemed pretty shocked by what was inside. He quickly put it away in his drawer when he saw me looking. I asked him if he was all right and he said he was fine. But he wasn't. He was moody and preoccupied for the rest of the day.'

'Did you ask him about the contents of the envelope or why he seemed upset?'

'No. I felt that if he wanted me to know he would have told me. I don't like to pry, you see.'

'Would the envelope still be in his drawer now?' Temple asked.

She shook her head. 'He took it with him when he left for the day. I noticed he put it in his briefcase as he walked out the door.'

'What about Mr Cain?' Temple said. 'Where was he on Friday?'

'He was covering the crown court,' she said. 'The agency has a contract with a couple of the national papers to monitor court proceedings. They file stories regularly. Vince normally goes because he enjoys it, but he's been tied up on some special feature on a local criminal.'

'You mean Joe Dessler?'

She was surprised. 'That's right. He runs an escort agency and lends money at extortionate rates to desperate people. The boys were keeping it close to their chests so I don't know much about it. But I know a couple of the tabloids had expressed an interest. It was Vince's project and he was spending a lot of time on it.'

'For your information, Miss Rowe, we've obtained a search warrant for the office. We'll be going through the files and computers.'

She was flustered by this. 'It's in a mess,

I'm afraid. We can't afford cleaners so I usually tidy up on Monday mornings.'

'Well, that won't be necessary this week,' Temple said. 'In fact you won't be able to gain access to the office for a few days.'

She shook her head again and put her fist against her mouth to stop herself crying.

'What kind of financial situation is the agency in?' Temple asked.

She lowered her fist and said, 'Dire.'

'You mean they've not been making much money?'

'That would be an understatement, Inspector. This past year they've really struggled. I was put on a four-day week three months ago and they were even talking about closing the office altogether to reduce their overheads.'

'And did this cause any friction between Mr Cain and Mr Mayo?'

'I don't understand what you're getting at.'

'Just answer the question, Miss Rowe.'

Her brow rumpled. 'But if you're suggesting that Danny killed Vince then you're very wrong. They were good friends. They looked out for each other.'

'We're not suggesting anything,' Temple said. 'But we have to explore every angle. Now please — did it cause any friction?'

'No, not that I was aware of,' she said. 'But I do know that Danny has been taking a lot of

184

flak from his wife because of their own financial situation. He told me she opposed the idea of starting the agency in the first place and was upset that they had lost most of their money.'

'So is it fair to say there are problems in their marriage?'

She nodded. 'I would say so, yes, but I don't know how serious they are.'

Temple spent another fifteen minutes questioning Miss Rowe and she left in a flood of tears. He then went back to the briefing room and told one of the detectives to check whether any large manila envelopes had been found in Mayo's cottage.

At the same time an excited DC Patel approached him with news that Danny Cain had been sighted near the city centre.

'When and where?' Temple asked.

'St Mary's,' Patel said. 'His description matches that of a man who attacked two youths with an iron bar a couple of hours ago, before we got the trace on his phone.'

Temple's jaw went slack. Hadn't one of the patrol car drivers mentioned the attack to him earlier?

'That doesn't make much sense,' he said. 'Where are the youths now?'

'They were taken to the general hospital, sir. A uniform who attended picked up a description of Cain that we circulated and realized they might be one and the same. So he called in.'

'But why would Cain assault two strangers?'

'The youths claim they don't know. That they were attacked for no reason whilst walking home.'

'Seems unlikely.'

'My thoughts exactly.'

'Then send someone over to the hospital to talk to them right away.'

'It's in hand, sir.'

'And check out the scene of the attack to see if there are any security cameras. While you're at it get someone to trawl the city centre CCTV network as well. If Cain has been wandering around town he might be on tape in more than one location.'

Temple went to his office and sat behind his desk. He didn't think he had ever felt so tired in all his years as a detective. He leant back and swivelled his chair so that it faced the window. Outside it was still dark, so he couldn't see the view of the park. But it would soon be dawn and a whole bunch of vibrant colours would grace the day.

But would he be able to shed his own light on what was going on with this case by then? Somehow he doubted it. New questions were being thrown up by the hour. Who was the man in the sheepskin coat watching Mayo's cottage? What had been in the mystery envelope that arrived at the agency's office? And if Cain did indeed attack two youths in St Mary's then what the hell was he playing at?

It didn't seem to make any sense, and what Temple didn't need were complications. He wanted this case to be simple and straightforward; he had a feeling it was turning out to be anything but.

21

The loft was cold and damp. Sounds played into the void from all around us. A constant drip, drip, drip into the cold-water tank. Joists and rafters cracked as the wood expanded and contracted.

My throat was already dry from the airborne fibres given off by the rolls of insulation laid between the floor joists. Where there was no chipboard the fibre-glass matting was fully exposed. I remembered reading somewhere that it didn't make for a healthy environment.

The kidnapper's rucksack had contained three pre-packed sandwiches and two large plastic bottles of water. I managed to eat a whole cheese sandwich and Maggie managed half of one with a ham filling. But Laura said she wasn't hungry or thirsty and when we made her take a bite of a sandwich she started retching.

She was in a state, there was no doubt about that; shocked and terrified, unable to really comprehend what was going on. She'd spent most of the time so far under the blanket whispering to Max. For the first time the presence of her invisible friend did not make me feel uneasy. He was keeping her occupied and that had to be a good thing.

Now, thankfully, she was sleeping between us. But it was a restless sleep. Her body twitched and turned and every now and then she called out Max's name.

The kidnapper had left us two hours ago and we'd heard him drive away. Maggie had told me what happened to them. The phone call soon after I left to go to Vince's place. Then how the man in the ski mask had turned up and forced his way into the house. Now she was sitting with her back to the wall, looking at me intently, fear haunting her expression.

'Do you think he was telling the truth, Danny?' she said. 'I mean, about the police suspecting you of killing Vince?'

'Probably,' I said. 'They might have seen me leaving by the back way when they arrived at our house. Or maybe someone saw me at the cottage. It could have been the guy who lives next door.'

'It's not fair.'

'I know that, but there's nothing I can do about it right now.'

Maggie bit on her knuckle.

'He's going to kill us isn't he?' she said.

I didn't answer.

'He can't afford to let us go,' she said. 'Not unless he wants to be a fugitive for the rest of his life.'

'Maybe he's made plans to disappear with a new identity,' I said. 'Go to South America where he can live the life of Riley with no questions asked.'

Maggie shook her head. 'He won't have had time to think about what he'll do with the money or where he'll go. Don't forget no one knew that Vince would have the winning lottery ticket. So whatever happened in that cottage was unexpected. The man in the mask is making it up as he goes along. He must be. But he's clearly not stupid. He must know that the sensible thing would be to take us out of the picture so there's no link between the lottery win and Vince's murder.'

'That must be why he left the cottage and came straight into town,' I said. 'He must have known that Vince called me. Presumably he wanted to stop me going to the cottage. But unbeknown to him I'd already left.'

'So why did he phone first?'

'You're sure it was him?'

'It must have been. He asked for you and when I said you had gone out he put the phone down. Then he turned up at the door.'

I shrugged. 'My best guess is he was hoping to catch me before I left. Somehow stop me

190

from going to the cottage. But when he discovered I was already on my way he was forced to improvise. He took you hostage and used it to threaten me.'

Maggie gave it some thought. 'But if he knew you were going to the cottage why didn't he wait for you there?'

'Who knows? Could be that he didn't know that I was on my way over, only that Vince had called to tell me about his ticket. Or it could be that he was never at the cottage. That he had an accomplice.'

'What do you mean?'

I told her about the car that was parked outside the church when I arrived at the cottage.

'When I left there it was gone,' I said. 'It might simply have been a coincidence. Or else whoever was in the car might have killed Vince.'

Maggie shook her head. 'But if that person was the killer then why didn't he stop you going into the cottage in the first place?'

I didn't have an answer because none of it made sense. That in itself annoyed me in my capacity as a journalist. I wanted to know the facts of the story even though I feared it would never be told. I didn't want to die. But the thought of dying without knowing the who, why and wherefore made the prospect even more horrendous.

I don't like unanswered questions, unsolved mysteries. They give me angst. I'm a reporter. I like searching for answers, finding them and then basking in the satisfaction of seeing my name in print. This mystery was magnified a hundred times over because I was part of it. I was the victim about whom the reporters would soon be writing their stories. The poor sod caught up in events that were completely out of his control. But by the time the truth came out I'd probably be dead, along with my wife and child.

I'd never know who he was, this masked man who had imposed himself on our lives. I'd never know what happened in the minutes before he — or maybe his accomplice — killed Vince. I'd never know if he went on to lead a glorious life as a multi-millionaire. I'd never know if it had anything to do with Joe Dessler.

'We have to find a way to get out of here before he comes back,' Maggie said.

It was a statement of the obvious but the task seemed impossible. There was no one around to hear our cries for help. I had checked for weak points on the chains and cuffs. There weren't any. There were no tools or sharp objects in the loft that might be used to extricate ourselves.

As I looked around, racking my brain for a means of escape, I felt Maggie's eyes on me. Willing me to come up with the answer. But I didn't turn to face her because I didn't want to disappoint her.

22

At eight o'clock on Sunday morning the hunt for Danny Cain went national.

A hastily arranged press conference was held at the central police station in Southampton. Temple sat alongside Superintendant Priest at a table at one end of the room facing an audience of about twenty reporters, photographers and TV camera operators. In front of them were foldaway boards emblazoned with the Hampshire police logo.

Priest kicked off the proceedings by confirming the identity of the man found dead in his home in the New Forest. He didn't have to mention that Vince Mayo had been the boyfriend of his only daughter. Most of the reporters already knew it. After a brief summary he held up a photograph of Danny Cain that had been taken from his house.

'This is the man we want to question in connection with the murder,' Priest said. 'His name is Danny Cain. He's a freelance journalist based here in Southampton and was, as you may already know, the victim's business partner. We believe he is with his wife and six year old daughter and we're very concerned about their safety. It is imperative that we find this man as soon as possible.'

Cain's photo and those of Maggie and Laura Cain had already been issued to the press and broadcast news outlets. Now they were going to make public CCTV footage that had been obtained in the last few hours.

Priest indicated the large TV monitor on a stand to his left. Angel stood next to it holding the remote.

'There are two short sequences,' he announced. 'The first shows a man we believe to be Danny Cain being attacked by two youths in Southampton city centre. The second was recorded about half an hour later in another part of town. This sequence appears to show the victim getting his own back by viciously attacking the two youths with an iron bar. We are taking the unusual step of releasing this footage because we fear that Danny Cain poses a serious threat to other people and we need the public's help in finding him.'

Priest gave the cue for Angel to run the tape.

Temple watched the black-and-white images for the third time that morning and still he could not believe his eyes.

As luck would have it there were several

CCTV cameras trained on the Bargate, one of them, mounted on a building just yards away, had captured in graphic detail the attack on Cain. It appeared to be unprovoked. The tape showed him walking into the archway whilst looking at his phone. Less than a minute later he reappeared and that was when the youths jumped him. It was a classic mugging. They punched and kicked him and made off after taking something from his pocket.

The camera dwelt on Cain as he struggled to his feet and staggered out of shot. By the time police arrived at the scene he was gone. Only to appear later in St Mary's. There the pictures were not as clear because they were from a private security camera mounted on top of a pole at the entrance to the flats. The action was very much in the background, but once the youths had confirmed that it was the same man they'd jumped earlier it was easy to see the resemblance.

Cain attacked the pair suddenly and savagely after running up behind them. He wielded the iron bar with brutal force, striking the two youths about their heads and bodies. It was no wonder their injuries included a broken nose, a fractured cheekbone and three lost teeth.

As the audience reacted to the footage with

predictable surprise Temple wondered yet again what had possessed Cain to do it. The youths had not owned up to the Bargate attack until they were confronted with the evidence by the officer who went to see them. Then they said they had attacked Cain because he had — in their words — 'annoyed them' by not answering his phone.

They were drunk, they said, and just lost their cool. Having stolen his phone and wallet they made off, believing they would never see him again.

Temple wondered how Cain had managed to find them so quickly? Was it pure chance or had he followed them from the Bargate?

But there were other more pertinent questions that needed answering. Like, what he was doing wandering around the city centre in the first place, having run away from his house? Was he looking for his wife and daughter perhaps? And why did he feel compelled to go after the youths? Was it to get revenge or was it because he was desperate to retrieve his phone?

It was strange behaviour, but Temple wasn't sure how much to read into it. Cain was hardly likely to act normal if he had just murdered his best friend. But even so there was something about the sequence of events that troubled him.

'I suggest you field the questions, Jeff,' Priest said, jerking Temple out of his reverie.

The tape had finished and the Q&A session began.

Do you have reason to believe that Cain might kill his wife and daughter?

What evidence links Cain to Mayo's murder?

Are you looking for anyone else in connection with the killing?

Do you know if Cain and Mayo were working on another exposé about police corruption?

Some of the local reporters knew Danny Cain and Vince Mayo personally. They had worked with them over the years. They found it hard to believe that the man they knew and liked had turned into a homicidal maniac. They were all aware, too, that the pair had enemies within the police, amongst them some of the detectives charged with finding Mayo's killer. Luckily none of them chose to pursue this aspect. They'd probably store it up for later when they were looking for a fresh angle.

'I must stress that Danny Cain has not been convicted of any crime,' Temple said. 'We want to question him about a murder and because of the circumstances we feel it necessary to name him.'

In truth the team were now convinced of Cain's guilt. In the past few hours they had received confirmation that Mayo's blood type matched the stain found on Cain's shoes and in his car. DNA tests were now being carried out. In addition they had found a carving knife in the kitchen sink at the cottage. It wasn't the murder weapon, of course, but the prints on it matched those belonging to Cain. So perhaps he had threatened Mayo with it before beating him to death.

But the real clincher for Temple and Priest was something that had been discovered by the officers who examined Mayo's mobile phone. There were a series of text messages that revealed what had presumably been a closely guarded secret.

If Cain had discovered that secret then he would have had a strong motive for killing his friend and partner.

★   ★   ★

'*It's me, hon. Danny's going to London on Monday to see the editor of the Mirror. But of course you know that. Can we get together early afternoon at your place? Call me.*'

'*It's me. I tried calling earlier but your phone was off. Let's meet in the usual place at lunchtime. I'm in the mood for some car sex in the forest.*'

Those were two out of five voice messages

that Vince Mayo had for some reason saved on his phone. They had come from Maggie Cain's mobile so it was reasonable for Temple to assume that it was her voice.

The service providers for both their mobile phones had also emailed a full list of text messages they had exchanged. Most were of an intimate nature. Lots of kisses. Talking about what they had done to each other and what they wanted to do the next time they met up.

It was clear that Mrs Cain had been conducting an illicit affair with her husband's partner for at least five months. But the last exchange of text messages between the two suggested to Temple that Cain might have got wind of what was going on.

Mayo to Mrs Cain: 'Are you sure that Danny doesn't know about us?'

Mrs Cain to Mayo: 'Positive. Why?'

Mayo to Mrs Cain: 'I think I'm being stalked. Jennifer saw a guy in the woods behind the cottage yesterday afternoon. He was watching the house and had binos.'

Mrs Cain to Mayo: 'Danny was with me.'

Mayo to Mrs Cain: 'So maybe he's hired a private detective.'

Mrs Cain to Mayo: 'You're getting paranoid, Vince. First the man with the camera and now this.'

Mayo to Mrs Cain: '*I told you the guy took a pic of us in the car. I saw him with my own eyes. And, just like the man behind the cottage, he was wearing a sheepskin coat.*'

Mrs Cain to Mayo: '*We were parked in the forest, Vince. He was probably snapping the wildlife. I told you.*'

Mayo to Mrs Cain: '*I'm still worried. If it has nothing to do with Danny then what's going on?*'

Mrs Cain to Mayo: '*Let's meet tomorrow. Call me from the office when you get the chance.*'

That final exchange had taken place a week ago. There were no text messages between the pair after that.

Temple was in Priest's office discussing the messages and their significance. They had not been mentioned at the press conference, but in terms of the investigation they were an explosive development.

But on a personal level Priest was shocked that Mayo had been cheating on his daughter.

'If the bastard wasn't dead already I'd probably kill him myself,' he fumed. 'This is just what my daughter doesn't need at the moment.'

'You don't think Jennifer suspected that Mayo was being unfaithful?' Temple asked tentatively.

Priest shook his head. 'No way. She would have told me. I'm sure of it. And even if she hadn't I would have sensed in her mood and behaviour that something was wrong.'

'We'll have to tell her, sir. Do you want me to do it or do you want to?'

'Of course I'll tell her. She's going to be inconsolable.' Priest sat back in his chair and looked at the ceiling. His rugged features were taut and sallow. He seemed to have aged ten years in as many hours.

'Well, at least we have our motive now,' he said. 'Cain found out about the affair and went to the cottage to confront Mayo. Something was probably said in that last phone call Mayo made to the Cain house.'

'Maybe his wife confessed and he got straight on the blower to confront Mayo. Tell him he was coming over.'

'I think it's more likely that he found out,' Priest said. 'Maybe the mystery guy that both Jen and Maggie Cain mentioned was indeed a private detective.'

Temple nodded. 'Let's hope Jennifer can help us with a description.'

* * *

The latest developments energized the detectives. The briefing room was loud and lively, despite the fact that many of the officers had been up all night working on the case.

The display boards now contained pictures of Cain and his family. There was also a large map of Southampton and the New Forest. Coloured pins showed Mayo's cottage, Cain's house and the sites of the two attacks involving the youths. A sweep of all the CCTV cameras in the city was still in progress, but so far there were no other sightings of Cain.

Temple asked the teams to provide updates. He learned that Mayo had a bank overdraft of £7,000. He also had a string of credit-card debts, as well as his other outstanding loan. Cain's finances were healthier but still in bad shape. The salary he was paying himself was barely covering his outgoings. The Southern News Agency was bringing in a small amount of income from some fixed contracts with newspapers, but it had almost used up its capital base. There was just a few thousand left in a business account with Santander.

Brayshaw had spoken to Maggie Cain's mother. She had no idea where her daughter was, but said she'd taken Laura out for the day on Saturday. When she took her home about five in the evening she didn't bother to stay because her daughter and Cain had been arguing.

'The mother said she didn't know that her daughter had been having an affair with Mayo,' Brayshaw said. 'She told me she found it hard to believe. And I must say she looked pretty upset.'

'So Cain and his wife had an argument only hours before he drove over to Mayo's cottage,' Temple said.

Brayshaw nodded. 'Her mother assumed it was over money. But of course she can't be sure. She didn't have a chance to talk to her daughter. But she did say that money has been an issue between the couple for sometime.'

More evidence had come to light confirming that Mrs Cain and her daughter had been at home on the previous evening. Apparently a neighbour — a Mrs Susan Troy — had dropped by to get a petition signed against a development of flats near by. The neighbour said Mrs Cain answered the door and let her in. Both Mrs Cain and her husband signed the petition and they seemed happy enough. Mrs Cain mentioned that they would soon be sitting down to watch the lottery draw on television.

'Then what the bloody hell happened after that to set things off?' Priest wanted to know.

'It must have been the phone call,' Temple said. 'The one made by Mayo to Cain's land-line. That was at eight forty-five — around the time the Lotto programme ended. We know that Cain went to the cottage soon after.'

'But what about the wife?' Angel said. 'Did she go with him to the cottage or did she wait at the house? And where was she when we arrived? The neighbour in the street behind saw a man who we think was Cain. But there's no mention of a woman and child.'

Brayshaw had checked out Joe Dessler's alibi. He'd managed to track down the owner of the Grand Casino, who was now in the process of obtaining all the security footage.

'He confirmed that Dessler was there last night,' Brayshaw said. 'He saw him several times playing roulette and blackjack. And he reckons he lost a large sum of money.'

The level of interest in Dessler had diminished however since the focus of the investigation had shifted to Danny Cain. But Temple wanted the loan shark to remain in the frame because of his threats against Mayo. And because of the story that Mayo and Cain had been working on, the one that was supposed to expose Dessler as a criminal.

'What about the computers we picked up?' Temple asked. 'Have we examined the drives yet?'

'We're expecting something through any minute,' he was told. 'They're password protected so it's taken a bit of time.'

In fact just an hour after the meeting in the briefing room ended a computer technician named Ben Crawley called Temple to say he had got into Mayo's computer and had managed to download the Dessler story, which was in rough draft form.

'You're not going to like it, Inspector,' Crawley said.

'Oh?'

Crawley read out one of the paragraphs that Mayo had written. The words sent a fast ripple through Temple's body and raised a whole new question about what the hell was going on.

23

Daylight filtered through the cracks along the eaves but the new day did not bring new hope for Maggie Cain. She was cold and terrified. Her soiled jeans had started to smell and the air in the loft had become thicker and more claustrophobic.

Danny and Laura were both sleeping, entwined in each other's arms under the blankets. Maggie had been watching her husband for the past half-hour. His face was a mess, with bruises and cuts and dried blood across his cheeks and forehead.

He'd told her what had happened to him, what he had done to the two youths. She'd listened with a strong sense of pride and admiration. But his words and appearance had increased her own sense of self-loathing.

At least if they died here in the loft Danny would never have to know about her betrayal.

The affair with Vince had been an escape from what she had come to regard as a dull, monotonous life. The passion had gone out of her marriage over a period. The catalyst was the realization that family life was not all it was cracked up to be. She'd embraced it with enthusiasm at the start and made a firm decision not to go back to work until Laura was at secondary school. She wanted to devote all her time to her daughter. She wanted to be the perfect mother.

And at first that's how it was. She enjoyed the whole baby thing, even the nappies and constant vomiting. But as Laura grew up so did the demands on Maggie's time and patience. But that was all right because Danny was bringing in a terrific salary and they had an affluent lifestyle. When Laura was at school she could go shopping or visit the gym. They had lots of expensive holidays and weekends away.

But then everything changed when Danny lost his job. Only ten of the editorial staff were made redundant and her hapless husband had to be one of them. It was grossly unfair.

She began to see things then in a new light. The total, unhealthy dependence she had on her husband. The lack of her own identity. The fact that they were suddenly struggling to make ends meet. She would have to go back to work, but for the wrong reason. Not because she wanted to but because she had to. She became bored, resentful, frustrated.

Vince had always had a crush on her, since the day she went to work in the ad department at the *Post*. But it was Danny, the bright, dynamic reporter, who had asked her out first.

For years Vince remained on the scene, though. He was the office flirt, flitting from one relationship to another, and in a way Maggie had envied his free spirit and devil-may-care attitude to life.

After she left the *Post* to become a full-time housewife and mother she continued to see him through Danny. He came to the house and they would go out as a foursome when he had a girl in tow. Usually there was more than one girl on the scene, since Vince liked to play the field and had a voracious sexual appetite.

But they probably wouldn't have got together if Danny had gone along to the staff reunion at the *Post* just over five months ago. He didn't go because he was feeling poorly that day and stayed at home to look after Laura. He insisted that she should go and asked Vince to take care of her.

That was how trusting he was. It would never have occurred to him that two of the people he loved most in the world would betray him.

After checking with his current girlfriend, Jennifer Priest, that it was all right, Vince took her to the party. He was the perfect companion. He fetched her drinks and danced with her. He told her she looked beautiful and that if she hadn't married Danny he would have snapped her up. It was the drink talking, of course, but nonetheless she was flattered.

The evening was drawing to a close when the banter and flirting turned into something far more dangerous. The last dance. A slow one. Vince held her close. She felt his erection against her stomach, his warm breath on her neck. And then he nibbled her earlobe. She closed her eyes and felt her pulse race. He ran his tongue over her cheek, whispered the words that changed her world.

'For years I've yearned to get this close to you, Maggie. You turn me on more than any woman I have ever known. Danny is a lucky man.'

Vince didn't take her straight home that night. Instead, the taxi dropped them at his cottage where they made love. It was intense and rushed, but it lit a fire inside her that she couldn't put out.

From then on they got together whenever they had the chance. It was a purely physical thing. Passion with a capital P. They were able to keep their emotions in check because neither of them wanted it to go beyond that. What they had was lust and not love. For both of them the affair satisfied a need. Maggie suddenly felt alive again. The aspects of her life that had been bringing her down no longer seemed so important, although she was careful not to let Danny know how she felt.

Vince was a distraction. He made her feel good about herself in a way that her husband no longer did. She liked the excitement, the danger. She liked the uncomplicated, uninhibited sex.

Vince, God rest his soul, was selfish and shallow. Even though he professed to love Danny like a brother, he was prepared to risk their friendship by sleeping with his wife. His offer to share his lottery win with Danny was almost certainly to assuage his own guilt.

Maggie thought back to their last face to face conversation. She had met him in town and over coffee they talked about his belief that he — or possibly they — were being stalked. And it wasn't without some justification. Two sightings of a mystery man in a sheepskin coat was perhaps more than a coincidence.

Maggie agreed that they shouldn't see each other for a while, but she couldn't help wondering whether Vince was using it as an excuse to extract himself from the affair. She had been expecting it, actually. Vince had become preoccupied with his personal problems. His debts were mounting and Jennifer was putting pressure on him because she wanted to move in to the cottage.

Now, of course, his problems were no more and Maggie was in no position even to grieve for him. As for her own perceived needs and wants prior to this nightmare, well they just seemed pathetic now. She longed instead to return to the life she'd had. The life she had put at risk.

'What are you thinking?'

Danny's voice startled her. Her eyes had drifted away from him and she didn't realize that he was awake.

'I'm thinking that I don't want to die,' she said.

Danny raised himself on one elbow, carefully so as not to wake Laura.

Maggie was desperate for him to reassure her, to tell her that they would survive this ordeal. But he just stared at her, his bloodshot eyes heavy with sadness.

For the briefest moment she thought that he was reading her mind and seeing what she had done. But then his chest heaved with emotion and he said, 'We don't know for certain that he's going to kill us. He said he would let us go.'

'We both know he's lying,' Maggie said.

'He can't let us go.'

Danny winced as he pushed himself to a sitting position. He looked down at Laura and stroked her hair. Then, turning back to Maggie, he said, 'We can't give up without a fight.'

Maggie held up her cuffed hand and rattled the chain it was attached to.

'But what can we do, Danny?'

She started to cry and Danny reached over and pulled her close to him.

'We have to find a way out before he comes back,' she said. 'There must be something we can do.'

He squeezed her harder. She felt his blood and sweat and tears. She also felt his unconditional love for her. A love she didn't deserve.

'We'll find a way,' he said, his voice breaking. 'We just have to keep thinking.'

24

Temple tapped his fist against the open door of the super's office. Priest was sitting behind his desk speaking into the phone. He waved Temple in as he continued the conversation.

'I agree this is a serious allegation against DS Jordan,' Priest said into the mouthpiece. 'At this stage we have no idea whether it has any bearing on the murder investigation. We're having trouble contacting the officer.'

Temple sat down on one of the chairs facing Priest. He was tired and sweaty. He rubbed both his cheeks, fingers scraping over a thick layer of stubble.

Priest, he knew, was briefing his superiors at Hampshire police headquarters on the latest development which had taken them all by surprise.

Detective Sergeant Ian Jordan was with the vice squad, which occupied an office in another part of the building. Temple knew him, but not well. He had been transferred from Portsmouth a year ago and was regarded as an arrogant shit, with a loud mouth and a short temper. By all accounts the Pompey lot were glad to get shot of him. It was why Temple had never made an effort to get to know him.

But now he had a reason to because, according to Vince Mayo, Ian Jordan was a bent copper. The article Mayo had been writing about Joe Dessler contained the blistering allegation that Dessler was paying Jordan a monthly retainer. In return for the cash Jordan was steering the vice squad away from Dessler's activities and tipping him off if trouble was brewing. There were other allegations — among them that Dessler was running at least two illegal brothels in Southampton and that he was also blackmailing a city counsellor who had been a regular client.

Mayo claimed he had proof, including an email from the councillor and statements from several prostitutes who had fallen out with Dessler for one reason or another. If it was all true then Dessler could potentially go down for a long time, which was apparently Mayo's objective in exposing him.

But it was the claim about DS Jordan that most concerned Temple and Priest. Another bent copper exposed by the same journalist who exposed George Banks. It couldn't be worse. If the allegations were to be proved it would be a major embarrassment. It would look as though they were presiding over a police department filled to the core with rotten apples.

'What's the latest on Jordan?' Priest asked when he was off the phone.

'He's not at home and he's not answering his phone,' Temple said. 'He's single and because he keeps to himself we don't know much about his private life except that he's a keen angler.'

'Have we come across this so-called evidence yet?' Priest asked. 'This email or the statements from the prostitutes?'

'Not yet, sir. We're still wading through his computer notes and files.'

Priest rubbed his eyes with his fingertips. 'Jordan will have to be suspended while we investigate the allegations. Meanwhile, I want his work station seized and his phone records checked. I also want Dessler questioned about this.'

'Dessler is due for another visit anyway, sir. I'm waiting to hear whether his alibi checks out.'

Priest heaved a sigh. 'This is all we fucking need on top of everything else. It's going to reflect badly on the rest of us.'

'I realize that, sir.'

'Is there any way we can contain it?'

'We can try,' Temple said. 'But I honestly think it's unlikely. In fact I guarantee it's already been leaked. It won't be long before we hear from the media.'

'This is one big mess,' Priest said. 'I mean, look where it leaves us with the investigation. We have Danny Cain in the frame for killing his partner and the evidence stacking up against him is pretty strong. And yet there's all this business involving Dessler and the mystery man stalking Mayo. Plus one of our own fucking detectives has now been added to the mix.'

Temple was about to respond when the office door was pulled open and Angel appeared clutching a sheet of A4 paper.

'I think you both need to see this straight away,' she said, as she crossed the room and placed the paper on the desk.

'The artist just arrived back from your daughter's flat,' she said to Priest. 'That's an impression of the man she saw watching Mayo's cottage.'

Temple stood up and stepped around the desk to look at the drawing over Priest's shoulder.

'If I'm not mistaken it bears an uncanny resemblance to someone we all know,' Angel said.

Temple saw it immediately and gave a sharp intake of breath.

'My God, it looks like Jordan.'

'I don't believe it,' Priest said. 'It can't be him.'

'Well, your daughter reckons it's a good likeness,' Angel said. 'Shaved head, protruding ears. And I know for a fact that he often wears a sheepskin coat.'

Priest went red in the face. 'This is totally fucking ridiculous. Why would one of my own detectives spy on Mayo's cottage?'

'Could he have been on official business?' Angel asked.

'Absolutely not. I would have known.'

'Then I'd like to take a photo of Jordan to your daughter right now,' Temple said. 'Get a more positive identification.'

'I'll come with you,' Priest said. 'It's time I told her about Vince and Maggie Cain.'

25

'That's definitely him,' Jennifer said when Temple handed her a photograph of DS Jordan half an hour later. 'He's the man who was watching the cottage.'

Temple felt a thud deep in his chest. 'You're sure about that?'

'If I wasn't I'd say so, Inspector. But I watched him for long enough to remember the face. It made me nervous at the time and I recall trying to describe him to Vince.'

'And did Mr Mayo have any idea who he might be?'

'He said he wasn't sure, but he might well have been lying about that.'

'Why'd you say that?'

'Because he hesitated when he said it. It just made me wonder, that's all.'

'We've identified him from the description you gave us,' Priest told his daughter. 'His name is Ian Jordan. He's a police officer. I'm his boss.'

Her eyes glinted in surprise. 'The police were watching us?'

'He wasn't there officially, Jen.'

'Then why? I don't understand.'

'Neither do we, but I can tell you that there's a link between him and Joe Dessler.'

'What kind of link?'

'It's possible Jordan was accepting money from Dessler in return for certain favours,' Priest said. 'So maybe Vince did indeed recognize him.'

Jennifer sat back in her chair and stared into her lap. She was still wearing her robe and it looked as though she'd been crying again. The flesh around her eyes was swollen and there was a pile of bunched-up tissues on the floor in front of her chair.

'There's something you need to know, Jen,' Priest said.

She raised her eyes to her father and in them Temple saw that she was drowning in a sea of emotion.

'There's no easy way to say this,' Priest said. 'And I really wish I didn't have to.'

Her brow creased. Her bottom lip quivered.

'What is it, Dad? What's wrong?'

Priest swallowed. 'Vince was having an affair.'

Jennifer's features froze. Her body went rigid.

After a moment she started shaking her head.

'Why are you saying that?'

'Because I'm afraid it's the truth,' he said. 'He'd been seeing Maggie Cain. We know because we've got voice and text messages that were exchanged between them.'

'Vince wouldn't have done that,' she said. 'I know because he was in love with me.'

Her father sat on the sofa and put his arm around her.

'I wish it weren't true, Jen,' he said. 'But it is.'

She stared at him for a few heartbeats, hurt and confused. 'How long had it been going on?'

'We're not sure,' he said, 'but we think it started months ago.'

She continued to stare at him, tears spilling on to her cheeks, her skin turning a shade lighter.

'Did you have any idea that something was going on between them?' Temple asked.

She looked at him as though offended by the question. 'Of course not. Why would I?'

'Were you friendly with Mrs Cain?'

'I've only met her a couple of times. She seemed nice enough. Vince didn't talk about her, but he was fond of the family, especially Danny. It doesn't make sense that he should do something like this to both of us.'

'These things happen, Miss Priest.'

'But not to me,' she snapped. 'We were

221

good together. Why would he go with another woman? An older woman at that.'

'I can appreciate how you feel.'

'I doubt that, Inspector. Not unless you've had it done to you. Right now I feel as though my heart has been ripped out of my body.'

Temple said nothing. He let her words hang in the air. He could see that her mind was churning with questions that might never be answered.

Outside an ambulance siren grew piercingly shrill, then fell silent.

'So what does the bitch have to say for herself?' Jennifer said suddenly.

The anger was to be expected. Her lips stretched back across her teeth and her eyes blazed.

'If you're referring to Mrs Cain, well, we still don't know where she is,' Temple said. 'We're trying to trace her and her husband.'

She scowled, her voice was strident. 'With any luck the bitch will turn up dead like Vince.'

It was an awful thing to say but Temple understood where it came from. This girl had just had all her hopes and dreams trampled into the ground. It was no wonder she was filled with a primal rage.

Her father went to make a pot of tea and Temple asked some more questions. But

Jennifer found it increasingly difficult to answer them. This latest blow had compounded her grief and she was struggling to cope.

Temple had a brief conversation in the kitchen with Priest, then left the flat to drive back to the nick. He checked on progress and was told there was still no sign of Danny Cain and his family.

More CCTV footage had turned up showing Cain's BMW crashing through a red light at about 10 p.m. on Saturday evening. This was on the main road out of the New Forest and even on the grainy tape you could see that he was alone in the car. His wife and daughter were not with him. The footage strengthened the case against the journalist, showing that having killed his partner he had fled the scene in a mighty panic with blood on his shoes.

Temple decided he had to get some sleep. He was struggling to focus now and his thoughts were fogging up. By the time he arrived at his small semi on the outskirts of the city his head was spinning and his eyes were heavy. The place still didn't feel like home. He'd bought it a year after selling the house he'd shared with Erin, but he was already wishing that he hadn't. At the time he'd thought it was what he needed to do.

The constant reminders of Erin and their life together had been torturing him and stopping him from moving on. But now he missed them and at the same time he knew that he hadn't really moved on at all. At least, not inside his head.

He made himself a coffee and carried it up to the bedroom. He undressed quickly and checked the time. It was coming up to midday. He put the alarm on for 3 p.m. and climbed between the sheets.

He was asleep in minutes, but it was a fitful sleep, plagued by an all too vivid dream. But this time it did not feature George Banks dangling from an electric cable.

In this one he watched as Danny Cain battered his wife and daughter to death with an iron bar.

26

As the day dragged on the temperature in the loft rose ever so slightly, but it remained cold.

The three of us stayed huddled beneath the blankets, growing more miserable and desperate with every passing minute. Laura was in the middle and Maggie and I had our arms around her to keep her warm. She kept whimpering, a low, pitiful sound that made my scalp crawl.

She hadn't eaten anything for almost fifteen hours and had managed to drink only a couple of mouthfuls of water. She was scared and confused. It broke my heart to see her like that.

I put my hand under her chin and raised her face to look at me. She was as pale as a Russian swimmer. Her wide brown eyes were devoid of expression. The skin around them was dark, almost bruised. I could see that she had retreated into herself, shrinking away from the terror. I felt the muscles in my throat tighten.

'I promise I won't let the bad man hurt you,' I said.

She blinked. Her top lip curled at the edges.

'Max and me want to go home,' she said, her voice shrill. 'We're cold and we don't want to stay here.'

'I know you don't, sweetheart. Mummy and I want to go home too. I'll soon think of a way to get us out of here.'

'But what will happen when the man comes back? He's wicked and he frightens me.'

I gritted my teeth. Tried to think of something to say that would reassure her. But whatever I said would not be truthful, just like the promise I had just made to her.

I leaned forward and kissed her forehead.

'Let me worry about what happens next,' I said quietly. 'I think the best thing you can do is go back to sleep. Maybe you'll have a really nice dream.'

We made room so that Laura could stretch out between us. She rested her head on my lap and covered her face with the blanket. Maggie massaged her legs and patted her back. We stayed like that, without talking, for about ten minutes, by which time Laura was asleep.

Then Maggie broke the silence.

'I'm certain we're going to die, Danny, but before we do I want you to know that I love you.'

She was looking at me, her features hard

and strained, her long hair in a glorious tangle. My chest heaved and I felt tears gather in my eyes. I reached out, put a hand on her shoulder.

'I love you too, honey. With all my heart.'

'I know you do. I've always known it.' Then she paused, tilting her head so that it rested on my hand. 'I just wish I'd been a better wife to you and a better mother to Laura.'

I grimaced. 'That's a ridiculous thing to say. You've been a great wife and a wonderful mother. You've made me happy and very proud.'

Maggie wiped a tear from her eye with a finger.

'That's not true, Danny. For much of the time I've acted as though I've been ungrateful. I've nagged an awful lot and I've not supported your business when I should have.'

'That's nonsense. You're scared and mixed up and you're not thinking straight.'

She shook her head. 'No, Danny. I know what I'm saying.'

I didn't get it. Why should she give herself such a hard time? Sure, we'd had our problems over the years but no more or less than any other married couple. If anyone should have felt guilty just now it was me. I was the one who had got us into a financial pickle. I was the one who wasn't able to protect his family.

I brushed a tendril of hair away from her forehead and stroked her cheek. Her skin was cold and moist.

'I'll say this only once, Maggie. And then I want you to stop this silly talk and concentrate on how we can save ourselves.'

I took a breath and felt the emotion stir inside me.

'I love you more now than I ever did. You've been a light in my life since the day we met. If we are going to die in this hellhole then I have one big regret and it's that I won't have more precious years with you and Laura.'

She started to say something, but then stopped herself. She reached out and took my hand, squeezing it with all the strength she could muster.

And that was when the dam burst and she broke down. I held her close to my chest and let her cry.

27

The kidnapper dropped the shovel and wiped the sweat from his face with his sleeve.

He was exhausted. Digging, he realized, was as hard as an intense workout on a rowing-machine.

But it had been worth it. The shallow grave he had dug was a necessary part of the plan he'd devised, a plan that followed on from his decision to kill the Cain family.

It was the right and sensible thing to do. He saw that now, having agonized over it for long enough. He would simply have to live with it on his conscience. He could do that. The money would help, and so too would the fact that they were strangers to him. He was engaging with them as little as possible and keeping his mask on to remain anonymous. It helped him to stay detached from them.

The child was the problem. She was sweet and vulnerable and the thought of ending her life was abhorrent to him. But he reasoned with himself that he had little choice.

The guilt would fade with time and since he did not believe in God he did not fear the wrath of Judgment Day. The world was full of murderers, after all, and most of them had never been punished. They went about their lives along with everyone else. Raising families. Watching football. Going on holidays.

Everyone knew that human life had long ago been devalued. It was acceptable to kill in all kinds of circumstances. You only had to look at the television and read the papers to know that.

He lifted his head and looked out over the fertile Hampshire countryside. From here he could see the house, just a five minute walk away. He had chosen this spot because to reach it you had to slug through a patch of thick woodland. Few people came here and those who did so in future would have no idea that they were standing on the grave of Danny Cain.

The kidnapper lit a cigarette and sucked smoke deep into his lungs through pouting lips.

Then he took out his mobile and made a call.

'I've come to a decision,' he said when it was answered. 'They're going to have to die.'

28

'Have you any idea who he is?' Maggie asked me.

'Not a clue,' I said. 'I wish I had. Maybe it would help explain what's going on.'

I'd chosen not to mention my suspicion that it might conceivably be Joe Dessler. She didn't need to know that and I didn't want her to think that Vince and I had brought all this on ourselves by trying to expose him as a crook.

We'd been talking to fill the time. Trying to make sense of what was happening. Laura was still sleeping, her breath ragged.

The same questions kept rolling around inside both our heads. Did the masked man know Vince? Was he at the cottage when Vince's lottery numbers came up? Was he listening in when Vince phoned me? Did he have an accomplice?

I didn't want to die without knowing the answers and I could tell that Maggie felt the same way. It was bloody frustrating. There was a bitter irony too. If the police did indeed think that I had killed Vince then my name would have become big news by now. It was a huge story and I could imagine what the papers and the broadcast news operations would be saying.

Freelance journalist Danny Cain goes missing after his partner is found slain. There's mounting concern for his family who have also disappeared.

Temple and the woman detective had probably come to my home last night to arrest me. Maybe someone had seen me leaving the cottage. The old neighbour perhaps. What was his name? Nadelson. Vince once described him as a busybody and said he was always poking his nose in where it wasn't wanted. Whatever the circumstances, I was apparently suspected of being a killer. Great. I wondered what Temple and his team thought about that. Vince's death had probably caused a stir among them for the wrong reasons. I was willing to bet that some, if not all of them, were secretly pleased.

And yet it was grossly unfair. George bloody Banks had been selling confiscated drugs. We merely exposed him. Sure, I felt bad about his son, but we weren't responsible. Banks was the instrument of his own destruction. Even Temple said as much that day he came to see me.

'*George has done a stupid thing,*' he'd said.

'He brought this on himself, but you know why so surely you can sympathize with him. All I ask is that you kill the story and let us deal with it internally. We'll sort him out.'

But we hadn't, and despite what had happened it was a decision I stood by.

'What do you think the bastard is doing?' Maggie asked, her frail voice snapping me out of my thoughts.

'I expect he's covering his tracks,' I said. 'He'll want to be absolutely certain that there's no link between Vince and the lottery win before he submits the ticket.'

The lottery ticket. I wondered if Vince had been murdered because of the ticket, or had he been killed for another reason and that little pink slip with the numbers on it was purely incidental?

It was another question to add to the mountain that was building up inside my head. And it wasn't one the police would be asking. I was pretty sure of that. They had no idea what was really going on and I very much doubted that there would be any evidence to point them in the right direction.

'What was that?'

Maggie's panic-filled voice jolted me.

'I heard something,' she said. 'Outside.'

We both listened.

'There,' she said.

This time I heard it too. A car on the driveway.

'He's back,' she said.

★　★　★

Five minutes after we heard the car outside the hatch opened and light flooded into the attic. As the ladder was unfolded out of sight I began to experience a rising sense of helpless panic.

Maggie grabbed my arm. I felt her body stiffen. Her breath made a harsh sound. Laura stirred between us, sensing that something was about to happen. I could hear my heart beating like a drum roll.

Was this the end? Was the bastard going to kill us and then go on to claim the lottery cash?

Suddenly he rose up through the ceiling. Head first. It was still covered with the ski mask. Then his body. Dark coat. Dark jumper. Black leather gloves to finish off the guise of Mr Nightmare.

He was carrying a bag which he held up for us to see.

'I thought you might need feeding,' he said.

I was taken aback. He wasn't going to kill us. At least, not yet.

He took several steps across the loft,

ducking to avoid a low rafter. Then he tossed the bag towards us. It landed just in front of me.

'How long are you going to keep us here?' I asked him.

He just stood there for a moment, staring down at us, and I couldn't help but wonder what he was thinking. He smelled earthy and there was wet mud on his boots.

'I told you before,' he said. 'Until I have the money. It won't be long now. I just need to be sure it's safe.'

Laura suddenly realized what was going on and pushed herself against me. I felt her shaking.

'You're going to kill us, aren't you?' Maggie said, her voice full of anger. 'Like you killed Vince?'

He took another step forward. He was a large, threatening figure, but there was no way to gauge his reaction beneath the mask.

'Not if you don't give me any trouble,' he said.

I noticed how close he was. I'd actually crawled that far across the chipboard floor before the chain attached to the stanchion prevented me from going any further.

'Why did you kill Vince?' Maggie asked.

He shook his head. 'No more questions. The least said between us the better.'

'Who are you, for God's sake,' she persisted.

He shook his head again. 'You're wasting your time, Mrs Cain. So just shut the fuck up.'

I mentally measured the distance between us, weighed up the odds on reaching him. They were not good but there was a chance.

'You're a wicked, murdering bastard,' Maggie yelled at him. 'How can you do this to us? It's not right.'

For some reason he didn't budge. He stood there staring down at her as though shocked by her outburst.

'Please let us go,' she wailed. 'We don't know who you are. We won't tell anyone what's happened.'

'Sorry,' he said, his voice so calm it was infuriating. 'That's just not going to happen.'

He started to turn.

It was now or never.

I took a deep breath and propelled myself forward. He was caught completely unaware, having misjudged his position relative to mine. He reacted by twisting his body away from me, but he wasn't quick enough to stop me doing a one-handed rugby tackle.

The chain was attached to my left wrist and this snapped taut as I stretched out as far as I could and wrapped my right arm around his legs. He let out a cry as he lost his balance and fell backwards.

His body crashed down on the floor. I heard Laura scream. I felt the metal cuff cut into my wrist as I clung desperately to his legs, my fingers getting a purchase on his trousers.

I needed to pull him closer so that I could bring my cuffed hand into play. But he started to kick out and I struggled to hold on.

From my sprawled position on the floor I saw Maggie jump to her feet and attempt to help out, but her own chain was shorter and she couldn't reach the kidnapper. She swore instead. Then I realized that the man had heaved his body up into a sitting position.

Shit.

He grabbed at my hair and yanked it hard. I tried to keep my head down, cheek flat against the floor, but the pain and pressure was unbearable.

Then he was digging his fingers into my arms, trying to prise them away from his legs. It quickly became evident that my assault had been misjudged. It was over almost as soon as it began. He knew that as well as I did.

He battered me until I was forced to let go of his legs in an attempt to cover my head and face. At once he was on his feet. Kicking me as though I was a dead carcass.

237

'You bastard,' he yelled, his voice distorted by rage. 'You fucking bastard.'

I tried to roll away from him but he didn't let up. I took a blow to the forehead. Another to the chin. Then suddenly he stopped. And I became aware of a curdled scream erupting from Laura's mouth.

It wasn't a normal scream. This was a hysterical, high-pitched cry like nothing I'd heard before or would want to hear again. I opened my eyes to look at her. Maggie was kneeling beside her, trying to calm her down, but Laura seemed unaware of this. Her eyes were closed, her mouth wide open, and the haunting sound that came out was chilling.

I shifted position and glanced up at the kidnapper. He'd stepped back from me, out of reach, and was staring at Laura.

'Please calm down, sweetheart,' Maggie was pleading.

I hauled myself across the floor towards them. Pulled myself up on to my knees and wrapped my arms around my daughter. Her body was as stiff as a mannequin. I felt the panicked rhythm of her heart inside her chest.

I squeezed her to me, pressing her face against my shoulder. Felt her gradually begin to relax. The screaming slowly subsided, to be replaced by huge, wrenching sobs.

Then the kidnapper said, 'You shouldn't have tried to jump me. I warned you.'

I eased my hold on Laura and turned to look at him as he backed away towards the hatch.

'What do you expect me to do?' I shouted. 'Just wait for you to kill us?'

He reached the hatch and paused.

'My daughter is terrified,' I said. 'Please don't let her suffer like this.'

He put one foot down through the hatch on to the top rung of the ladder.

'Let us go,' Maggie said. 'You don't have to do this.'

He put his other foot through the hatch. Then he paused again and said, 'It's not that simple. If you knew why this was happening you'd understand. I'm sorry, but there's no going back.'

And then he descended the ladder and closed the hatch behind him.

29

Temple came awake at two. He checked his phone but there were no messages, which meant there had been no developments in the case. He heaved himself off the bed and went downstairs.

He made himself a bacon sandwich and sat at the kitchen table to eat it. On the radio the press conference was the lead story. That was good. At this stage they wanted as much coverage as possible.

The second item in the running order was about Saturday night's lottery draw. The holder of the winning ticket still hadn't claimed the prize.

He remembered that he'd bought three lottery tickets himself on Thursday. They were around somewhere so he went looking for them. He found them on the coffee table in the living room, checked the numbers on TV text and sighed when he discovered that not a single one matched those numbers in the winning combination.

Still, he thought, some lucky bastard was going to have a fabulous Christmas as soon as he or she realized they'd won.

Temple showered and shaved, then locked up the house and headed for the station. The sun had disappeared behind a thin layer of grey cloud. There was a hint of rain in the air. The streets had a grim pallor and an ugly feel. Temple sensed it. As he drove into the city he thought about Danny Cain, their chief suspect in the murder of Vince Mayo.

Cain was a desperate man and that made him dangerous and unpredictable. Temple recalled the CCTV images of his brutal attack on the two youths. It convinced him that Cain was a man who was capable of extreme violence. But what would he do next? Would he kill his family and then himself, if he hadn't already done so?

If they were very lucky Cain would come to his senses and realize that he couldn't run for ever. He'd give himself up without harming his wife and daughter and then seek to explain why he'd killed his friend. But Temple had a feeling that it wouldn't happen like that. No, his instincts told him that the outcome of this case was going to be pretty messy and perhaps even bloody.

★ ★ ★

When Temple got back to the nick he was summoned straight to the boss's office.

'It looks like Joe Dessler told you a porky,' Priest said.

'What do you mean?'

'I just took a call from DC Patel. He's seen security footage from the casino. It shows that Dessler left the premises at about seven o'clock. He didn't return until eleven.'

'He told me he was there all evening,' Temple said.

'Well he wasn't. The manager might have thought he was, but he slipped out. And that's not all. You'll recall he also told you that he phoned Mayo to tell him he wouldn't be coming over.'

'That's right.'

'Well, as you know, there was a call to Mayo's landline that evening from a pub in town, the Duke of Wellington. Patel's been there too and checked it out. He's coming back with digital footage on disc which shows Dessler in the pub using the landlord's phone.'

Temple pondered this for a moment. Why had Dessler lied about being at the casino? Where had he spent the rest of the evening?

'We need to look at the footage,' he said. 'When is Patel due back?'

'In about twenty minutes.'

In the event Patel was back in the building half an hour later. They gathered in Priest's office to view the footage.

'I've cued up the relevant sections,' Patel said. 'First the disc from the casino.'

Patel ran the tape and pointed to a tall man in a dark coat who was strolling towards the exit. Just before reaching it he was stopped by someone who wanted to talk to him. And as he turned Temple caught sight of his face.

'That's Dessler,' he said.

Patel fast forwarded.

'This shows him leaving the casino and walking to his car,' he said. 'Note the time — four minutes past seven.'

They watched Dessler get into the car and leave the car park. Then the disc fast-forwarded again to a point where Dessler was seen returning to the casino. The time was 11.15.

Patel then put in another tape.

This one, in black-and-white, was from the pub. It was timed at 7.25 p.m.

It showed Dessler with a young woman at the bar. She was thin and plain and wore a short red coat and knee-length white skirt. Temple guessed that she was one of his working girls. They were chatting away to each other and sharing a bottle of wine.

'Watch this,' Patel said.

They saw the girl pull something from her handbag. It looked like a white envelope. She handed it to Dessler and he put it in his pocket.

The pair talked at the bar for another ten minutes. Then the girl left the pub.

'I'll print off a frame and get it circulated,' Temple said. 'We need to know who that woman is.'

'No doubt one of his escorts,' Priest said.

Temple nodded. 'Which probably means that vice can ID her.'

On screen Dessler took out his phone but it looked as though he couldn't get a signal. He held it up and moved along the bar, but then said something to the barman, who promptly produced a landline which he placed on the counter.

Dessler then made a call, presumably to Mayo.

The call lasted less than a minute. After Dessler replaced the receiver he rushed straight out of the pub.

'So where the hell did he go next?' Temple said.

'He had plenty of time to drive to the forest and back before he turned up at the casino,' Priest said.

Temple agreed. 'So it means we have another suspect. Dessler is now firmly in the frame again, alongside Danny Cain.'

30

An hour later Temple was sitting behind his desk chewing on a sweet and watching the news. The hunt for Danny Cain was still the top story. That was because it had captured the public's imagination.

Cain was a suspected murderer and he now posed a serious threat. Were his family on the run with him or had he already killed them? There was drama, jeopardy, mystery. All the elements of a story that ensured it remained prominent in the minds of the news editors and producers. A feeding frenzy was well under way, only this time hacks were scrambling for information about one of their own.

They wanted to know everything there was to know about him. His state of mind. His financial affairs. His hobbies and habits. They wanted photographs. Interviews with friends and neighbours. Quotes from the police, his parents, his secretary, his accountant.

The news reports included clips from the press conference. There were shots of Mayo's cottage and Cain's house. There were police outside both. A BBC News reporter did a piece to camera in front of the police station, in which he talked briefly about the link between Superintendent Priest and the murder victim. He also mentioned George Banks.

'The police still have no clue about the whereabouts of Danny Cain,' the reporter said. 'And they continue to express their concern about the safety of his wife and daughter.'

It seemed to Temple that there was a veiled criticism in what the reporter said. But then perhaps it was justified. After all, they were no closer to apprehending Cain than they had been twelve hours ago.

Anyone watching the coverage would have been left in no doubt that Danny Cain was a killer. Temple still believed that to be the most likely scenario, but the revelations involving Joe Dessler and DS Jordan had prompted him to consider a full review of all the evidence. The forensic findings from the murder scene and Cain's home; the statements from Jennifer Priest and Marsha Rowe; the notes on Mayo's computer, the messages sent between Mayo and Mrs Cain; the interview with neighbour Bill Nadelson and the man who'd seen Cain running away from his home.

What did it all add up to? Temple

246

wondered. Was he missing something? Something vital? A piece of the puzzle that would make sense of what was going on?

Innocent men don't flee from the scene of a crime or leg it from the police. Yet that was exactly what Cain did after going home and removing his bloodstained shoes. Seldom had Temple worked on a case where the evidence against an individual was so strong. Everything pointed to Danny Cain being a cold-blooded murderer. Something inside him must have snapped, sending him over the edge.

But then where did Dessler fit into it? Why had he lied about his alibi and where had he spent the evening after leaving the pub? It was a real brainteaser and the more Temple thought about it the more his head ached. To cap it all Dessler had disappeared. He wasn't answering his phone and Brayshaw, who'd been to Dessler's flat in Ocean Village, had been told by the security guard that Dessler had left with a suitcase earlier in the day. So was that a sign of guilt? Why else would he bugger off?

Temple could feel the pressure building inside his head. He was about to search for a painkiller in his desk drawer when Angel appeared in the open doorway of his office.

'There's been a development, guv,' she

said. 'Jordan has just turned up at his house. He didn't expect anyone to be there but we were waiting. We're now bringing him in.'

★ ★ ★

DS Ian Jordan was brought to the station at 7 p.m. According to the officers who fetched him he had been ranting and raving all the way and had threatened to make an official complaint.

Temple spoke to Jordan's boss in Vice, DCI John Halliwell, and explained the situation. Halliwell had already been briefed about the allegation and wanted to have a go at Jordan after Temple had finished with him.

'If he's been on the take then I'm going to roast the bastard,' Halliwell said.

Interview room one was oppressively hot. Two radiators pumped heat into a space just twelve-by-twelve feet wide. There was a metal table, a wall mirror, a video camera mounted on the ceiling and four moulded plastic chairs.

By the time Temple sat down Jordan was calm but remained indignant.

'What the fuck is this all about, Jeff?' he demanded to know. 'I'm one of you, for pity's sake.' His voice had an abruptness to it, a strident quality.

Temple was not aware that he and Jordan had ever been on first-name terms. It put his back up and set the tone for what was to follow. He explained that it was not a formal interview so there were no lawyers or recorders. That would come later if it was deemed necessary.

Jordan was pale and unshaven, his skin damp with a sweaty sheen. There were black circles beneath his eyes. He was wearing a denim shirt and matching jeans and his sheepskin coat was on the back of his chair. Temple wondered if it was a permanent accessory.

'We've been trying to contact you,' Temple said in a flat monotone. 'Where have you been?'

Jordan licked his lips nervously and shook his head. 'What's that got to do with you? I've been off duty, so where I go and what I do is my business.'

Temple could see why he was so unpopular in the nick. He was an arrogant git of the first order.

'Just answer the question, Detective Sergeant.'

Jordan's lips were pulled back against his teeth. He had narrow eyes and protruding ears. His hair was shaved to within half an inch of his scalp and he was a dead ringer for the face in the drawing Temple had seen earlier.

'I've been night fishing,' Jordan said after a moment. 'I go every other weekend when I'm not working. Since when is that a frigging crime?'

'What time did you go?' Temple asked.

Jordan drummed his fingers on the table. 'I got there about six on Saturday evening. Left at lunchtime today and went straight home. Two bloody uniforms were waiting outside for me. And let me tell you those fuckers will regret talking to me the way they did.'

'Where did you go?' Temple asked.

'The front at Warsash.'

'Anyone with you?'

'No. I always fish alone. Have done for yonks.'

'Did anyone see you there?'

'Nobody except the fishes. Now are you going to tell me what this is all about? I'm a detective, not some scumbag off the street.'

Temple pursed his lips and stared Jordan hard in the eyes.

'Where's Joe Dessler?' he asked.

Jordan tried to act surprised by the question but it didn't come off.

'How should I know?' he said.

Temple heaved a sigh. 'Look, I can do without the bullshit, OK? Tell me where he's hiding out. We want to question him about the murder in the forest last night.'

Jordan arched his bushy brow.

'Are you talking about Vince Mayo? That piece of slime had it coming. Shouldn't it be a cause for celebration around here?'

'Remarks like that are not helpful,' Temple said.

'But it's true and you must know it. Wasn't George Banks your best mate?'

'Forget about Banks. Right now I'm interested in finding a killer.'

'I thought Mayo's toerag of a partner was in the frame for that,' Jordan said. 'I heard about the press conference on the car radio.'

'There've been some developments,' Temple said. 'For one thing we discovered what you'd been up to.'

Jordan moved his head to one side. 'What are you on about?'

'Just tell us where Dessler is.'

Jordan sat back and folded his arms across his chest. He tried to project an air of confidence but it didn't work.

'I have no idea where he is,' he said. 'Why should I?'

Temple leaned forward, locking eyes on Jordan. 'Because we know that you're in his pocket.'

Jordan blinked a couple of times.

'I don't know what the hell you're talking about,' he said. 'But I do know it's a serious fucking accusation. What's Halliwell say about this?'

'He's pissed off. We all are. You see, we have proof that you've been on Dessler's payroll for some time. Within the hour I'll have the go-ahead to delve into your bank accounts. So you might as well come clean.'

Jordan started to get to his feet but Temple roared at him to stay put.

As he sat back down his jawline pulsed and he suddenly lost some of his swagger.

'Listen to me, you pathetic shite,' Temple said. 'One person has already been murdered and whatever's going on I believe you're in it up to your neck.'

Jordan's eyes skittered nervously up to the video camera. 'Don't be ridiculous. I'm not involved in any of that.'

'Is that so? Well, let's just look at what we've got so far.'

Temple held up his fingers and started counting them off. 'First, we've got you for corruption. You're a bent copper and that makes you lower than the low in my book. Then we've got you stalking Vince Mayo, who happens to have been the murder victim.'

'Fuck off. I'm no stalker.'

Temple jabbed a finger at him. 'You were

252

identified by Jennifer Priest as the person spying on Mayo's cottage through binoculars. I can tell you that her father — Superintendent Priest — is not happy. You were also seen taking photographs of Mayo in a car with Mrs Maggie Cain. So you see why you're high up there on our list of suspects?'

'I didn't kill anyone,' Jordan said, his face flushed.

'Then try to convince me of that,' Temple said. 'Tell me what's been going on. Why were you watching Mayo? Where's Dessler? And what do you know about Danny Cain?'

Panic flared in Jordan's face. He rested his arms on the table, fingers splayed.

'I want a fucking lawyer,' he said.

31

Jordan's reaction came as no surprise to Temple. He was after all an experienced copper. He knew the rules, even if he wasn't prepared to play by them.

While they waited for a lawyer to turn up Temple went back into the briefing room for an update.

There had been more than thirty alleged sightings of Danny Cain. They were spread across the country and would all have to be followed up. The Chief Constable of Hampshire was hounding Priest for a result. The papers were hounding the press office for more information. A local radio reporter had learned that a vice squad officer had been arrested. She wanted to know the details.

Temple went to his desk, checked his emails, then called Priest to update him.

'Not much so far, sir,' he said. 'Jordan has demanded a lawyer.'

'So what's your impression, Jeff? You reckon the allegations in Mayo's article will stand up?'

'I'm afraid I do. Jordan is a sleazebag and I don't understand why he hasn't been rumbled long before now.'

'There'll have to be an investigation. We'll get to the bottom of it.'

'Yeah, and a fat lot of good it will do,' Temple said.

The lawyer who turned up to represent Jordan was well known to Temple. His name was Irwin Applebaum and he was with one of the best legal firms in town. Tall, jogger-trim and in his forties, he had a reputation for being ruthless but straight. Most of the officers who needed representation called on his services.

After a private consultation with his client, Applebaum announced they were ready to resume the interview.

If anything Jordan looked paler and more nervous than before. That was probably because the gravity of the situation had sunk in. Applebaum was a smart brief and he would have convinced his client that co-operating with his accusers on Dessler might play well when and if they eventually charged him with corruption.

At first Jordan continued to deny everything, but when confronted with some of the facts in Mayo's article he began to crack.

The article included dates and places where Jordan had met Dessler and money had changed hands. There were also statements from two of Dessler's girls who claimed they had 'entertained' Jordan for free.

Temple then introduced new evidence — bank statements picked up in the last hour on a warrant from Jordan's flat which showed regular monthly cash deposits of £2000 into his account. How did he explain them?

Jordan was astute enough to realize that he was in deep shit. He was also bright enough to know that if he wasn't careful he'd end up so far in that there would be no way out.

So he finally opened up.

★   ★   ★

'It started about a year ago,' Jordan said. 'I called up Dessler's agency and got them to send a girl over to my flat.'

'You mean a prostitute?'

'Yeah.' Sheepishly.

'Go on.'

'Well, the girl that the agency sent was a stroppy cow. She was crap in the sack and mouthy. I wasn't happy so I refused to pay. We got into an argument and she took a swing at me with a bottle. I lost my temper and punched her in the face. It wouldn't have happened if I hadn't been a bit drunk. I didn't mean to hit her so hard. I broke her nose.'

Temple would have liked a pound for every copper whose career had hit the rocks because he got involved with a prostitute. It had been a common occurrence back in the seventies and it was happening again. The soaring divorce rate among coppers was partly to blame, plus the fact that the government insisted on cracking down on the oldest game in the world. It meant that coppers were dealing with working girls and their pimps far more frequently. So there was far more temptation and many more opportunities to seek out a cheap thrill.

Jordan was flustered and embarrassed now. He drank tea from the plastic cup in front of him and didn't flinch even though it must have been cold.

'After she ran out screaming I knew I was in the shit,' he said. 'I called the agency and asked to speak to whoever was in charge but she had already been in touch with them. They sent a car to take her to the hospital. Then about thirty minutes later Dessler and two of his minders turned up at my house. They were going to give me a kicking before they realized who I was. It changed things. They saw an opportunity. Said if the girl made an official complaint my career would be over. I didn't need to be told that. So they made me an offer. Work for them and they'd put things right. They'd pay me a retainer and give me regular free sessions with the girls.'

'And that was an offer you couldn't refuse,' Temple said, his voice dripping with contempt.

'It was either that or end up on the fucking dole with a conviction for ABH.'

Temple felt the urge to reach across the table and pile a fist into his ugly face. He wondered how the bastard had got away with it for so long. Why had it taken a freelance journalist to expose him as a crooked cop and a sleazebag? Why had it not been bloody obvious to all of his colleagues in Vice?

There was a whole list of questions relating to his day job that would now need to be answered. Like how many times had he tipped Dessler off about operations? How much confidential information had he disclosed about Dessler's enemies?

But all that could wait. Another time and place. Right now they had to focus on a murder investigation.

'So tell me why you started stalking Vince Mayo,' Temple said.

Jordan was sweating profusely now. As he spoke his right eye developed a twitch. His breathing became laboured.

'Mayo owed Dessler a pot of cash,' he said. 'Dessler was getting fed up waiting for it. So he threatened him a couple of times. He also talked to me about fitting him up for something just to scare him into paying.

'Anyway, Dessler then got wind that Mayo was going around asking lots of questions and delving into his affairs. Even a few of his girls were approached. I think the one I hit gave Mayo some information. She was still pissed off that I'd got away with it.

'Then someone told Dessler that Mayo and his agency were putting together a news exposé on his activities. He was going to pay him a visit and sort it out but he was worried that if things were in writing and if Danny Cain was party to it, then it would get out anyway.'

'So what did he do about it?' Temple asked.

'He called me. Asked me to dig up what I could on Mayo and to follow him around. See what he had. He said he'd pay me a few extra grand. So I said I'd do it.'

'What did you do exactly?'

'Dessler wanted me to break into their office and access their computer, but I wasn't prepared to go that far, although I told him I'd try to. Instead, I followed Mayo. Spied on him if you like. I took pictures and watched his home. I didn't really expect to find anything but within days it became obvious that Mayo was shagging his partner's wife. It was a result. I got photos of them together.'

'Did you know that they saw you?'

He shrugged. 'I know they did on one occasion when they were in his car. But there was another time when they didn't see me. I photographed them through the French doors at the cottage when he was giving her one on the sofa.'

'What did you do with the information?'

'I took the photographs to Dessler,' he said. 'Told him he should use them so as to get what he wanted. From what I knew about Mayo's relationship with Cain it was clear he wouldn't want his partner to find out. They were supposedly best mates. Went back a long way.'

Temple thought about the envelope that Marsha Rowe had mentioned. The one that seemed to upset Mayo.

'Did Dessler send the photos to Mayo's office in a manila envelope?'

Jordan nodded. 'I put them under the door myself. There was a note in there too. It warned him that they would be shown to Cain if he didn't stop work on the article and pay the money he owed.'

'And did Mayo respond?'

Jordan shrugged. 'The pictures were delivered on Friday. Dessler called me on Friday evening to say he'd spoken to Mayo.

He said Mayo had agreed to pay him some money and stop writing the article. He'd arranged to collect some cash on Saturday night.'

'And is that what he did?'

'How the hell should I know? I didn't speak to him after that. I'd played my part. I didn't want to be involved any more. I went fishing to clear my head. I was tired and stressed out. Then in the early hours of this morning Dessler called me. Said that Mayo had been murdered and he'd been questioned. He was in a panic.'

'Why? Because he killed Mayo?'

'He said he didn't, but he feared he'd be dragged into it and maybe even get fitted up. He warned me to keep my mouth shut, said he was going to disappear for a bit until things cooled down. Then he hung up and I switched off my phone so I could give myself some breathing space and try to work out what to do.'

'And what about Danny Cain?' Temple said. 'Where does he come into this? We know he was at the cottage last evening. His wife's affair gave him a motive for murder. Now he's on the run. Could he be in cahoots with Dessler?'

Jordan shook his head. 'I don't see how. Cain never really figured in anything except he was Mayo's partner and therefore they were both effectively working to bring Dessler down.'

Temple had to repress the anger that bloomed in his chest. He would have paid good money for just half an hour alone with Jordan. The man was a dirty, slimy disgrace and he'd given more ammunition to those who were critical of the police.

'Do you think Dessler went to the cottage and killed Mayo?' he asked.

A frown wrinkled Jordan's brow. 'I don't know. It's possible. Dessler is a ruthless fucker and he has a fierce temper. I'd say he's capable of killing anyone who poses a threat to him and his little empire.'

32

Temple questioned Jordan for another hour, by which time he was sure he'd told them all he was going to.

He informed him that he'd be formally charged in the morning. Meanwhile, he'd be held in custody and was duly sent, shame-faced, to a cell for the night.

As Temple headed back to the briefing room he knew that they had to fully reassess the case. There were more elements to it now. The photographs. Blackmail. Betrayal. Two suspects on the run.

Now they knew that at least three people had a motive for killing Mayo. Cain, because Mayo was screwing his wife, and Dessler, because Mayo owed him money and was writing an incriminating article about him. Then there was Jordan, who also had a motive. He must have been fearful that the story Mayo was pulling together would involve him and threaten his future — maybe even his freedom.

But still the strongest piece of evidence involved Cain. He had Mayo's blood on his shoes. That in itself would be enough to get him convicted by a jury.

Temple explained to a room full of CID officers that Jordan had confessed to being bent. They all expressed their outrage because they knew it would mean another huge internal inquiry into which they would all be drawn in one way or another. More bad publicity. More passing the buck. And no doubt more unsavoury revelations about what certain police officers in the Hampshire Constabulary were up to.

'We have a warrant to search Dessler's flat,' Patel said when Temple started to assign new tasks.

'Go over there and check it out then,' Temple said. 'See if he's left any clues to his whereabouts.'

Then, just minutes after the meeting broke up, another bombshell dropped.

Brayshaw banged a mug on his desk to get everyone's attention. 'I just came off the blower to the lab,' he said. 'They've now run all the fingerprints from Mayo's cottage and there's a little surprise.'

'What is it?' Temple said.

'There were a couple of prints on the plastic handle on Mayo's bedside drawer. The one we believe he kept his mother's jewellery in.'

'And?'

'Well, they match those of his neighbour, Bill Nadelson.'

33

If you knew why this was happening you would understand. I'm sorry but there's no going back.

The kidnapper's words bounced around inside my head. I wanted to know why he'd said that. What did it mean? It was really bugging me.

After he descended from the loft we heard him drive away in his car. It then took us the best part of fifteen minutes to calm Laura. I had never seen her in such a terrible state. It had all finally got too much for her. The fear had built up inside her until she could hold it in no longer.

Now she was lying between us again. Exhausted, nearly catatonic. Her breath loud and hoarse. And she was still shaking. She couldn't stop shaking.

If you knew why this was happening you'd understand.

How could he possibly think that? He seemed to be suggesting that his actions could somehow be justified. But only a complete psycho would think that. And the masked man did not strike me as a complete psycho. He'd brought us food and drink. He'd refrained from making our ordeal any worse than it was through abuse and torture. Complete psychos did not act like that. At least, I didn't think they did.

'You're reading too much into it, Danny,' Maggie said. 'He killed Vince so he could get his hands on the lottery ticket. That's obvious. It doesn't matter how he came to be at the cottage. All that matters now is that he's desperate to cover his tracks and that means we're going to die whatever he says.'

She was right, of course, but that did not satisfy my curiosity.

'There must be something we can do,' she said tearfully. 'Please, Danny. Get us out of here.'

She wrapped her arms around her knees and started rocking back and forth. A sob bubbled in my throat as I watched her. Once again I was going to disappoint the woman I loved. I felt the despair flowing through my veins. I should be able to protect her. But how? I was chained up like a fucking dog.

In the silence that followed the guilt set in. It came at me in unforgiving waves. I experienced a fresh bout of anger too. I wanted to kill the animal who was doing this to us.

Who was he, for Christ's sake? Where was

he now? Did he have a job? A wife? A family? Even a bloody name?

Right now he was just a man wearing a ski mask. Tall and strong. A voice with no discernible accent. He was economical with words, careful and resourceful. I guessed his age at anywhere between thirty and sixty. It was impossible to be more precise.

Was he Joe Dessler? I had never met the man, only seen a photo that Vince showed me. Sure, the agency had been working on an exposé of his illegal business interests, but it had been Vince's baby. My own involvement had been minimal. He had done all the research and started writing the first draft. For him it had been personal and I had warned him to be careful.

When he told me what he had I could see it would make a cracking piece in one of the Sunday red tops. There was everything to titillate and shock. Underage prostitutes from Poland and the Ukraine. A bent detective. A couple of illicit brothels. A bully-boy loan shark. Its publication would have triggered a major police investigation into Dessler's activities and that, surely, was something he would have wanted to stop happening.

But Maggie was spot on when she said that the kidnapper's identity was irrelevant anyway. It wouldn't change anything. He would still be intent on claiming the lottery money. And he would still be determined that he should get to spend it without fear of ending up in jail.

34

Bill Nadelson was not at home. There was no car on his driveway. Temple found this immensely frustrating. Since they had no idea when he'd be back Temple called in for authority to search the house.

While he waited for the go-ahead he went and had another look around Mayo's cottage. A uniformed officer was still stationed outside because the forensic sweep was still in progress upstairs.

He took a call from DC Patel who said that they were searching Dessler's flat but there was no sign of the man himself.

'Any indication where he might be?'

'Not so far. We'll keep looking and I'll keep you posted.'

Temple glanced at his watch. Another sleepless night ahead. Almost twenty-four hours since the murder and what did they have to show for it? Three suspects but nothing concrete. Not very impressive. Then a thought struck him. He called Angel at the station.

'The girl Dessler met in the pub,' he said. 'Have we identified her yet?'

'I don't know,' Angel said. 'We sent a uniform to the pub with a printout from the CCTV footage. I'll check.'

Temple hung up and wandered outside. He tried to pull his thoughts together. He was confused and frustrated. The case was getting to him.

Cain. Dessler. Nadelson. Jordan. All of them were connected to Mayo. All of them were suspects. But the picture was still as blurred as ever. He just couldn't get a handle on it. The questions were taunting his tired brain.

Where was Cain? What had happened when he came to the cottage last night? Did he simply confront Mayo over the issue of his wife's affair? Or was there more to it? Where did Dessler go after leaving the pub and where was he now? Why were Nadelson's fingerprints on Mayo's bedside drawer? And did detective Jordan know more than he was letting on about Mayo's murder and events leading up to it?

Then there were the two questions that needed answering more urgently than all the others. Where were Maggie and Laura Cain? And were they safe? He was desperately worried about them.

Temple's phone rang. It was Angel.

'We've got a name and address of the

woman Dessler met in the pub,' she said. 'Colleen Wild. Aged twenty-five. She's a working girl and well-known to Vice. They believe she shares a house with two other girls and they use it to service clients. Dessler runs it and Vice have raided it twice but each time the house was clean. Now they know why.'

'Jordan?'

'Almost certainly.'

Temple hung up and then took another call, this time from Priest with the go-ahead to search Bill Nadelson's house. A unit was on its way with a ram for the door.

Thirty-five minutes later they were inside the house and a team of officers started the search.

'As well as the jewellery we're looking for a pile of cash,' Temple said. 'And, of course, anything that might have been used as the murder weapon, including a large granite pestle.'

Temple thought back to his conversation with the neighbour. He'd seemed genuinely shocked and upset by what had happened. He'd said he saw Mayo's body and then phoned the police straight away. No mention of going upstairs and opening Mayo's drawers. And no mention of a pile of cash on the worktop.

Temple recalled how anxious Nadelson

271

suddenly became when he was told his prints would be taken for elimination purposes. His face had registered alarm, which Temple had put down to shock.

'I've got something, sir,' one of the officers called from upstairs after only ten minutes.

The officer had pulled a suitcase out from under a bed. It was unlocked. Inside there was a bundle of notes that totalled £3,000. There was also a leather jewellery box and inside that a collection of brooches and bracelets that had almost certainly been worn by Vince Mayo's late mother.

35

Temple left an officer in Nadelson's house and asked for a scene of crime team to be sent over. He then called Angel and told her to put out an alert for Nadelson.

'Meanwhile, I intend to drop in on Colleen Wild,' he said. 'What's her address?'

They found the house in a street that was desperately in need of a facelift. The pavements were lined with wheelie bins. Most of the tiny front gardens were littered with rubbish. The property façades were shabby and in various states of disrepair. Broken gutters. Dirty brick walls.

The patrol car parked across the road. One of the uniforms went off to check the rear of the property and the other followed Temple up to the front door.

Temple rang the bell. The door was opened after about fifteen seconds by a skinny, dishevelled girl who looked barely out of her teens. She was wearing faded jeans and a red T-shirt. Her bob of blond hair was completely lifeless. She didn't seem surprised to see them, but that was probably because she was spaced-out on drugs.

She said nothing, just stared at them, her expression empty.

'Is Colleen Wild in?' Temple asked.

'Who are you?' she replied.

'We're the police. Can we come in?'

'What for?'

'We want to speak to Colleen.'

'I didn't say she was in.'

Temple was in no mood to mess around so he pushed open the door and strode into the house.

'Hey, you can't do that.'

'I just have,' he said. 'Now, where's Colleen?'

The girl shook her head. 'She's not here.'

'Then where is she?'

'I don't know.'

At that moment they heard floorboards creaking above them.

'Check down here,' he said to the officer. Then he hurried upstairs.

The landing had a grey threadbare carpet. The walls were painted an ugly shade of purple. A powerful waft of marijuana hung in the air. There were three doors. One was open and revealed a toilet. Temple opened one of the others and peered in. A bedroom. Double bed and cheap-looking wardrobe. No sign of life.

He heard a noise beyond the other door

and pushed it open. In this one the large double bed was occupied by two naked bodies. A woman riding a man, her heaving buttocks facing the door.

She did not become aware of Temple's presence until he cleared his throat with a rattling cough. Then she stopped thrusting her hips and turned around. He recognized her as the woman on the CCTV footage.

'Colleen Wild?' he said. 'I'm DCI Jeff Temple of Southampton police and I want a word with you.'

Shocked, she rolled off the man and jumped off the bed. Without bothering to cover her nakedness she glared at Temple.

'What the fuck do you think you're doing? You can't just barge in here.'

The man on the bed sat up. Thin. Pigeon-chested. His milky flesh was covered in sweat.

Temple flashed his warrant card. 'Sorry to spoil your fun, but I suggest you get dressed and leave. I have some business to conduct with the lady of the house.'

Colleen Wild then started mouthing obscenities. Temple picked up a dressing-gown from the floor and tossed it to her.

'Put that on and come downstairs.'

'Go get fucked,' she yelled at him.

'And if you don't co-operate I'm going to

arrest you for running a brothel,' he said. 'So why not make it easy on yourself and do as I ask?'

She stood rooted to the spot, her mind working, and Temple found it hard not to look at her body, which was in great shape.

The punter struggled into his clothes and hurried out of the room without saying a word. Temple wondered if the poor sod would expect a refund.

Colleen slipped on the dressing gown. 'OK, let's get this over with. Then you can fuck off.'

The second uniform was in the living room with the girl who had opened the door to them and a middle-aged woman wearing a green sweater and a short, tight, black skirt.

'Meet Dawn and Anna,' the officer said.

They were sitting on an overstuffed sofa looking bored. The older woman, Anna, was plump, with a pale doughy face and bright-red lipstick. It turned out she was Polish and spoke little English.

Temple asked Colleen to sit on the sofa with them and then got straight down to business.

'Right. If you tell us what we want to know we'll leave straight away and let you get on with your business,' he said. 'If you don't you'll all spend the night in a cell.'

'Just get on with it,' Colleen said, her voice clipped and impatient.

Temple stood in front of them, hands on hips. He suddenly felt self-conscious as three pairs of eyes stared up at him. He personally did not have a problem with prostitutes and therefore he felt obliged to treat them with respect. Theirs was the world's oldest profession and if that was how they chose to make a living then good luck to them. But his attitude towards the men who exploited them was different. He felt nothing but contempt for people like Joe Dessler.

These girls probably felt the same way, but would never admit to it. To them Dessler was a man to be feared. Their pimp, protector and abuser. Temple knew they would not want to upset him.

'Tell me where I can find Joe Dessler,' he said.

'Who?' This from Colleen. The others didn't respond.

'Look, we know he runs this place,' Temple said. 'We also know you must be scared of him. But I don't care. We want to question him about a murder. He's done a runner and if you conceal information then you'll be implicated too.'

'We don't know anyone named Dessler,' Colleen said.

'Yes you do. He's the one you met in the pub last night. You gave him an envelope which I assume contained his commission. We have the transaction on tape.'

Colleen gritted her teeth. 'You bastard.'

'We don't care about the money,' Temple said. 'Or you. We just have to find Dessler and since you work for him I'm betting that you have some idea where he's gone.'

Colleen shook her head. 'Even if we knew we wouldn't tell you.'

'Then you're obviously more stupid than you look. This man is dangerous. We intend to put him away, if not for murder then for living off immoral earnings and running brothels. He'll be banged up for a long time and so will you if you don't help. So if you want to avoid arrest tell us where he's likely to be hiding out.'

They remained silent. Colleen started biting her nails. She looked worried. Anna, the Pole, looked confused. The skinny one just looked out of it.

Temple told the two officers to search the house. As they set about the task he started questioning the women again. But they continued to insist that they knew nothing of Dessler's whereabouts.

That was until one of the uniforms discovered a bag filled with cocaine. Several thousand pounds' worth. Temple held it up in front of them. All three women stared at it.

'There's a lot of stash in here, ladies,' he said. 'More than enough to put you inside for a spell. Is that what you want?'

They looked at each other. The skinny one was suddenly more alert. Clearly they didn't warm to the prospect of spending time behind bars. But even so they were not directly forthcoming. It took another fifteen minutes of cajoling and threatening before Colleen rolled her eyes and said, 'All right. You fucking win. There's only one place I can think of. It's a house. We've been to parties there. It's near Winchester and Joe has always told us never to talk about it.'

36

A house near Winchester.

It would have been a promising lead were it not for the fact that Colleen Wild and her two friends professed not to know the address. They were taken there at night, they said. It was dark and they drove along various country lanes. None of them could remember the route or any particular points along the way.

Temple had brought them back to the station and spent the best part of an hour questioning them individually about Dessler and the house in the country.

They told him about the parties where Dessler's girls would entertain high-spending clients. There was always lots of booze and drugs and sex.

Temple got them to look at a map of the Winchester area but they were not able — or willing — to elaborate on what they'd already said. He decided to keep all three in custody overnight. He'd have another go at them in the morning and give thought to whether he should charge them with drug-related offences.

Then it was back to the briefing room

where Priest told the team about Jordan's confession. He also updated them on Dessler and Bill Nadelson. Priest then handed over to Temple, who talked about Colleen Wild and co.

'The house she mentioned is a long shot,' he said. 'But it is possible that Dessler has gone there to stay out of sight. So we need to find out where it is.'

He went on to assign new tasks to the team who'd be working through the rest of the night. Those who'd been on since the previous evening were instructed to go home and get some sleep.

Then Priest took Temple to one side.

'You need to get some rest too,' he said. 'You look absolutely shattered.'

'I went home and caught a nap earlier,' Temple said. 'Besides, I don't like to ease up when things are moving so fast.'

'We've got good people in place,' Priest said. 'And they've all been given their assignments.'

Priest was about to go back to his office when DS Patel suddenly appeared at his side. The officer looked worried.

'Sir, I've just taken a message for you. It's about your daughter.'

Priest gave him a quizzical look. 'What about her?'

'I'm afraid she's been involved in a car accident, sir. The officers who attended the scene recognized the name and called it in.'

Priest blinked at him. 'Are you sure? My daughter's at home.'

'The officers are positive, sir. Your daughter was injured but I don't know how seriously. An ambulance took her to the General.'

'But it must be a mistake,' Priest said.

Patel shook his head. 'I don't think so, sir. It's her car and it happened very close to where she lives.'

Priest looked at Temple, puzzled. 'I don't understand. Where the hell was she going at this time of night?'

'You should go straight to the hospital,' Temple said.

Fear and confusion suddenly rippled across the super's features. For a couple of seconds he didn't move. He just stood there, mouth open, shaking his head.

Then he suddenly came out of his trance and said, 'You're right. Let's go.'

37

Fifteen minutes later Temple and Priest arrived at the hospital. The patrol car dropped them outside the accident and emergency department and Temple followed Priest inside.

Temple had never seen his boss in such a distressed state. He was beside himself with worry and had hardly said a word during the ride from the station.

It was a busy night in A&E, but Priest's commanding presence ensured he had everyone's attention as soon as he burst through the swing doors. He didn't bother approaching the reception desk. Instead, he went straight up to a nurse with a clipboard who was talking to one of the patients waiting to be seen.

'You've just had a car accident victim in named Jennifer Priest,' he said. 'Where is she?'

The nurse pointed. 'You'll need to check in at the desk, sir. The receptionist will be able to help you.'

'There's a queue. I haven't got the time. Just tell me where to go.'

The nurse started to speak but at that moment Temple noticed two uniformed police officers walking along the corridor towards them. He took Priest by the elbow and steered him away from the nurse.

'The uniforms are here, sir. They'll know.'

As Temple suspected, the uniforms were the ones who had attended the accident and called it in when they realized that the super's daughter was among the injured. They'd been expecting Priest to show and were ready to tell him all they knew.

'Your daughter is in a treatment room,' the taller of the pair said. Temple recognized him as Constable Todd Fleming. 'She has a number of injuries and remains unconscious. But her condition is not critical.'

'I want to see her,' Priest said.

'Then come this way, sir.'

Temple followed the group back along the corridor. A nurse greeted them, asked them to wait outside the treatment room whilst she talked to a doctor. Soon after the nurse appeared again and invited Priest into the treatment room. The rest of them waited outside. Temple dug out some loose change and got three coffees from a vending machine, handing them to the uniforms.

'OK,' he said, when they were seated in the waiting area. 'What happened?'

The details were still sketchy, but it seemed that Jennifer Priest was lucky not to have been killed. The accident had happened at a road junction only yards from her block of flats. She had apparently driven into the junction at some speed without stopping. A car coming from the left had slammed into the passenger side of her VW, crushing the door and sending both vehicles into a spin. They ended up careering across the road and into the wall of a house.

A middle-aged couple in the other vehicle had both escaped with minor injuries. Jennifer was still strapped to her seat when the officers arrived on the scene and they helped paramedics to extract her and put her in the ambulance.

'Any witnesses?' Temple asked.

'Only one, sir,' Constable Fleming said. 'It happened to be one of Miss Priest's neighbours in the flats. He said Miss Priest ran past him as he was going into the block. He said hello to her but she ignored him and dashed to her car. He watched her get behind the wheel and screech away from the kerb. He kept watching because, in his words, she drove like a maniac. So he actually saw her cross the junction and get hit by the other vehicle. He was the one who called the emergency service.'

Temple jotted down the neighbour's name and address.

He wondered where Jennifer had been going and why she was in so much of a hurry to get there. He was still thinking about it when Priest came out of the treatment room.

'How is she?' Temple asked.

'She's still not awake,' he said. 'She has two broken ribs and her left leg is fractured. She's also concussed and they're concerned about some internal bleeding.'

'Shit.'

Priest choked back tears. 'But at least she's breathing normally. They say she's serious but not in danger.'

Constable Fleming handed Priest a fresh coffee from the machine. As he sipped it he started shaking his head.

'I can't believe it's happened,' he said. 'She could have died.' Priest's eyes were sagging, his voice raw and ragged.

Temple suggested to him that he should sit down.

'I'm going to stay with her,' he said. 'Will you get someone to bring my car over?'

'No problem,' Temple said. 'Is there anything else I can do for you?'

'No. I'll be fine. I'll just be glad when she's awake.'

'I'm sure it won't be long, sir.'

Temple then told Priest what the officer said about the accident.

Priest frowned, his face radiating a dozen questions. 'I don't get it? What made her leave the flat? I spoke to her earlier and she didn't mention that she might be going out.'

Temple shrugged. 'Maybe she just got upset and needed to go for a drive.'

'The poor girl has had a nightmare time of it,' Priest said. 'First, Vince. Then the affair with Cain's wife. And now this. Jesus, it's not fair.'

Priest was on the verge of tears. Temple didn't know what to say. It was one thing dealing with members of the public in this situation, but quite something else when dealing with your boss.

'I'd better go,' he said. 'Are you sure you're going to be all right here, sir?'

Priest nodded. 'Of course I will. Call me if you need to.'

38

Jennifer's car was being lifted on to a recovery truck when Temple got to the junction where the accident happened. The other car involved had already been taken away.

Temple had a few words with the officers at the scene but learned nothing that he didn't already know. Then he walked to Jennifer's block and looked up the neighbour who saw the accident, a Mr Raymond Noye.

Temple rang his security buzzer. A voice responded almost immediately and he explained who he was. A minute later he stepped into a top floor flat where Noye lived with his girlfriend. They were still up drinking coffee and talking about the accident. Noye looked pretty shaken. They were both student types in their twenties and Noye was happy to describe what he saw after pouring Temple a coffee.

'She was sobbing as she came bounding out the block,' he said. 'I tried to speak to her but she ignored me completely. She was in a real hurry and she looked scared.'

'Scared?'

'That's right. As in terrified. It was like she

was desperate to get somewhere and her life depended on it.'

'Did you see anyone else?'

'No, there was nobody else around, although I have to say I can't be absolutely sure because I didn't come straight into the block. When I saw the crash I ran over there.'

Temple thanked him, finished his coffee and left. Out of curiosity he went downstairs to Jennifer's flat, not really expecting to find anything untoward, but checking it out nonetheless. What he found surprised him. Her front door was ajar. He paused outside, wondering if she had left in such a hurry that she had simply neglected to close it. Or was there someone inside?

He should have played safe and called for back-up from the officers waiting in the car. But instead he ventured into the flat.

The lights were on.

'It's the police,' he called out. 'We're coming in.'

He stood in the hall, tense and alert. No sounds reached him so he started to explore the flat and soon discovered it was empty. Everything appeared to be in place. There was no mess. Nothing broken. No sign of a struggle.

The landline phone was on a side table in the living room. He picked it up and dialled

1471. He wondered whether maybe she had received a call that spooked her and sent her running, scared, from the flat. But the last call had been from a mobile that Temple recognized as belonging to her father. And that had come in much earlier in the day.

Temple replaced the phone and left the flat, making sure to close the door behind him. He got the patrol car to take him back to the station. On the way he called Priest on his mobile. 'How's Jennifer?' he asked.

Priest sounded solemn. 'She's still unconscious, but the doctors tell me they're quietly confident that she'll make a full recovery.'

'That's good.'

Temple told him that he had dropped in on Jennifer's flat.

'She must have left the door open,' he said. 'I looked around but everything seems to be in order. I also checked her landline — she hasn't received any calls this evening. Might be worth taking a look at her mobile if she has it with her.'

'So what the hell happened to make her rush out of the flat and get behind the wheel of her car when clearly she was in a state?'

'I spoke to the neighbour who saw her,' Temple said. 'He described her as being in a hurry and looking scared when she bolted past him.'

'What was she scared of?'

'He didn't know. He didn't see anyone chasing her, either.'

'Then I don't get it.'

'Like I said before, maybe it all got too much for her, sir. She needed to get away from the flat to unwind.'

Priest issued a heavy sigh. 'Shit, Jeff. All my life I've dealt with victims and their families. But now I know what it feels like to be one of those people. And I can tell you it's pretty scary. I feel as if I've lost control of everything. That being a policeman counts for nothing. I can't protect my daughter even though I thought I could.'

Temple said nothing. He didn't feel the need to. After a moment he told Priest that he'd call back in the morning. The patrol car took him back to the station.

He didn't go up to the office. Instead, he picked up his own car and drove straight home.

39

I could tell it was morning because of the light that slipped in through the vents in the eaves. But it wasn't enough to bring fresh life to the grim loft space. It had been a dreadful night. I'd slept for brief periods but for the most part had lain awake, cuddled up to Maggie or Laura, listening for the sound of our nemesis downstairs in the house.

My body ached and there was a constant throbbing behind my brow. I was now sitting up, back against the wall, knees up to my face. Maggie and Laura were curled up together next to me under the blankets. I wasn't sure whether they were sleeping or just lying there, dreading what the new day would bring.

I'd woken, sweating, from a dream about half an hour ago. In the dream I was back at the *Mail* before they'd sacked me. The high-flying reporter. On top of the journalistic tree. The big stories. The big salary. Front page bylines. It was what I had always wanted and for a spell I had it. And it was great.

But now, given our circumstances, I realized how unimportant it all was. And how fragile. Like every aspect of our lives. Who can ever know what will happen from one day to the next?

My breath caught in my throat as I looked around our prison: at the slanting roof with its layers of black insulation material; the thick timber joists; the cobwebs and dust and bare brick walls.

Were we going to die here? Would he leave us to rot? There was no food left and only a few drops of water in the plastic bottle. If the kidnapper did not come back how long would we survive? A week? Maybe two?

Pictures skipped in my head, a series of vivid stills of our three bodies decaying. Turning into skeletons as this house eased from one season to the next without anyone ever coming into the loft. I found myself hoping that he wouldn't leave us to die in that way; that he would make it quick, perhaps with shots to the head. Execution style.

Laura rolled on her back, peered at me above the blanket. I forced a weak smile, felt tears leak from the corners of my eyes.

'Have you thought of a way to save us, Daddy?'

I felt my skin tighten, my mouth go dry.

'Not yet, sweetheart, but I soon will. So don't you worry about it.'

And I was determined to stick to my word,

despite the fact that being a journalist hardly qualified me as someone with the brains and brawn to get out of a life-threatening situation. The closest I'd ever come to such a thing was to write about people who've done it.

A couple of stories I'd covered in the past came to mind. The young soldier who survived weeks of torture at the hands of Islamic terrorists and then somehow escaped and made it back to his family. And the guy who trod water in shark-infested seas off Florida after his boat sank. I interviewed him by phone after he was rescued and he said he told himself that if he just kept moving his legs he might get lucky and live through his ordeal.

Well, now I had to force myself to be inspired by what they had done. I had to use their stories and others like them to pull myself out of the quagmire of defeatism. After all, you don't have to be a cop or a secret agent or a fictional hero to pull yourself back from the brink. You just have to look into your daughter's eyes and know that you'll do whatever it takes to keep her alive.

40

Temple was back in the briefing room just before ten on Monday morning, having managed just four hours' sleep. He'd been churning over scenarios and possibilities, trying desperately to pull all the strands together and make sense of them.

The night crew gave him an update which amounted to very little. There was still no sign of Cain, although the papers were full of the hunt for him and his family. Detectives were still busy contacting friends, relatives and associates of both Cain and Mayo. But there were no new leads.

Then there was Joe Dessler. Nobody knew where he was, or if they did they weren't saying. And to top it off Bill Nadelson still hadn't turned up. Where the hell had that lying bastard snuck off to?

Temple stood in the briefing room staring up at the evidence boards. The anger and frustration tried to shake itself out of him. But it wasn't enough. He wanted to yell at someone, anyone, just to release the pent-up emotions.

Instead he decided to have another chat

with the three prostitutes. He asked for Colleen Wild to be brought up first and taken to an interview room. He also asked for Jordan to be taken to another room when his lawyer showed. It was time to charge him formally and see if the rat was holding anything back.

Then Temple called Priest.

'Good morning, sir,' he said. 'What's the news on Jennifer?'

'She's conscious at last,' Priest said, 'but I haven't spoken to her yet.'

'Is she stable?'

'Yes, thank God. The doctors have stopped the internal bleeding. Thankfully it was not as serious as they first thought.'

'Well I'm glad to hear that her condition is improving. Hopefully you'll be able to talk to her soon and find out what happened last night.'

'What about your end, Jeff? Any progress?'

'Not so far, sir. I'm just about to have another go at Colleen Wild. This house in the country she mentioned is our only lead to Dessler and it's not much.'

'Well, keep me posted.'

Temple then went to the interview room. A WPC greeted him, then stood with her back to the door.

Colleen was already at the table with a duty

solicitor. She was angry and restless. The morning light streaming through the window was not kind to her, revealing as it did the lines in her face and the hollow expression in her eyes.

'I hope you slept well,' Temple said as he sat down facing her.

Colleen scowled. 'Very funny. I've had enough of this. You are well out of order, so charge me or let me go.'

Temple put his coffee on the table. 'We need to have another conversation first, Colleen. I'm sure a night in the cell has refreshed your memory about this house you mentioned. The one where the parties were held.'

'I still don't remember where it is,' she said. 'Like I told you it was dark every time I went there and I wasn't paying attention.'

'But you were driving so you must have some idea.'

'Who said I was driving? Most times I was driven there by one of Joe's guys.'

'The problem is I don't believe you,' Temple said. 'I find it hard to imagine that you didn't know where you were going.'

'Well, it's a problem for you, then. Not for me. Besides, I don't know why you're so obsessed with that place. He's probably not there anyway. He could be anywhere, even abroad by now.'

'Then how about telling me where else he might be. We know he left his apartment block carrying a suitcase.'

She threw her head back and sighed. 'Bollocks to this. Look, I know my rights and I don't have to stand for any more of your shit. Charge me with possession if you want. It's no big deal. Otherwise let me go.'

He continued to press her. How long had she been working for Dessler? How many brothels did he operate? Was he a violent man? Could she remember any of the punters who attended the parties?

But her answers were vague and unsatisfactory. She'd worked for Dessler for about a year, she said. Yes, he could be violent, and she had seen him attack and bully the girls on several occasions. She wasn't sure how many brothels he ran but she was pretty sure the premises would not be in his name. And no, she couldn't remember the names of any of the punters who went to the house parties.

'Look, I honestly don't know much about anything,' she said. 'That's the way Joe operates. He doesn't tell us much. When I went to the parties I was usually off my head. Everything was a blur. I was either filled up with booze or dosed up with coke. All I can remember is that the house was in the country and pretty remote.'

After half an hour Temple sat back, disappointed. He'd already decided he wasn't going to charge any of the three women. They were small fry and the drugs in their possession didn't really amount to much. Why create more work for themselves when there was so much else going on?

He downed the rest of his coffee, said, 'OK Colleen, you're free to go. But I'll be talking to your friends next.'

'Well, don't build your hopes up,' she said. 'They're not the brightest matches in the box.'

Temple got up and opened the door. As Colleen breezed through it he said, 'It goes without saying that if you do find out where Dessler is I want you to call me straight away. That's if you don't want to land yourself in serious trouble.'

She snorted as she walked out of the room. At that moment a uniformed officer was leading a handcuffed DS Jordan along the corridor.

Colleen stopped and looked at him. He returned her stare, a slight frown creasing his features.

'Hey, I know that guy,' Colleen almost shouted. 'I thought he was a copper.'

'He is,' Temple said drily. 'How'd you know him?'

'Because I met him once. In fact I gave him a blow job. A freebie.'

'Charming. Where was this?'

She hoisted her cheeks into a wide grin. 'At one of the parties I told you about. That bloke was one of the guests. I bet he'd know where the house is.'

★ ★ ★

'Right, now listen up,' Temple said, addressing his team of detectives. 'We have a possible location for Joe Dessler. It's a house near Winchester where he's been staging sex parties for clients.'

He'd got the address from DS Jordan, who had consulted his lawyer before imparting the information and admitting that he had attended two parties at the house earlier in the year as a guest.

The property was a secluded four-bedroom house a mile from Winchester, the ancient cathedral city that lies just north of Southampton. It was part of a property portfolio owned by a development company, but rented out to an associate of Dessler's named William Noakes. Dessler paid the lease and all the bills but had never wanted the place in his name, for obvious reasons.

'We have no idea if Dessler is in the house,'

Temple said. 'But there is a distinct possibility. We understand that Noakes lives there. And he may not be the only one. A records check has revealed that Noakes has form. He's been inside once for GBH and did community service for burglary. He's one of the heavies Dessler employs to put the frighteners on people who don't pay their debts. We should have his picture in the next few minutes.'

Temple went on to say that he had got the go-ahead from Priest to descend on the house with an armed response unit.

'We tread carefully,' he said. 'This might be a complete waste of time. On the other hand, if he's there it might turn nasty.'

41

The atmosphere in the loft was heavy and airless. The light from the overhead bulb was growing weaker, flickering more frequently.

Maggie's head was resting in the crook of my arm and I was running my fingers through her ravaged hair. Laura was still sleeping, her breath soft and fragile.

It might have been any ordinary lazy Sunday morning, like hundreds of others we'd shared as a family. It was hard to accept that we were actually sitting here in a cold, dank loft waiting to die. Waiting for the dreaded sound outside of tyres on gravel. Waiting for the hatch to open and the kidnapper to appear.

But that was the truth of it.

'You've got to do something,' Maggie said, her voice hoarse and tired.

I knew that, but what?

There has to be a way, I told myself.

Think, think, think.

I had to *think*.

I had to unscramble my brain and concentrate on saving my family from certain death. I looked around, letting my senses soak up everything in sight.

The slanted roof. The eaves. The cobwebs. The joists. The water tank. The exposed rolls of insulating lagging.

I'd never thought of a loft as a prison before. But it can be a pretty effective one, especially when it's at the top of a house in the middle of nowhere.

Sweat moistened my entire body, pasting my jumper to my skin. I tried to shut my mind to the sobbing sounds that Maggie kept making. I looked again at our surroundings, willing myself to see something that I had so far missed. Something obvious or not so obvious. Something that my tired mind could latch on to and be inspired by.

The roof. The joists. The rafters. The water tank. The chains. The cuffs. The exposed insulation.

But it was a struggle. My name is Danny Cain, not Harry Houdini. I'm a reporter, not an escapologist.

I thought about the loft hatch. Maggie told me she'd already tried to get Laura, who was able to reach it to open it from the inside, but she'd struggled with the mechanism and hadn't been able to work it.

The clock was ticking faster than my own heartbeat. My watch said one o'clock. Sunday-roast time. But not for us the comforts of a lovely meal and a warm fire. We were cold, scared and desperate.

I told myself to concentrate. Don't get distracted. There's no time for that.

Just *focus.*

And *think.*

Think harder than you have ever had to think in your life.

The roof. The joists. The chipboard floor panels. The lagging. The water tank. There has to be . . .

The lagging.

I looked again at the fibre strips tucked between the joists, where there were no chipboard panels. Beneath the strips were the ceilings of the rooms downstairs. Ceilings made of plasterboard.

The golden rule when moving around in a loft space is never to step between the joists because the ceiling won't hold your weight and you'll crash through. It's a universal rule and plenty of people have come unstuck by ignoring it.

As I stared at the exposed roll of lagging nearest to me an idea began to form. I moved away from Maggie and shuffled across the chipboard to the spot, grabbed the lagging and pulled it up to reveal the back of the plasterboard ceiling.

And that was when hope was revived. I saw

a way out of our prison. But it wouldn't be easy. In fact the odds against it succeeding were astronomical. But it was our only option.

I turned and saw that Maggie was staring at me.

'I think I've found a way out,' I said.

★   ★   ★

I roused Laura from her sleep. She moaned a little and smacked her lips together. Then caught her breath when she was fully awake and realized that she was back in the nightmare she had sought to escape from.

'I want you to go downstairs for me, sweetheart,' I said gently. 'I'm going to lower you through this floor and I want you to help us get out of here.'

I was asking a lot of a six-year-old, but it had to be done. It was the only way out. Laura wasn't chained up to a joist like her mother and me. We couldn't go anywhere, but she could.

She stared at me, terror etched firmly into her features. She was so young, so innocent, so unable to comprehend the magnitude of what was happening.

But for all our sakes she had to summon up the courage to do what I asked of her. I had to persuade her to go downstairs into this strange house; a tall order for a little girl who had already been traumatized by a series of horrific events.

'You'll be safe,' I told her. 'The man isn't in the house.'

'But I don't want to go,' Laura said.

'I know, sweetheart, but you have to.'

'But it's dark and I don't like the dark.'

'It won't be dark downstairs. It's daytime. And anyway you can turn on the lights.'

She pulled away from me, clung to her mother.

'Can't you see she's absolutely terrified?' Maggie said. 'I don't think she can do it.'

'There's no other way,' I said. 'And she has to do it now, before he comes back.'

Maggie wiped the dampness from Laura's brow.

'What exactly is it you want her to do?'

I got up and stepped over to where I'd pulled back the lagging.

'I'm going to kick a hole in the ceiling here. It shouldn't take long because it's just plasterboard. Then I intend to lower Laura into the room below. I'd do it myself if I didn't have this bloody chain around my wrist.'

'And then what?' Maggie said.

'I want her to go down the stairs and look

306

for a phone,' I said. 'She can dial the three nines. She knows how to do that. Then she can either try to talk to the police or leave the phone off the hook and they'll respond.'

'What if there isn't a phone? After all, it's pretty clear there's nobody living here now.'

'Then she can go outside and try to get help. There must be a village close by.'

'It's a lot to ask,' Maggie said.

'I know, but she can do it. I know she can.'

Laura clung even more tightly to her mother.

'Don't make me do it, Mummy. Please don't make me.'

I felt bad. The last thing I wanted was to upset my daughter even more. The raw fear she was feeling was evident in her expression. But I knew I had to hold firm. I had to bully her into submission or stand by and watch her be killed.

'We can't make her do it,' Maggie said.

'We can and we will,' I shouted, making both of them jump. 'Unless you can think of a better plan, that is. And if you can't then just shut up and don't make this any harder for me than it already is.'

Maggie was shocked by my outburst and Laura reacted by bursting into tears.

'You can be the one to save us, sweetheart,' I said in a gentler voice. 'And when we go home you can tell your friends that you were the bravest of us all. Everyone will be so proud of you.'

I decided to let it sink in for a few seconds. Laura needed to calm down and I needed Maggie's support. A unified approach was the only way this was going to work.

I reached down again and this time I cleared all the insulating lagging from a small area. Then I stood with my feet on two parallel joists. Between them was the ceiling of the room below us.

'I'm now going to make a hole in the plasterboard,' I said. 'So brace yourselves for some noise.'

I pulled up the slack in the chain and used it to give me support. Then I stamped down hard on the ceiling with my right shoe.

CRASH!

It was easier than I'd expected. My foot went crashing through it but the rest of me followed suit. A large section of plasterboard collapsed in an explosion of white dust and jagged grey particles.

I dropped through the opening like a man on the gallows. For a second I thought I would fall all the way into the room below, but then the chain snapped taut and my arm was almost ripped out of its socket.

I was left dangling through the ceiling with the cuff around my wrist cutting deep into my skin. The pain was excruciating and it rippled through my entire body. I clamped my eyes shut and bit into my lip.

Maggie was saying something to me but I couldn't make out the words. Then I felt her hands on my shoulder and I knew she was trying to pull me up out of the hole.

I looked down and saw a small pool of light on the carpet from the loft. Over to the right was a double bed with a bare mattress that was now covered with bits of plasterboard. I could also see a wardrobe and a chair in one corner. The room was dark so the curtains must be closed.

'Are you hurt, Danny?' Maggie was saying. 'Take my arm and I'll help you out of there.'

I placed my hands on the joists and heaved myself back up into the loft. My wrist was throbbing but I was sure it wasn't broken.

I glanced up at the joist in the hope that my weight had somehow dislodged it. But no such luck. It was still in place and looking as sturdy as an iron girder.

'Are you all right?' Maggie said.

I nodded. I took a couple of deep breaths, coughed, and then retched into my hand. The fall had shaken me up pretty badly. My heart was in overdrive and my vision was blurred around the edges. The muscles in my back, arms, shoulders and neck were screaming.

But that didn't matter. I was doing something and it felt damn good.

'Sit down and steady yourself,' Maggie said.

'There's no time for that.' I turned to Laura, who made a faint guttural sound as I beckoned her towards me. She didn't move.

'Come on, sweetheart. Please be brave and do this one thing for Daddy. All you have to do is go down and look for a phone. Dial nine, nine, nine. That's the number for the police. If there's no phone then I want you to go outside. Run down the lane and try to find a house or even someone out walking. Tell them where we are and to call the police.'

Her panic-filled eyes darted towards her mother. Maggie started to say something but held back. I had her support now which was a relief. She knew we had to force our daughter to confront her fears. There was no other way out of this hellhole.

'There's nothing to be afraid of,' Maggie told her. 'Just turn the lights on and walk down the stairs. It'll take you a few minutes at the most. Nobody will harm you. I promise.'

But Laura was having none of it. The fear was buried too deep and no amount of gentle persuasion was going to uproot it.

There was only one thing for it — I had to make her fear me more than she feared the house.

42

'Get off your backside and come here, young lady. Don't make me come and get you.'

Laura wasn't used to me shouting at her so I wasn't sure how she would respond. I worried that she might become completely hysterical and maybe even hyperventilate.

But in the event my booming voice and angry face did the trick. She started crawling towards me across the floor, her face white and wet, her body quivering with every pathetic sob.

I felt awful. Piling further pressure on my little girl was like driving a stake through my own heart.

'Please don't make me do it, Daddy.'

I reached for her hand, pulled her to her feet. Held her close to me for about half a minute, hoping my body would calm her nerves.

'Just think what it will be like once we get home,' I said. 'You can play with your toys and meet up with your friends. You can have ice cream and watch the Disney Channel.'

'I want to stay with you and Mummy,' she said.

'And you will, honey. We'll be right here. But you've got to do this one thing for us first.'

'Take Max with you,' Maggie said. 'He'll look after you and make sure that you're safe.'

'Max is scared too,' Laura responded. 'He doesn't want to go.'

'Well, he doesn't look scared to me,' I said. She frowned at me. 'You can see him?'

'Of course I can. Now tell him to go with you and take care of you.'

She looked around, her eyes focusing on a spot to my right. Was she actually seeing her imaginary friend? Was he speaking to her? Telling her to ignore her father and stay put?

I looked over her shoulder into the hole I had created. It was gloomy and forbidding, but I tried not to think about that.

I let go of Laura. Maggie put an arm around her. I lowered myself on to the chipboard and lay flat out so that I could peer into the bedroom below. I could just see the door, which was closed.

I got back up and said to Laura, 'The light switch is very close, sweetheart. As soon as you're down you can turn it on.'

As Maggie whispered reassuringly to Laura, I applied my mind to how I'd get her down there. I'd have to use my right hand and lean as far into the hole as possible. It was going to be tough — and painful.

'OK — let's do it,' I said. 'The sooner it's done the better.' I pointed to one of the joists. 'Laura, I want you to sit there and take my hand. I'm then going to lower you slowly into the bedroom below us. I won't let go until you've almost reached the floor.'

In truth there would be a drop of several feet, but I didn't think that would be a problem since Laura was young and supple. It would be no different from leaping off the sofa at home, something she did all the time. The bed, unfortunately, was just too far over to allow me to lower her on to it.

She was looking at me warily now as she clung to her mother. It was clear that I hadn't persuaded her to do this willingly. She was frightened and confused and she was hoping that I would change my mind.

I could shout at her again, but I wasn't sure what that would achieve, other than to wind her up even more.

So I just grabbed her hand and tugged her towards me. She screamed out and tried to jerk herself free.

'I'm sorry, sweetheart,' I said, 'but I have to make you go down there. Max will be right behind you. I promise.'

She started to react with her body and I realized there was no way she was going to sit on the joist and allow me to lower her gently. So I didn't bother to try. Instead I swung her towards the hole in the ceiling until she was hanging above it. The strain this put on my arm was almost unbearable. It was made worse by the fact that she was kicking and screaming the whole time.

'Keep still, for heaven's sake,' I shouted.

But she was terrified. Her mind hadn't matured enough to grasp the significance of the threat we all faced. To her the worst thing that could happen was to go down into that scary room.

'Be careful, Danny,' Maggie yelled. At the same time she reached out and tried to grab Laura.

'No,' I snapped at her. 'Leave her be. I've got this.'

With all the strength I could muster I held on tightly to my daughter as I dropped to my knees. Keeping my arm rigid was the real problem at this stage. The pain was agonizing. The tendons in my arms looked as though they might burst through the skin.

Laura grabbed on to one of the joists with her free hand and I yelled for Maggie to prise it free. But she hesitated.

'Just do it, will you?' I screamed at her.

They were both hysterical now, as Maggie seized Laura's wrist and lifted her hand away from the joist. I let my arm drop more quickly and Laura's body sank down into the hole. But the pressure on my muscles became too intense. I was struggling to hold on.

Laura was now flailing around like a fish on a hook and she was clawing at my hand with her fingers. My face was now above the hole. I was supporting myself by pressing down on one of the joists with my cuffed hand. My arm was at last at an angle and Laura's head was now below the level of the ceiling. Her feet were dangling about five feet above the bedroom floor.

My arm was on fire. And so were the muscles across my chest.

Just hold on.

Don't let go yet. If you do she'll be hurt.

I lowered her another few inches. And then another.

Eventually I had to release my grip because the pain and pressure were too much.

Laura fell the rest of the way to the floor — a drop of about four feet.

'Oh my God,' Maggie screamed.

But thankfully Laura wasn't hurt. No sooner had she struck the floor than she was on her feet again, frantically looking up at us and holding out her arms.

The relief blotted out the crippling pain I felt in my arm and chest.

'The light,' I said. 'Go to the switch next to the door and turn it on.'

I had to say it several times before Laura finally got the message that we weren't going to pull her back into the loft. She stood there for a few seconds, looking around the bedroom, her body stiff with fear.

'The light,' I said again. 'Switch it on.'

At last she hurried over to the door and turned on the light. Blinking into the sudden glare, I took in as much detail as possible. It was a small room with dark furniture. The carpet was threadbare and there was a wicker chair in the corner.

Laura stood with her back to the door, her eyes wide and her face flushed. She looked so small and helpless and frightened. I forced myself to ignore the wave of guilt that washed over me. 'That's great, sweetheart. Now you can see that the room is empty. There's no one in the house other than us. So what you have to do next is open the door and go out on to the landing. Find the light out there and turn it on.'

But she didn't move. She was frozen to the spot.

So I switched back into angry father mode.

'Open the frigging door and go outside,' I yelled.

She moved quickly then. She turned

around and gripped the bulb of the door handle with trembling hands. Then she pulled it open and looked out on to the landing, her little body framed by the doorway. Thankfully it wasn't dark out there on the landing. The curtains must have been open.

'Go on, sweetheart,' I urged. 'Go out on to the landing.'

But suddenly she took a step back and started shaking her head.

'It's OK, Laura,' I said. 'You can do it.'

She turned her head to look up at me and her terror-stricken face caused my heart to lurch.

'Don't make me.'

'Just do it, Laura.'

She choked back more tears and ventured out on to the landing.

★   ★   ★

Once she was out of the room, I shouted to her, 'Now go downstairs and look for a phone. If there isn't one, then go outside. See if there's another house close by.'

'Supposing the front door is locked,' Maggie said.

'What?'

'The front door. If it's locked from the outside then she won't be able to open it.'

I hadn't thought of that.

'Let's just wait and see,' I said.

Then I called out. 'Are you OK, sweet-heart?'

She replied instantly.

'I'm on the stairs, Daddy. I'm scared.'

'I know you are, babe. But the worst is over.'

Maggie rested a hand on my back.

'Do you think we can do it?' she asked. 'Do you really think we can get out of here before he gets back?'

'We'll know soon enough,' I said.

We waited anxiously as Laura went downstairs. We heard nothing for at least five minutes. Then she suddenly appeared in the doorway to the bedroom below.

'I can't open the front door,' she said. 'I tried but it won't open.'

'OK,' I said. 'What about the phone? Did you check the kitchen and the living room?'

'The doors were shut,' she said. 'I was scared to open them. Max said the man might be behind them.'

I was becoming impatient now. We had come this far and there was no going back.

'Don't listen to Max,' I said. 'Just go back downstairs and look for a phone. And see if there's a back door that's open. Please, Laura. Hurry up.'

She went back down and I made a silent promise to myself that if we got out of this I would buy her anything she wanted. A noise reached us from down below. I couldn't make out what it was but it sounded like something being knocked over.

'Laura, can you hear me?' I shouted. 'Are you all right?'

I strained my ears to listen, but the only sounds now were the normal groans and creaks of an old house. Floorboards shifting. Water rushing through rusty pipes. The wind sneaking through the eaves around us. Then I heard footfalls on the stairs. Laura was coming back up. My body tensed. A moment later she came bursting into the bedroom, panting. She came and stood directly below us and looked up.

'There's no phone,' she said between gasps. 'But I found these. They were on the kitchen table. The man used them to put the chain on Mummy. I saw him.'

She held up a small bunch of keys and an overwhelming sense of elation swept through me. I couldn't believe it. I didn't doubt for a single second that they were the keys to the handcuffs. Small and silver, they were the miracle I'd been praying for.

'You'll have to throw them up to me,' I said. 'I'll catch them.'

It took two attempts before I actually had the keys in my sweaty palm. There were three pairs in all and I wasted no time checking to see if they fitted the cuff on my wrist.

The first one didn't. The second one didn't.

With a high degree of apprehension I tried the third.

Bingo!

The cuff snapped open with a loud click.

'Jesus, we've done it,' Maggie shrieked as I handed her the keys. Within seconds she'd removed her cuff and was rubbing her sore wrist.

Together we scrambled over to the hatch. I found the internal lock mechanism and realized why Laura had not been able to open it. There was a metal clasp that had to be raised and then turned. A tiny bit complicated for a six-year-old. But I had it undone in seconds. The hatch opened downwards, taking the ladder with it.

I let Maggie descend first and by the time I stepped on to the landing she had Laura wrapped up in her arms.

It was a sight to behold and I waded straight into the embrace. Despair had turned to delight, thanks to our astonishingly brave little girl. We were almost home and dry now. All we had to do was get the hell out of the house.

* * *

'You've been terrific, sweetheart,' I said to Laura. 'You're so good and brave and I'm so sorry I had to shout at you.'

I picked her up and kissed her on both cheeks. The salty tang of her tears mingled with the warm sweetness of her sweat.

'We'll make it up to you,' I said. 'When we get home I'm going to buy you lots of presents.'

She smiled weakly and pressed her face against my neck.

'We'd better go,' I said to Maggie. 'Follow me downstairs.'

My body throbbed, my eyes stung with fatigue and the cut on my forehead was prickling. But I was driven now by a sudden boost of energy and hope.

The house was old and creaky. There were damp patches on the walls, dust everywhere.

We passed a window and through it I could see an area of woodland beneath a grey, oppresive sky. It was the middle of the afternoon but the day was already losing its lustre. It wouldn't be long before it was dark.

We reached the downstairs hallway and I tried the front door. It was locked, just as Laura had said.

We went into the kitchen. The curtains

were closed and although it wasn't dark I switched on the light anyway. There were wooden beams and wooden floorboards. It was a large kitchen with all the usual stuff: fridge, dishwasher, cooker. Everything looked old, but clean.

'There's no side door here,' Maggie said.

'Look for a key,' I said. 'And a phone.'

But just then I heard a noise outside. Like a car crunching over gravel.

Panic seized me. I grabbed Laura's arm and switched off the light.

'Oh my God,' Maggie said. 'He's back.'

43

The house was easy to find. It was set back from a road that clung to the southern perimeter of a small wood. The front had open views over fields that rolled towards the ancient city of Winchester.

Temple was in the lead patrol car as it swept up the short driveway. He quickly took in the scene. A large detached property that looked grey and uninviting. Trees surrounded it. There was an outbuilding to the left that might once have been a barn or a stable. There were no cars in sight and this caused Temple's heart to sink. But there was a garage attached to the house, its wooden doors painted a dull green.

Tyres crunched over stones as the three patrol cars slowed to a halt. Temple climbed out, cold air snapping at his flesh. The sky was a sullen shade of grey and the promise of rain had given way to a thin drizzle. He strode towards the front door, signalling to others to go round the back. The curtains inside the downstairs windows were closed, but through the cracks he could see that there were lights on. He rang the doorbell and braced himself for the unexpected. Whoever was in the house must have seen or heard the cars approach. So they would be ready to respond. But how?

He rang the bell again. No answer. He was about to give the order for an officer to ram the door open, but at that moment there came shouts from the back of the house.

Temple pointed to the uniforms behind him. 'You stay here and cover the front.'

Then he dashed round the back to where an officer was standing in the rear garden. The officer pointed towards the woods and Temple saw two armed officers in padded jackets running across a small area of open land.

'We spotted people entering the woods,' the officer said. Then he gestured towards a rear door that was open. 'Looks like they just left the house in a hurry.'

Temple broke into a run towards the densely packed gloom of the woods. He scrambled through clumps of low bracken, the ground soft and heavy going. Mud spattered his suit trousers and it wasn't long before he was panting like a dog.

He just made it to the woods before he was forced to stop and catch his breath. He leaned up against a large oak, a cold sweat prickling his forehead as he took big gasps of air. And that was when he heard the shots. Two of them in quick succession. He pushed himself away from the tree and hurtled into the woods, dodging branches and leaping over fallen logs. His stomach was cramping with exhaustion. Voices came at him from out of the gloom. He saw movement ahead, lumbered towards it.

He came to a small clearing. Three armed officers were pointing their guns at the ground. Temple stopped, his eyes following the direction of the weapons. He saw three figures lying face down in the dirt.

'They're not hurt,' one of the officers told him. 'We fired warning shots.'

Temple stared down at the three bodies sprawled on the ground. The one in the middle cranked his head to the left, exposing his face.

It was Joe Dessler.

'Have you searched them?' Temple asked.

'Yes, sir. They're clean.'

He wiped a sleeve across his sweaty brow.

'Then get them up and march them back to the house. Let's find out what they have to say for themselves.'

44

Five minutes had elapsed since the car drew up outside the house. The three of us were now huddled behind the sofa in the living room. The patio doors were locked, blocking our exit.

The lights in the kitchen and hallway would have alerted the kidnapper to the fact that something was wrong. I reckoned he was out there, circling the house, trying to determine whether we were still in the loft or someone else had broken in.

The sofa lay square across the room, facing the glass doors that gave access to the garden. It shielded us from the gap in the curtains which allowed the fading light of the winter afternoon to filter into the room. I should have had the presence of mind to close the curtains all the way after checking the locks. But I'd been in too much of a panic, not knowing what to do or how best to protect my family.

There was something else I should have done in those few crucial seconds after we heard the vehicle outside. I should have armed myself before rushing out of the kitchen. A knife. A rolling pin. Even a fucking saucepan. Anything that could be used to defend us against the maniac in the ski mask. As it was I had nothing. Crouched down between the sofa and the living room wall, we were like lambs hiding from the big bad wolf.

Maggie and Laura were either side of me. I could feel their bodies trembling. Feel their hearts pumping. My skin was hot. There was a heaving in my chest and stomach. I had a real urge to vomit. We held our breaths, listened to the oppressive silence of the house. Where was the bastard? Did he have his gun? Had he come back to kill us?

Maggie turned to look at me, her eyes sending me a question.

Aren't you going to do something?

But what could I do other than wait it out? The kidnapper was still in control. He had the power, the weapon, the advantage of knowing we couldn't make a run for it without his seeing us. And who was to say he wouldn't shoot the first chance he got?

The situation was different now. We posed a serious threat. We'd put at risk his plan to claim the lottery winnings. He was —

We all stiffened at an indeterminate sound that came from beyond the glass doors. It could have been a shoe scuffing across the concrete patio, or a side gate opening.

'Oh God, he's out there,' Maggie said in a hushed voice.

Laura started to shake more violently. I sensed that she was about to cry out.

'I've got to get a weapon of some kind,' I said.

'Don't leave us,' Maggie pleaded.

'Just stay put. I'll crawl to the kitchen. If I keep low he won't see me from outside.'

There was no carpet, just floorboards. That made it easier for me to slide my body towards the open door into the hallway. Here I was more exposed. I glanced up at the front door. There was no one outside it. I crawled across the hall into the kitchen. It was still empty and the curtains were closed.

I jumped up and looked around. I saw stainless-steel knives in a rack on the counter. I grabbed one with a big, serrated blade and squeezed the handle until my knuckles turned white. I moved back into the hall and paused for a second to listen. The house stayed silent and the front door remained closed. I got back on the floor, crawled into the living room. Maggie and Laura were just where I'd left them. Maggie's eyes widened at the sight of the knife.

'Have you heard anything more?' I said.

Maggie shook her head.

I raised myself up and peered over the top

of the sofa. I could see the sky through the gap in the curtains. Below it a wall of dark trees. Then suddenly the view was obscured by the man in the mask. He appeared as if out of thin air and stared at me through the window, his head and body black as the darkest night.

Instinctively I tightened my grip on the knife. In that same instant there was a crash of glass as the kidnapper put a boot through one of the doors. Maggie screamed and my stomach lurched. I watched the tall, dark figure step through the shattered door as though in slow motion. I stood up quickly and stretched out my right arm, displaying the knife in a threatening gesture. But it did not stop the kidnapper from striding towards me, his boots crunching over fragments of glass.

'Put the knife down,' he yelled.

I could barely hear him. Maggie was still screaming and the explosion of broken glass was ringing in my ears.

'If you don't drop it I'll fucking shoot you.'

He was now directly on the other side of the sofa, both hands holding the revolver that was pointing straight at my chest. My heart thumped so hard it resonated across my ribs. I felt sure he would pull the trigger if I didn't comply. But if I did we'd be back where we started. At the mercy of this lunatic.

Maggie was shouting at me.

'Do as he says, Danny. Please.'

I ground my teeth together and slowly lowered my arm.

'Drop it on the sofa.' His voice was quieter now, with a measured menace.

I loosened my grip, let the knife fall on the cushion.

'Now don't move a muscle,' he said.

Stepping forward, he picked up the knife with his free hand and put it into his jacket pocket. Then, without warning, he reached out and grabbed my jumper and pulled me across the back of the sofa. I tried to stop myself falling, but it happened too fast. As I landed face down on the cushions, I felt a blow to the back of the head.

Then another.

I heard him swear. I heard Maggie yell for him to stop. I heard Laura scream. And then I felt the explosion of pain behind my eyes. It sent me hurtling into oblivion.

45

Temple stood with his back to a wide brick fireplace. The fire had burned itself out and there was a pile of ash in the grate.

It was the focal point of a large, L-shaped living room. Like the rest of the house the room was packed with furniture. There was a glass-fronted bar at one end, stacked with drinks. Two white leather sofas faced each other across a black glass-topped coffee table. Temple had noticed that the same light and dark theme was evident throughout the rest of the house. He had looked in all the rooms. Four bedrooms. Two bathrooms. Kitchen. Utility room. Dining room.

There were two cars in the garage. One belonged to Dessler, the other to his minder, Noakes.

The third man had identified himself as Tony Weekes, another of Dessler's henchmen, who had been living in the house.

The preliminary search had revealed that the property was not just used for outlandish parties. One of the bedrooms was like a mini studio with two video cameras mounted on tripods on either side of a king-size bed.

There were also a couple of arc lamps on stands. In the converted loft they found a digital editing suite and a stack of DVDs, all with the same label; it read *Sluts and Slappers.*

It seemed that Dessler wasn't only into loan sharking and prostitution. He was also in the business of producing his own brand of porn.

Now the three men who had fled into the woods were seated on one of the sofas, their wrists cuffed, their faces suffused with righteous indignation. Dessler was in the middle, head and shoulders above the other two. Noakes was a short, stout man in his thirties with a square face and blotchy skin. Weekes was bald and powerfully built, everyone's idea of a punch-drunk boxer. Temple had listened to their protestations and their demands to know what was going on. He'd refused to allow Dessler to phone his lawyer and had told him they would shortly be taken to Southampton central police station to be formally interviewed.

But first there were some questions.

'Why are you hiding out?' Temple said, addressing himself to Dessler.

The big man shrugged. 'I'm not hiding. I rent this place. Often stay over when I'm bored with the city.'

'That's a lie. Your bent copper friend Jordan told us you were in a panic over what we had unearthed. So you decided to disappear for a while.'

'That arse doesn't know what he's talking about.'

'We've seen a draft of the article that Mayo was writing,' Temple said. 'It's extremely incriminating. We also know about the photos that you sent to Mayo.'

'He owed me money,' Dessler snorted.

'And so when he wouldn't pay you decided to kill him.'

'That's bollocks.'

'You arranged to visit his house on Saturday night. Jordan told us. And so did Mayo's girlfriend.'

'I didn't go. I swear.'

'Then maybe you sent one of these morons.'

The other two men looked suitably outraged.

Noakes said, 'Don't fucking lay that one on us. We had nothing to do with it.'

Temple jabbed a finger at Dessler. 'You told me you were at the casino all Saturday evening. But it wasn't true. We have security video showing that you left early and didn't return until much later. We also have a tape of you at a city centre pub. You called Mayo from there.'

Dessler nodded. 'Look, I called Mayo on Friday to ask him what he thought about the photos. They had him worried and he agreed to stop writing that fucking feature about me. He said he'd square it with his partner by telling Cain that the evidence he'd gathered wasn't safe and therefore they should drop the piece. He didn't think Cain would have a major objection to it.'

'And what about the money?'

'He agreed to pay me an instalment of a few grand. I said I'd collect it on Saturday. But I got involved so I called from the pub to cancel. Said I'd pick it up on Monday.'

'So where did you go after leaving the pub? There's a gap of several hours during which Mayo was murdered.'

Dessler shook his head. 'I was doing the rounds. Collecting money from the girls. You can ask them. I've got names. I dropped in on two more houses and a pub. It's what I do every Saturday night. I didn't have time to go to the forest.'

'So why come here?' Temple said. 'And don't give me bullshit about being bored.'

'Look, when you turned up at my flat I was gobsmacked to hear about Mayo. Honest. But straight away I could see where it was going. I knew I'd be a prime suspect and you would start digging into my affairs. I reckoned it was only a matter of time before you hauled me in and I'd be banged up on a raft of fucking charges. I was also worried that once you had me you'd try to pin the murder on me and lose interest in catching the real killer. So I decided to lie low for a bit and sort out a few things.'

Temple had to admit he sounded convincing, but then the really smart criminals always did. It was their nature. Part of their makeup.

'Where's Cain?' Temple said after a moment.

Dessler shrugged expansively. 'I have not the slightest idea. I've never even met the guy.'

'But he knew as much as Mayo did about your activities,' Temple said. 'They worked together. He was involved in the article that was going to expose you.'

'That maybe so, but my gripe was with Mayo.'

'So you have no idea where he's gone?'

'None, but from what I've heard he's the one who whacked Mayo and you know it, so I don't know why you're hassling me.'

Temple sucked in air through his nostrils. He felt his anger mounting. This wasn't going well.

'Did any of you lot pay a visit to Jennifer Priest's flat last night?' he said, knowing it was a shot in the dark.

The three men exchanged glances. It was Dessler who spoke. 'Why would we do that?'

'Maybe you've taken the view that she's inherited her boyfriend's debt.'

'Don't talk crap.' Dessler said. 'None of us has been near the Priest girl.'

'Is that a fact?'

'It's a fact, Inspector. And I can tell you now that you won't get another word out of any of us until I've spoken to a lawyer.'

Temple knew there was no point continuing, at least not here. 'Then I'm taking you all down to the station,' he said. 'You can call your lawyers from there before the formal interviews.'

'You'll be wasting your time,' Dessler said.

'We'll see about that.'

Temple signalled to the uniforms to take the three men out. He followed them, his mind in turmoil, a queasy hollowness in the pit of his stomach. To say that he was disappointed with the outcome of the raid would be an understatement.

On the way back to the station he reflected on what Dessler had said. It was clear that he had threatened and blackmailed Vince Mayo. But it was unlikely that he'd killed him. His alibi would be checked out, of course, and they'd seek to bring a variety of charges against him, but it was almost certain that a murder charge wouldn't be one of them.

Temple stared out of the window of the squad car, his mood matching the gloomy grey of the sky. So what now? he asked himself. Was it time to concentrate all their efforts on finding Cain and forget about chasing down other leads? It was the obvious route to take. The reporter was still the only viable suspect and the evidence against him continued to stack up. But there were still too many loose ends. Too many unanswered questions. Maybe jealousy wasn't the motive. Maybe Cain hadn't acted alone. Temple racked his brain going back over the evidence and all the interviews they'd conducted. What hadn't they done?

He took out his notebook and started making a list of questions. Was Dessler telling the truth? Was DC Jordan more involved than he was letting on? Who or what had caused Jennifer to flee from her flat?

This last question triggered a snap of electricity in his brain. He recalled checking Jennifer's landline to see if someone had phoned her during the evening. But he wondered whether anyone had checked her mobile. Maybe she'd received a call on that and it had spooked her. He recalled that he had mentioned it to her father, but Priest was in such a state at the time that he probably didn't take it in. Temple whipped out his phone and rang Angel.

'I was just about to call you, guv,' she said.

'I'm on my way in,' he told her. 'I want you to do something for me. Get the call log on Jennifer Priest's mobile phone. See if she had any calls last night before she bolted from her flat and had the accident.'

'I'll get on to it right away, guv. Meanwhile there's something you should know. Bill Nadelson turned up at his cottage a short time ago. He's been arrested and they're bringing him in.'

46

When Temple got back to the station he told the duty inspector to process Dessler and his crew and put them in the cells until he was ready to begin formal interviews.

'And let them call their lawyers,' he said.

He went to the briefing room. It was half-empty. Angel was seated at her desk poring over documents.

'Have you managed to get Jennifer's phone log?' he asked.

She looked up and nodded. 'Just going through it now, guv.'

'And?'

'Well, no joy really. She didn't receive any calls all day yesterday on her mobile.'

'Shit.'

Feeling tired and bad tempered, Temple stalked along to his office and helped himself to a couple of painkillers. His head was buzzing and he could feel a gnawing in his stomach. He checked his watch, conscious of the fact that with every minute that passed there was an increased chance that things would not turn out well for Mrs Cain and her daughter.

After a few minutes he was told that Bill Nadelson had arrived. The old man was assigned a duty solicitor named Parker, a tall, thin guy in his thirties. Nadelson looked tired and nervous when he was led into the interview room to face Temple. He started chewing on his fingernails and refused the offer of a cup of tea. He was wearing a rumpled white shirt with a frayed collar and looked haggard and stooped.

'Where have you been today, Mr Nadelson?'

He raked a hand through his thin grey hair. 'I went to my son's. I was too upset to stay at my house. What is it I'm supposed to have done? What's all this about?'

'I think you know that,' Temple said.

'No I don't. I arrived home and was arrested before I even let myself in. The officers refused to say what it was about.'

And so the grilling began. Temple watched Nadelson's face as he questioned him about the money and the jewellery that had been found in the suitcase under his bed. His shocked expression was a picture. He bit his bottom lip and furrowed his brow. His face lost colour and he clearly had a problem swallowing.

'We know it doesn't belong to you,' Temple said. 'We know you took it from Mr Mayo's house.'

340

The sheen of fear in Nadelson's slate-grey eyes was unmistakable. At last he cleared the obstruction in his throat and said, 'I didn't kill Vince. I swear. I found him just like I said I did.'

'But why should we believe you?' Temple said. 'You lied to us. You stole the money and jewellery, didn't you?'

Nadelson drew air through his teeth and clamped his eyes shut. Pearls of sweat popped up above his top lip.

'I've a mind to charge you with murder right now,' Temple said.

Nadelson opened his eyes, alarm writ large in his expression. He threw a glance at his solicitor, but Parker just shrugged his shoulders.

Temple narrowed his eyes at Nadelson, studying his face. 'I meant what I said. You're facing a charge of murder. The motive: robbery.'

And that did it. Nadelson started talking. What he'd told them before was all true, he said. He'd seen the dark car speed away from his neighbour's cottage. He'd gone to investigate. Found the body. Called the police.

'But when I was in the house I saw the money,' he said. 'It was on the worktop in the kitchen. A wedge of twenty-pound notes.

341

I don't know what came over me. I went back inside and picked it up, put it into my pocket. I thought you would assume that the killer took it. It was a mistake. I know that now.'

Temple leaned forward. 'And what about the jewellery?'

He crimped his lips and placed his hands flat on the table, palms down.

'Vince showed me his mother's jewellery a while ago,' he said. 'You see, I'm a retired jeweller. He wanted me to give him a rough valuation. I told him it was worth in total about five thousand pounds. I advised him to put it in a safe-deposit box after he told me he kept it in his bedside drawer and I told him that was foolish.'

'So you decided to take it along with the cash?'

He nodded. 'I knew both his parents were dead. I didn't think anyone would notice.'

Temple angled his head slightly. 'How do we know that you didn't kill Mr Mayo to get your hands on the money and the jewellery?'

'He was dead when I found him,' he insisted. 'That's the truth. I had a moment of weakness. I'm deeply ashamed of myself. But I'm not a killer.'

Temple believed him. All the same, he questioned Nadelson for another fifteen minutes, going over his story in minute detail, pushing and probing at his explanation and his character. Had he stolen anything before? What had he been going to do with the jewellery?

Nadelson looked a wreck by the time it was over, his face ashen. But that served him right, Temple thought. What he'd done was shameful but what he clearly hadn't done was kill his neighbour, which meant that the focus of the inquiry remained firmly with Cain.

Shoulders slumped, Temple walked out into the corridor where Angel was waiting to speak to him. She held up a sheet of paper.

'I was just coming to get you, guv,' she said. 'I've found something.'

'I hope it's good,' Temple said. 'Because I'm feeling monumentally pissed off just now.'

'This is a print-out of Jennifer Priest's mobile phone record.'

'So? I thought you said she had no calls yesterday.'

'She didn't, guv, but I had the feeling that there was something not quite right about the list of calls and a minute ago it came to me.'

'Well, come on, detective. Don't keep me in bloody suspense. What is it?'

47

'Don't fucking move,' the kidnapper yelled. 'Just stay where you are.'

Maggie froze. She had been about to rush around the sofa to where Danny was lying on the floor, blood seeping from a gash on the back of his head.

But now her attention was focused on the revolver in the kidnapper's hand which he had used to beat Danny unconscious. The gun was levelled at her chest and she didn't doubt that he'd pull the trigger if she gave him cause. Laura was clinging to her mother's waist, her fingers digging into the flesh above her belt.

The kidnapper stepped over Danny. He grabbed Laura by the arm and jerked her towards him. Laura gave a startled yelp and tried to hold on to her mother. But her fingers lost their grip and as Maggie attempted to pull her back she found herself staring into the muzzle of the gun.

'Stop there,' the man said.

The muzzle was inches from Maggie's forehead. The man's hand was shaking. There was a feral anger in his eyes. Maggie felt her blood run cold as he put his hand over Laura's mouth and pulled her close. Her little girl's eyes almost popped out of their sockets and she grabbed frantically at his sleeve.

'Be sensible, Mrs Cain,' he said. 'I will hurt her if you don't do as I say.'

Maggie put up her hands, palms out.

'Please don't. You're scaring her.'

He nodded towards the door.

'Go and get the cuffs. Bring them to me along with the keys.'

Laura stopped struggling. He took his hand away from her mouth and put his arm around her neck. She was stiff with fear.

'Mummy,' she cried, terror distorting her features.

'Be still, sweetheart,' Maggie said. 'I won't be long.'

Maggie threw a glance at Danny. He was still sprawled on the floor, face up, eyes closed.

'Do it now,' the kidnapper yelled.

Maggie had to think about it. Where were the handcuffs? They had taken them off in the loft. She hurried upstairs, ascended the ladder into the loft. She retrieved the two pairs of cuffs, releasing them from the chains that had secured them to the stanchions. When she walked back into the living room she saw that the kidnapper had tied Laura's hands in front of her with duct tape. She was sitting on the floor just inside the door.

'Come here,' he told Maggie.

He put the cuffs on her wrists and ordered her to sit next to Laura. Then he pulled Danny's hands across his chest and put the other pair of cuffs on him. He straightened himself and stared down at Danny. Slowly he raised his weapon and aimed it at Danny's face.

'I should blow his fucking brains out here and now,' he snarled through the mask.

'Please don't,' Maggie pleaded. 'He's my husband. I love him.'

The kidnapper lifted his head, his dark eyes locking on to hers.

'Is that a fucking joke?' he yelled. 'If you cared about him you wouldn't have been screwing his partner.'

Maggie felt her heart stop. Her breath snagged in her throat.

'Don't act so surprised,' he said. 'I've seen pictures of you and Mayo at it. You'd been having an affair for months. Shagging behind your husband's back. And then you have the front to act like the loyal, caring wife.'

Maggie was dumbstruck. How did he know? What was going on?

Then she remembered the man with the camera in the forest.

346

'In fact I can let you in on a little secret,' he said. 'Those pictures were the reason your boyfriend was killed. And it's why you and your family are here now. So it follows that you, Mrs Cain, are ultimately responsible for all that's happened. How does that make you feel?'

Maggie's head started to spin. A pain erupted in her chest. Oh God, she thought, this can't really be happening. It's too awful. She turned to Laura. Her daughter was staring at her, wide-eyed and confused. She wanted to say something to her. Anything. But the words wouldn't come. In that moment Maggie felt ugly and vile and wicked. She didn't think she could possibly feel any worse.

But she was wrong.

As she wrenched her gaze away from Laura, she looked instinctively at Danny, lying on the floor.

His eyes were open and he was looking up at her with a stricken expression on his face.

48

Temple went straight to A&E when he got to the hospital. He was told that Jennifer Priest had been moved to a private room on the first floor. He hurried up the stairs. The hospital was busy with scores of people milling around. Visitors. Medical staff. Patients in dressing-gowns, some of them wheeling around intravenous drips.

At the first-floor reception he identified himself to a plump nurse with bleached blond hair.

'I'm a police officer. You have a patient, Jennifer Priest. Where is she?'

The nurse eyed his card. 'She's in a room down the corridor on the left.'

'I need to speak to her.'

'I'm not sure that's possible. I'll have to page the doctor.'

'Then do it now.'

As she reached for the phone Temple checked his watch. It was 4.15 p.m. It was almost forty-eight hours since Vince Mayo had been murdered. They were two days into an investigation that had taken more twists and turns than he cared to think about.

A white-coated doctor appeared. He was

tall and ungainly with slightly hunched shoulders and untidy brown hair.

Temple asked him how Jennifer was.

'She's recovering well,' the doctor replied. 'I'm hoping that she'll be able to go home in about a week. Her injuries looked more serious than they actually are.'

'I need to talk to her right away,' Temple said. 'It's urgent.'

'That shouldn't be a problem as long as she feels up to it.'

'Shall we find out?' Temple said.

★   ★   ★

Jennifer Priest was sitting up in bed staring at the ceiling. She was wearing a flimsy hospital gown and looking rather pathetic. There were dark rings under her eyes and her lips were dry and cracked. She stiffened visibly when she saw Temple.

'Hello, Miss Priest,' the doctor said. 'The inspector here would like a word with you. Are you feeling all right?'

She didn't respond. Instead, she stared at Temple. She was still attached to a drip. There was a bandage around her forehead. Another around her left arm.

After a beat, she said, 'I want my father. Where's my father?'

'He isn't here,' the doctor said. 'But I'm sure he'll be back soon. Would you like us to try to contact him?'

'Yes. Yes, I would.'

'Then I'll get right on to it and leave you to speak to the officer.'

'I don't want to talk to him,' she said as the doctor turned to go.

'You don't have a choice, Miss Priest,' Temple said. 'There are some questions I need to ask you.'

Temple looked at the doctor and signalled with his eyes for him to leave the room. The doctor hesitated a moment, then complied, closing the door behind him.

Jennifer squeezed her eyes shut and swallowed. She's nervous, Temple thought. And extremely uncomfortable.

'I won't keep you long, Miss Priest,' he said. 'But it's really important that you clear something up for me.'

She opened her eyes, looked at him. Her mouth was tight and bloodless.

'If it's about the accident you should talk to my father,' she said, her voice croaky. 'I've told him everything I can remember.'

'It's not about that,' Temple said. 'Although I would like to come to that in a moment.'

'Then what is it you want? I'm tired and I need to sleep.'

Temple ran his tongue over his teeth and took a deep breath through his nose.

'You told us that on Saturday evening you were with your father,' he said. 'You had dinner with him at his house.'

'That's right.'

'And you were there between about four p.m. and eleven p.m.?'

'I think so. My father will know the precise times. Why are you asking me again if you already know?'

Temple took the calls print-out from his pocket and held it up.

'It's because of this,' he said. 'It's a list of the calls you made on your mobile on Saturday evening. There were two calls, at nine p.m. and ten p.m.'

'So?'

'So they were to your father's home phone. And what I'd like to know is why you called your father from your mobile if you were right there in the house with him? To us it doesn't make any sense.'

The muscles tensed in her jaw. Temple wondered whether she had a simple, honest answer. She'd popped out to an off licence or a shop and needed to call her father to check something. Or maybe she had been testing her phone. There were any number of bogus reasons she could have come up with, providing she had already agreed it with her father. Which she clearly hadn't because suddenly her face collapsed in anguish.

'I told him we shouldn't do it,' she shrieked. 'I knew we'd be found out. Oh dear God, I'm so sorry.'

Her shoulders heaved and she started to cry. Temple felt a rush of heat flare across his skin. He leaned forward, rested his hand on Jennifer's shoulder, waited for her to calm down a little. It took a minute or so. She wiped her eyes, blew her nose.

'I'm so sorry,' she said. 'I didn't mean for it to happen like that.'

Temple kept his voice low, gentle. 'Start at the beginning, Miss Priest. Tell me what it is you did and why.'

49

The kidnapper grabbed the cuffs and hauled me to my feet. He pushed me up against the wall, aimed the gun at my face.

'How the fuck did you get out of the attic?' he spat.

I heard the question but I couldn't respond. My mind was still reeling from what I had just heard. I felt a sharp ache in the pit of my stomach.

'I asked you a fucking question, Cain.'

Ignoring him, I turned to look down at Maggie. She was on her knees, staring up at me, her face the colour of putty.

A thousand thoughts and images flashed through my mind.

Vince.

An affair.

Sex.

What the hell was I supposed to say or do or think?

'I'm so sorry, Danny,' she murmured, her voice breaking as she spoke. 'Please forgive me.'

Her face went out of focus as a huge ball of grief tried to blast its way out of my chest.

I heard the kidnapper repeat his question and I heard Maggie respond on my behalf. I was in shock. Despair gnawed at my mind and body like a hungry rat. It took the butt of the kidnapper's gun across the side of my face to bring me back to my senses. It wasn't hard enough to knock me over, but it hurt like hell.

My vision blurred for a few seconds, then steadied. The room came back into focus. My eyes settled, not on Maggie but on Laura, and I suddenly realized that I couldn't let go. The other stuff could wait. Right now it didn't matter that my heart was broken, that my wife had been unfaithful with, of all people, my best friend and partner. What was important just now was our survival. The kidnapper was talking again, his tone strident.

'I came to take you away from here anyway,' he said. 'You're going to a place that's more comfortable. You can stay there until I collect the lottery money. Then I'll vanish and tell the authorities where they can find you.'

Was he telling the truth? Would he really let us live? If only I could see his face, I thought. Maybe his expression would be more revealing than his voice.

'Why should we trust you?' I said.

He snorted. 'I don't care if you trust me or not. That's what is going to happen so I suggest you show some fucking gratitude.'

He gestured for Maggie and Laura to stand up. I noticed for the first time that Maggie was also wearing cuffs and Laura's wrists were bound with duct tape.

'This other place is very close,' the kidnapper said. 'Just a few minutes in the car. So let's get moving. Outside.'

Maggie went first, with Laura holding her hand. We walked across the hallway. The front door was locked but the kidnapper stepped in front and unlocked it with a key he produced from his pocket. We stepped outside. There was a slight drizzle. The cold air smelled of leaf-mould and pine. The sky was growing dark. The trees around us were alive. I could hear the autumn wind prowling through them. There was a grey car parked on the driveway. A Mercedes. The kidnapper used his key fob to remotely activate the boot, which sprang open.

'You know the routine, Cain. Get in. This time I won't clobber you unless you give me a reason to.'

I turned to look at him as a fresh wave of fear swelled up inside me.

'What are you going to do?'

'I told you,' he said. 'I'm taking you somewhere else. Another house near by. We have to leave now.'

'So why do I have to get in there?'

'Because your wife is going to drive and I'll be in the back seat with your daughter. It's the only way I can make sure that nothing will go wrong. Now stop talking and get in.'

I reached out with my cuffed hands and touched Laura's head. 'Be brave, sweetheart,' I said. 'I'll see you in a bit.'

'Don't leave us, Daddy.'

'I have to, sweetheart.'

I looked at Maggie and her expression implored me to say something. But I couldn't. Instead, I turned and climbed into the boot.

A second later he slammed it shut behind me.

50

Jennifer Priest wanted to get it off her chest. That became obvious to Temple as she spoke. She was a mental as well as a physical wreck, unable to live with what had happened, her mind ravaged by guilt and remorse.

'Vince was subdued all Saturday afternoon,' she said through a steady stream of tears that dribbled down her cheeks. 'Something had upset him. He wanted me to go and spend the evening with a friend or my father. He said he had some business to take care of. But I kept on at him until he told me that Dessler was coming round to collect some money. He said it would keep Dessler happy for a while. He showed me the cash and left it on the kitchen worktop. He said he'd won the money earlier in the week.'

Temple pulled up a chair and sat down.

'So you didn't go to your father's for dinner?' Temple prompted.

She shook her head. 'No I didn't. I lied about that. We both did.'

Temple's heart started to pound inside his chest.

'Go on,' he said.

Jennifer cleared her throat. 'Later in the evening, about seven o'clock, Dessler phoned to say he wouldn't be coming over after all. Vince seemed relieved but he was still stressed out.'

She stopped there and closed her eyes, squeezing out some more tears.

Then she continued, 'Everything changed when he checked his lottery numbers.'

Temple frowned. 'What's that?'

She swallowed. 'He started shouting that he had won the jackpot.'

Temple stared at her, open mouthed. 'Are you being serious?'

She nodded. 'He had all six numbers. He was so excited. I couldn't believe it was happening. He was jumping up and down like a lunatic.'

Temple was taken aback. A lottery win. It was totally unexpected. He recalled that there had been an £18 million jackpot and that the winner had yet to claim the prize. Now, according to Jennifer Priest, Vince Mayo was that winner.

'Vince then insisted on phoning Danny,' she said. 'He told me to go and open a bottle of champagne. There was one in the fridge. So I went into the kitchen while he made the call. But I made a mess of popping the cork. The champagne spurted out and a good deal of it landed on Vince's briefcase, which happened to be on the floor.

'It was half-open and I saw that the contents were soaked. So I put the bottle down and picked up the case. I took out a pile of documents, mostly hard copies of various reports and invoices. There was also a large envelope. It was dripping wet so I tipped out what was inside.'

Temple recalled the envelope that Marsha Rowe had mentioned. The same one that Jordan had slipped under the office door.

'They were photographs,' Jennifer said. 'Five of them. They showed Vince with Danny's wife Maggie. There was also a handwritten note clipped to them. It said that if he didn't come up with the money he owed and drop the article he was writing then the photos would be sent to Danny.'

Jennifer took a deep breath and phlegm rattled in her throat. By now her nightgown was drenched in tears. Her cheeks were red, her eyes tinged with veins.

'What happened then?' Temple asked.

'Vince came into the kitchen,' she said. 'He told me Danny would be coming over. He looked so pleased with himself that it made me feel sick. I confronted him with the photos. He was surprised, but that's all. Almost immediately he grinned and said it was nothing and I shouldn't worry. I asked him to explain himself, but he shrugged it off and said he didn't want to talk about it. He was too excited about the lottery. He couldn't understand why I wasn't as jubilant as he was.'

'So what did you do?'

'I lost it,' Jennifer said. 'I was furious that he was smiling. I grabbed the lottery ticket out of his hand and told him I would destroy it if he didn't come clean. I expected him to at least calm down and speak to me. But instead he took hold of my wrist and pushed me against the wall. He acted like a man possessed. I tried to hold on to the ticket but he bent my fingers back and retrieved it. Then he told me to go home and calm down. Said that he would talk to me about the pictures tomorrow.

'That's when he turned away from me. I was incandescent with rage at that point. I hated him and I wanted to hurt him. I couldn't think about the lottery ticket and what it might mean. I could only think that he'd betrayed me, and I realized too that once he got his money I'd be history.

'I had my back against the worktop. I saw the pestle and mortar and grabbed the pestle. I didn't think. I just hit Vince over the head. He stumbled against the worktop and turned towards me. That's when I hit him a second time and he fell to the floor.'

Jennifer closed her eyes again, distraught. Temple handed her a glass of water from the bedside table and suggested she should drink it. She managed two mouthfuls.

'So you killed Vince,' he said.

'I didn't mean him to die,' she said. 'I just wanted to hurt him. I was mortified when I realized he wasn't breathing.'

'We didn't find a lottery ticket in the cottage,' Temple said.

'That's because I took it. My father told me to.'

'Your father? How did he get involved?'

'I called him. As soon as I knew I'd killed Vince. I didn't know what else to do. I was scared and I was crying. So I told him what I'd done. That I'd murdered my boyfriend. At first he was too stunned to say anything. Then he asked me what had happened. I told him about the photos and the lottery ticket. He got me to pick up the ticket and read out the numbers.

'Then he told me that if I was convicted of murder I would go to prison for a long time. He said he couldn't let that happen. He would have to cover it up. He told me to leave the house and to take the pestle, the photos and the lottery ticket with me. He also told me to wipe my prints from the champagne bottle. I said I didn't want to go through with it but he said he would not let his daughter go to prison. He said he'd go over to the cottage himself later and clean up to ensure there was no evidence to incriminate me. He said he would be my alibi. We'd say we had dinner together.'

'And you agreed to all this?' Temple said.

'I didn't know what else to do. My mind was a shambles. I wasn't thinking straight.'

'So you left the cottage?'

'Not right away. I'd forgotten to tell my father about Danny. When I told him that Danny was coming over to the cottage he swore out loud and said he needed a few minutes to think it through. I stayed on the line. When he came back he said I was to leave the cottage and drive to the nearest point where I could see Danny arrive but be sure he couldn't see me. As soon as Danny arrived I was to call him.'

'And you did this without knowing what he had in mind?'

'He said it was a precaution. He was going to try to stop Danny before he left his house. He knew he couldn't get to the cottage in time, so he drove straight over to Bassett, where Danny lives. It's only ten minutes by car from my father's house in Botley. When he got there he saw that there were no cars on the driveway. He phoned the house from a call box, so that his own number wouldn't show up. But Danny's wife said he was out.'

'So what did he do?'

'That was when I called to tell him that Danny had arrived at the cottage. I was parked opposite the entrance to the lane, outside the abandoned church. I saw him turn off the road.'

'So what happened?'

'My father went up to Danny's house and took his wife and daughter hostage. He told me he had no other choice. He called Danny from there on his wife's phone. He told him that if he informed the police about the murder or the ticket they'd be killed.

'He told Danny to go home and wait for him to call. My father then took Mrs Cain and her daughter to a place where he could leave them. An empty house in the country near to his home.'

'Who does the house belong to?'

'Some people he vaguely knows who are away.'

'And he has a key?'

'No. He broke in. Then found a key inside. He put Maggie and Laura Cain in the attic. Then he called Danny and arranged to meet him in town. He took him to the same place and that's where the family have been.'

'But what about the calls you made to Mayo during the evening?' Temple said. 'You phoned both his mobile and his landline before going to bed.'

'My father told me to do that so it would add weight to my claim that I wasn't there.'

★   ★   ★

Suddenly it all fell into place. Danny Cain had discovered the body. Hence the blood on his shoes. Then he'd raced away from the cottage and the neighbour saw him. He went home and when he saw the police arrive he left by the back door because he'd been warned to keep quiet.

Temple saw now why Cain had to retrieve his phone from the youths. He also realized that Superintendent Priest must have picked Cain up in the city centre and been responsible for putting the two mobiles in the plastic carrier bag, which he attached to the van.

'So your father intends to claim the lottery money and cover for you,' Temple said.

Jennifer nodded. 'At first he told me he was going to let the Cains go free after he got the money. He said that we would have to go and live abroad somewhere. And I really believe that that was his intention at the time. But then later he said that he'd have to kill them so that they'd never talk about what happened. He told me it was the only way to avoid us both going to prison or spending the rest of our lives on the run.'

'And you went along with it?'

'I was terrified. It was an awful thought, but I knew he was right. I was sorry for what I'd done, but I knew I couldn't face going to jail. And I even convinced myself that Maggie Cain had it coming because of what she'd done to me. But last night I changed my mind. I was at the flat and I'd been thinking about it. I'd got myself worked up and realized I couldn't go through with it. So I rushed out of there. I was going to see my father and tell him. But I wasn't concentrating and crashed the car.

'When I came around today my dad was here. He listened to me but said it was too late. That he had already killed the Cains. I was devastated. He begged me not to say anything because it wouldn't change things except we'd both go to prison. He said he'd fixed it so that the police would think that Cain had murdered his wife and daughter as well as Vince.'

She fell silent and looked up at Temple, her expression hollow. He was speechless for a

365

while as a rush of nausea passed through his system.

'I'm not sure I believe him, though,' Jennifer said, breaking into his thoughts.

'Come again?'

'When my father told me he had killed them,' she said. 'I've been thinking about it. I'm not sure it was true.'

'Why?'

'Because he might have said it just to stop me speaking out. You see, he argued that since they were already dead there was no point in confessing.'

'So they could still be alive?'

'I don't know. He left here in a hurry. Said he was going back to the office. But maybe he didn't.'

'Then where are they being held? Where's this house in the country?'

She shook her head. 'I don't know. He never said. He told me only that it belonged to a couple he knows in his local pub in Botley who are spending the winter in South Africa, where they have a second home.'

'So who are they? Tell me what you know.'

'Their names are Peter and Anne Salmon,' she said. 'I remember that.'

51

Seconds after the kidnapper slammed the boot shut I knew that something was wrong. I heard Maggie speaking and then Laura called out 'Daddy'. But then the kidnapper shouted something, after which the voices began to fade. I listened carefully, curled up in the blackness of the boot. The car doors didn't open or shut. The engine didn't start.

I began to panic.

'Maggie,' I called. 'What's going on?'

But my voice bounced back at me in the confined space and my body started to heat up with anxiety. Where had the bastard taken them? Why weren't they in the car? I started kicking at the bodywork. Punching the boot lid with the sides of my fists. But it achieved nothing other than to cause my arms and legs to ache.

I was helpless. Again.

The moments stretched into minutes and after an agonizing wait I heard shoes on gravel. I started to shout again, half-expecting the boot to be wrenched open. But a door was opened instead. Then closed again. The engine fired up and the car began to move.

And I knew that Maggie and Laura had been left behind.

The panic grew inside me. I lay still, my body numb, my mind in disarray.

The car journey lasted just a few minutes. Then came a squeal of brakes. A door opened. I waited. Tense. My pulse went off the scale. The boot lid was pulled open and the kidnapper ordered me to get out. He helped by grabbing my arm and pulling. Then I was standing beside the car facing him. I looked around. Stared hard into the lighted interior of the car. No Maggie or Laura. We were at the end of a narrow dirt track. There were trees behind me. Ahead, fields rolled away into the distance.

'Where's my family?' I said.

He was still holding the gun and pointing it at me.

'They're back at the house,' he said. 'I'm afraid you won't be seeing them again.' His voice was pure steel and those words cut into me like a razor blade. I felt my legs go weak and the blood roar in my ears.

'But you said you were going to let us go.'

'I know what I said, Cain. But you're not stupid. You've always known that you would have to die. It's the only way we get to have a life.'

'Who's *we*?'

He held it a beat and said, 'My daughter. Jennifer Priest.'

I felt my throat constrict. 'Vince's girlfriend?'

He said nothing. He didn't have to.

'You're a fucking copper?' I blurted.

'I've had to protect my daughter, Cain. That's how this all started. The lottery ticket was just an added incentive.'

If you knew why this was happening you'd understand.

'Are you saying that Jennifer killed Vince?'

'He deserved it,' he said. 'The bastard was betraying her as well as you. Now turn around and walk into the woods. If you don't I'll shoot you right here.'

I took a step back, held up the cuffs in a defensive gesture. 'I want my wife and daughter. Please let me go back.'

'It's too late for that.'

He motioned with his head and I looked back in the direction we'd just come. At first I didn't see it. But then I noticed an orange glow in the sky above a clump of trees. I frowned, not quite sure what I was seeing.

'I'm sorry about your daughter,' he said. 'But your wife deserves to die for what she did. The bitch is a two-timing slut.'

And then it dawned on me.

'My God,' I yelled. 'You've set fire to the house.'

'And the police will assume that you did it, Cain. And you won't be able to reveal the truth because you won't be around.'

I felt a pain of anguish explode inside my chest and spread through my body. Instinctively, I threw myself forward, ignoring the gun, but he stepped to one side and struck me across the shoulder with the butt. I fell to the ground, rolled on my back. He stared down at me.

'At least let me die with them,' I begged him. 'Please.'

He shook his head. 'I've already dug a shallow grave for you just over there in the woods. If I left you in the house they'd find out that you weren't responsible. I know about forensics. The cuff marks, your injuries. The fire might destroy all the evidence, but then again it might not. This way they continue to believe that you killed them.'

I watched him reach inside his jacket and pull out the knife he'd taken from me in the house. Its serrated blade glinted in the light from the car. A gun in one hand and a knife in the other. What the hell was he planning to do? My mind raced, driven fast by terror. And as he took a step towards me I sensed he was going to stab me because he wanted to avoid the sound of a shot being fired. This presented me with an opportunity, albeit a fleeting one. I tensed my muscles as he took another step closer. Then I kicked out at his left shin. Contact was solid. He yelped and lurched off balance. I rolled to the right and swept the same leg out from under him.

He went down with a heavy thud, letting out a loud, shocked groan.

I leapt to my feet and dived forward on to his outstretched arm. With my cuffed hands I managed to wrestle the gun from his grip. Then I rolled away from him, took aim and fired.

Click.

The gun failed to go off. I pressed the trigger again.

Click.

By now Priest was back on his feet.

'It's a replica, you fucking idiot,' he screamed at me. 'I never planned for a bullet to kill you. Too risky and too noisy. You were going to suffer the same fate that was inflicted on your partner. But now that I have the knife it'll be even easier.'

I threw the gun at him and rolled across the ground. I managed to haul myself up and stagger away from the car. I was aware of the burning house in the distance; the glow of the flames was clearly visible in the darkening sky. I headed towards it. Priest came after me. I struggled to stay on my feet. Terror ripped through me as I ran. There was no way I could reach my family. I realized that now. But I ploughed on regardless, ignoring the fact that he was closing in.

And then I tripped on a boulder and went crashing to the ground, bits of dirt and grass sticking to my cheek.

It was over for me now. That much was obvious.

I was once again at the mercy of the man who was going to kill me. I no longer had the strength to get to my feet, let alone keep on running.

The earth beneath me was cold and damp. I was trapped and disoriented. My lungs were on fire and my breath was coming in great heaving gasps.

The cuffs on my wrists were cutting into the flesh, dripping blood on to the soft dirt and the dead, soggy leaves.

I wanted to plead with him to let my wife and daughter live, but I couldn't form the words. Instead, I could only lie where I had fallen and look up as he approached me. He was still wearing the black ski mask and he was still carrying the knife in his right hand.

I was going to be murdered by this man who had entered our lives just two days ago and whose face I had never seen.

Two days.

Long enough for the life I had known to be shattered like a light bulb hitting concrete. And I couldn't help but wonder why it had happened to us.

'It's the end of the road, Cain,' Priest said. 'No point resisting.'

I was too weak to do anything other than brace myself for what was to come. Pain racked my body from the beating I had taken earlier. Exhaustion numbed my senses and the sheer terror of what was happening had paralyzed my mind.

He reached down. Grabbed my shirt front. Pulled me roughly off the ground.

He started speaking again, his mouth wrestling with the fabric of the mask, but his words were now just a jumble of sounds. I felt myself being pulled away from the present into the comfort of my subconscious.

I saw Maggie and Laura. I was actually back in our home on the day it all started. I felt safe and warm and . . .

His knee landed on my chest, jolting me back to the present. I glimpsed the knife above me in his raised hand. Instinctively, I grabbed his wrist with both my hands, stopping the downward thrust of the knife. I then used all the strength I could muster to heave his body off me and roll away from him.

Thankfully, he was slow to react. I was on my feet before he was. I kicked out with my right foot. Caught his face full on. There was a crack of bone beneath the ski mask. I followed through with another kick. This one smashed into his chest. He cried out.

He had lost the advantage. He'd also dropped the knife, but I couldn't see where it was. I kicked him again, in the kidneys. He fell back. Limp. Then I rammed my shoe into the side of his head. It made a sickening thud and sent him sprawling on to his face. I stood for a few seconds, gasping for air. I contemplated searching him for the keys to unlock the cuffs but I knew there was no time. If Maggie and Laura were not dead already then they soon would be.

I had to get back to the house. I looked back along the track to where the car was parked. Would I be able to drive it with my hands in cuffs? I decided I had to try. I'd never get there in time on foot.

52

It was easier than I thought because the car was an automatic. I jumped in behind the wheel. Through the windscreen I saw Priest struggling to his feet. I felt like stamping my foot on the accelerator and running him down.

Instead, I engaged reverse and screeched backwards along the track and eventually came to a country lane. There was a moment when I didn't know whether to turn left or right. But then I saw the now familiar orange glow in the sky so I went to the right.

The blazing house soon came into view, although I had to turn into another lane to reach it. By the time I screeched to a stop on the driveway it was well on fire and I feared I was too late to save my family. The fire had taken hold downstairs and flames were spitting out of all the windows. One of the upstairs rooms was also engulfed, but there were two that were not. Smoke billowed out of one of them where the glass had shattered.

I seized on this as a glimmer of hope, although I knew that the odds on them being in either of those rooms were slim. The room on the far right had another window at the side of the house, overlooking the flat roof of the garage. I saw that it offered a way in and without hesitation I drove the car at the garage door, ramming into it so hard that the door flew off its hinges and crashed to the back of the garage.

I jumped out of the car, leapt on to the bonnet, and then on to the roof. From there I was able to haul myself up on to the top of the garage. The explosion of heat took me by surprise. I reeled back, rubbed my eyes and covered my mouth with my arm.

I reached the window and smashed it with the cuffs. I pulled myself over the ledge and into the bedroom. I held my breath to keep from inhaling smoke. Through the swirling black clouds I could make out two single beds.

'Maggie. Laura. Are you here?'

My shouts were no match for the flames that raged through the house. I ventured across the room. The door was open and I stepped out on to the landing. The hot air blasted my lungs and it was like breathing in a furnace. A couple of steps took me to the next room along. Beyond it was the stairwell and the ladder leading into the loft. The whole lot would soon be an inferno. The door next to me was closed. I pushed it open and looked in. A rolled-up sheet had been placed against the bottom of the door to keep out the smoke. This gave me hope.

'Maggie. Where are you? Talk to me.'

Someone cried out. It was Maggie. I squinted through the billowing smoke. After an agonizing moment I saw them. They were crouched in a corner between the bed and the broken window.

Maggie's cuffed wrist was attached to the wall mounted radiator. Without hesitating I started pulling and kicking at the radiator. It was old and the fixings were not in good shape. It took about thirty seconds to wrench the radiator an inch or so away from the wall. Then the pipe moved and the fixing snapped off, sending a stream of cold water into the air.

Laura had passed out. She was wrapped in Maggie's arms. I could see that Maggie was struggling to breathe.

'There's a way out,' I shouted. 'Can you walk?'

Maggie coughed and nodded at the same time.

'I'll take Laura,' I said. 'Stay close to me.'

I put my cuffed hands over my daughter's head and gave her a fireman's lift. Maggie grabbed hold of my belt and we moved into the hall. The stairwell was now engulfed in flames and they were moving quickly towards us. We could barely see. The smoke, black and dense, swirled around us, willing us to submit to it. Acrid cinders caught in our throats, making us retch. A step at a time. Feeling my way. Choking on the smoke. But we managed at last to get to the side window, which was sucking smoke out into the open air.

I climbed out with Laura. She was still unconscious. I put her down gently on the garage roof. Then I helped Maggie out. Together we managed to get Laura down on to the driveway. Maggie was coughing and retching, but Laura was pale and limp. I laid her out on the stones and as I did so I realized that she wasn't breathing.

Panic swelled inside me. Her chest was still and spittle foamed at the corners of her mouth. I leaned over, grabbed her shoulders, shouted her name. But she didn't respond.

As Maggie started to scream I covered Laura's mouth with my own. I forced my breath into her, prayed that it would ignite the spark of life.

'Oh my God, she's dead,' Maggie yelled. 'She's dead.'

And I knew that she was right. There was nothing there. No life. No breath. No pulse. I reared up then and threw back my head. A grief-stricken howl tore its way to the surface from the very depths of my being. So intense was the moment that I didn't see Priest bearing down on me until he was so close that I could hear his shoes crunching on the gravel.

My body went into lockdown. The scream died in my throat and every muscle inside me turned to stone.

Priest was maybe twenty feet away. He was no longer wearing the ski mask but he was still carrying the knife. His face was streaked with blood and his features were contorted into an ugly grimace. As I watched him close in I knew I was going to die. I knew also that it was what I wanted. There was no longer any reason to live.

He got to within about ten feet of us when the shot rang out. I saw his torso convulse and his chest open up. He stopped dead, as though hovering on the edge of a cliff. The knife fell from his hand on to the ground and he dropped to his knees.

Smoke curled out of the hole in his chest and he let out a primal scream before toppling forward on to his face. His body went in to a violent spasm, then he lay still.

My muscles unfroze. I twisted my neck and saw a man with a rifle. A police officer. Kevlar vest. Dark goggles. Dark helmet. He was standing next to a white patrol car. Its blue light was flashing and all its doors were open. There were two other uniformed officers next to the car and there was also a heavyset man in a dark suit.

DCI Jeff Temple.

A fierce rage flared inside me and I cursed out loud. My anger was directed at Temple as well as the officer who had fired the rifle. I wanted to kill them both because I knew that I'd never forgive them for what they'd done. They should have let Priest get to me. They should have let me die alongside my beloved daughter.

53

The funeral took place at the crematorium in Southampton. It was a cold day and the sky was a moody gunmetal. The chapel was full and outside in the street the media gathered. Reporters, photographers, camera operators. There were even a couple of satellite trucks for relaying live pictures back to the television news studios.

Maggie and I sat together in the front row. We held hands and bowed our heads and the emotions that swirled within us were mixed. A minister with a bald head read the eulogy, which was short and somewhat impersonal. He'd asked me if I wanted to do it but I declined. It was all too raw, I said.

The coffin entered the furnace to an organ rendition of *Morning has Broken*.

It was what Vince had wanted, along with a request that his ashes be scattered across an open moor close to his cottage in the New Forest.

Epilogue

In the weeks that followed Vince's funeral I struggled to come to terms with what had happened. I soon realized that I probably never would. DCI Temple talked to me at length. At the first informal interview he surprised me with an apology.

'I want you to know that I'm sorry, Mr Cain,' he said. 'A lot of bad apples have taken root in the force and we need to find them and turf them out. You were right to expose George Banks for what he did. And my colleagues were wrong to victimize you because of it. We should encourage zero tolerance no matter what the circumstances. Jordan and Priest have brought further shame on us and it's something we all regret. But I want you to know that we're not all bad.'

I told him I couldn't get my head around how a man like Priest could suddenly turn into a killer who was prepared to wipe out an entire family.

'It happens,' Temple said. 'You should know that better than most since you reporters are always writing about such creatures.'

The papers called Priest a fiend and a

madman. They called me a hero. In fact one paper, a popular tabloid, asked me to write the full story of our experience. It ran over four full pages. What's more, the editor liked it so much that he offered me a contract as a reporter. It was a surprise and came as a great relief since I'd decided not to carry on with the agency. That had died along with Vince.

So what about my marriage? Was that dead too?

Maggie and I finally got around to talking about it eight days after the fire. We had purposely avoided it until then because our priority was Laura. She had to be taken care of.

Thankfully a police officer trained in first aid had managed to revive her with CPR at the scene, despite the fact that she had effectively 'died' in my arms. We would have lost her for sure if it hadn't been for Temple and his team. Their swift, professional reaction when they realized how bad she was saved her life. It was touch and go for a while, but by the time the ambulance arrived her lungs were functioning and her heart was beating.

After leaving hospital Laura started to recover with remarkable speed. The doctors and psychiatrists who treated her said that she was a strong little girl. They were impressed that she could talk about it and not retreat into herself for long periods of time. I was very proud of her. But it did seem as though she'd blocked out what Priest had said about her mother and Vince. She acted as though it never happened.

I wasn't so lucky. Priest's words echoed in my head every second of every hour. Talking about it didn't help. It just intensified the pain. Maggie begged me to forgive her. She said she loved me and had made a terrible mistake. Our ordeal had made her realize what a fool she'd been and how much she had put at risk.

We both cried a lot but I didn't allow the anger in me to surface because I felt that we had all been through enough. Instead, I told her that I would try to forgive and forget what had happened between her and Vince. But the truth is I'm not sure I can.

Jennifer Priest eventually went on trial. The jury rejected her plea of manslaughter and she was sentenced to life for murder. Dessler faced a variety of charges and ended up getting a three-year jail term. DS Jordan was kicked out of the force and given a two-year sentence on corruption charges. Nadelson was ordered to do some community service.

The lottery commission decided to give Vince's jackpot win to charity. I told them that Vince had intended to share it with me but this fell on deaf ears, as I knew it would.

Temple told me I wouldn't face charges for assaulting the two youths. To keep them quiet he would bring lesser charges against *them*. I thanked him for that and I also thanked him for saving our lives.

'It was a team effort,' he said. 'Every one of my people did a good job.'

★ ★ ★

So a new phase of my life has begun. I'm once again a salaried hack and loving every minute of it. The paper has already got me working on a major investigation that will cause quite a stir when it's eventually published. But that's another story for another day.

Meanwhile, I spend a lot of time wondering if my marriage will survive. You see, things are not the same now. I feel differently about Maggie and she knows it. So we'll just have to see. After all, none of us can ever really know what is going to happen from one day to the next.

And that, I suppose, is why life is really just one big lottery.

We do hope that you have enjoyed reading this large print book.

Did you know that all of our titles are available for purchase?

We publish a wide range of high quality large print books including:
Romances, Mysteries, Classics
General Fiction
Non Fiction and Westerns

Special interest titles available in large print are:
The Little Oxford Dictionary
Music Book
Song Book
Hymn Book
Service Book

Also available from us courtesy of Oxford University Press:
Young Readers' Dictionary
(large print edition)
Young Readers' Thesaurus
(large print edition)

For further information or a free brochure, please contact us at:
Ulverscroft Large Print Books Ltd.,
The Green, Bradgate Road, Anstey,
Leicester, LE7 7FU, England.
Tel: (00 44) 0116 236 4325
Fax: (00 44) 0116 234 0205

RESURRECTION

Raymond Haigh

The Prime Minister has been murdered. At Chequers, under police protection, his widow, Helen Cosgrave, discovers her husband's private and damning bank statements. Samantha Quest knows the late Prime Minister's secrets, and, despite the risk, agrees to talk to Helen. Virtually imprisoned, she enlists Quest to contact the person her husband has been secretly paying. When there are more deaths and a prostitute is reported missing, the situation threatens the private lives of politicians. Mrs Cosgrave's life is a priority, but can Quest be persuaded to take a chance and stop the country's slide into panic and political disaster?

A NARROW RETURN

Faith Martin

Ex-Detective Inspector Hillary Greene returns to Thames Valley to work on cold cases. No longer a professional, she must cope with being a civilian — and she also has a stalker. Her superior Superintendent Steven Crayle, uncertain that she should be on his team, hands her a twenty-year old murder file that's as cold as a blizzard. Who would want to slaughter a housewife and mother of three in her own home? The original team couldn't make a case, what chance of justice now? Greene, with something to prove — to herself and her new boss — knuckles down to catch a killer . . .

A FATAL FALL OF SNOW

Joyce Cato

Spending Christmas in a country farm-house, snowed-in and cooking her favourite traditional, seasonal food, seems like a dream come true for travelling cook Jenny Starling. But the Christmas spirit evaporates because of the family she's cooking for: a rebellious teenage daughter and two resentful sons at loggerheads with their arrogant father. And then Jenny finds a corpse with a knife in the chest sitting at the kitchen table, and the farmer accuses her of the deed. She must act quickly and find the real killer — especially since the assigned police officer seems reluctant to be taking on his first murder case.

THE DEATH DETECTIVE AND THE SKELETON

John F. Rice

In Southfield, when a skeleton with a ligature around its neck is unearthed by a hungry fox, the Death Detective, DI Essach Wangdula, is brought in to investigate. The Detective Inspector is Sherlock Holmes's descendant; his assistant is DS Flora L. Hughes. Identification of the body by facial reconstruction leads the pair to London where they learn that the victim had been involved in a suspicious death. Then another body is discovered in Southfield and it's reported that there are now two missing people. Suddenly, Wangdula knows that he's up against a committed serial killer.

COMING TO THE EDGE

Theresa Murphy

DCI Mattia is struggling with a case that involves politics, big business and a psychopathic killer. He's depressed: the combination of his current investigation into the murder of a young girl singer, his rocky relationship with his girlfriend, and his infatuation with a sexy private detective are all having an effect. But as members of his team are attacked, it looks like he might be onto something. Will he succeed in clearing the murder victim's husband, whom he believes to be innocent, or will his police career end in ignominy and the loss of the woman he now knows he loves?

THE SECRETS MAN

John Dean

When DCI John Blizzard visits a friend in hospital, he is intrigued when an elderly villain in the next bed reveals much about Hafton's criminal gangs. These revelations attract a series of sinister characters to the ward. Blizzard wonders if they are seeking to silence the old man, but fellow detectives believe that the pensioner is suffering from dementia. It's only when people start dying that his colleagues take the DCI seriously. Blizzard faces a race against time to save lives, and must face a part of his past he's tried to forget — and with the one man he fears.